Make Mine Turbulence

Dorlon L. Pond Jr.

Copyright © 2022 Dorlon L. Pond Jr.
All rights reserved
First Edition

PAGE PUBLISHING
Conneaut Lake, PA

First originally published by Page Publishing 2022

ISBN 978-1-6624-5961-0 (hc)
ISBN 978-1-6624-5960-3 (digital)

Printed in the United States of America

CHAPTER I

THE TAXI I'D called for over an hour ago was late.

"What took you so long?" I admonished the cab driver when he arrived.

"Hey lady, it's not my fault the weather turned bad. Everybody and his little brother wants a cab in conditions like this, and driving seems to be getting worse by the minute. Where're you headed?"

"To the airport. I'm going to be late for my first day of work."

"Are you one of them stewardesses?" he asked.

"The term is *flight attendant*. And yes, I'm one of them or will be if we ever get there."

"We'll get there. It's just a matter of time," he said.

Rolling my eyes, I said under my breath, "Time is something I'm short on right now."

About a mile from the airport, we passed a huge billboard that advertised, "*Angel Air*—come fly with the Angels." Because of this lousy weather, my nerves were on edge. Maybe I'd be able to blame it on the taxi being late. The problem with that notion is that I'm sure my boss would tell me I should've called for a taxi earlier.

This weather couldn't make up its mind between rain or snow, which included strong winds.

When we neared the terminal building, traffic bogged down because of heavy congestion. The slush, created by the inclement weather, didn't help as it slowed our forward movement even more.

"You can let me out anywhere near the Angel Air Sky Cap station," I told the cabbie.

When we stopped, the driver said, "That'll be twenty seven fifty."

For me, that was an expensive but necessary ride. I reached into my purse for my wallet, and in haste, my clumsy hands dropped it. After retrieving it, I fished out thirty dollars and handed it to the driver.

"Keep the change."

"Thank you, Ma'am," he acknowledged and stuffed the money in his pocket.

By the time I returned my wallet to my purse, the cabbie had gotten out and gone around the car. I grabbed my tiny suitcase from the back seat just as he opened the door. At that moment, a gust of wind almost pulled me out of the cab. I'd planted my feet on the ground, turned toward the building, and almost instantly my feet began to slide like I'd stepped onto a sheet of ice. I lost my balance and fell face first between two parked cars, banging my left knee on a sharp chunk of ice that had dropped from the fender of a vehicle.

"Ow, my knee!" I hollered to no one in particular.

Luckily my coat received most of the water damage while the hem of my skirt soaked up some of the mire as well as my hands and face. I started to get up when a couple of strong gentlemen came over to rescue me. One was the taxi driver, and the other happened to be in a pilot's uniform. Both men were over six feet tall. I'm five foot two, with blue eyes and chestnut hair.

"Thank you, gentlemen," I acknowledged, feeling a little embarrassed.

"Are you all right?" the cabbie asked.

"Yes, thank you." Tears began to sting my eyes.

The pilot said, "Let me help you negotiate the slush between these cars. You're new here, aren't you?"

"Yes, Sir." My nerves were doing the mambo.

"I'm Captain Ross Morton," the pilot said.

"Cinnamon Shaffer—I'm one of the new flight attendants." A few tears spilled over the dam.

"Are you all right, Cinnamon?" he asked.

"Not really. This is my first day and now look at me. I'm a mess."

"Don't worry about it. This could have happened to anyone."

"Thank you, Captain."

"My pleasure, Cinnamon," he said as he led me into the building and to the employee door of Angel Air. Like a true gentleman, he held the door for me.

Dressed in my brand new sky blue uniform, I'd wanted to make a good impression on my boss and coworkers. It took a long time last night to get my uniform ready. Now it was a total disaster.

Pearl Bacon, my new boss, greeted us just inside the door.

My face turned candy apple red with embarrassment at the scowl on her face.

"You're late, Shaffer, and look at you. What did you do, go swimming in a mud puddle?"

Some of the other flight attendants and pilots snickered or laughed across the room.

"N…n…no." My stammer came out in a nervous whisper. "The wind knocked me down when I got out of the taxi, which caused me to slip on some ice. Captain Morton and the taxi driver helped me up. It didn't occur to me that the bad weather would make me late for work."

"You should've called the taxi earlier," Pearl mentioned, just like I'd thought she'd say.

"I didn't know it'd be this bad" came my reply. My nerves shook even worse.

"You're lucky the weather has delayed our flight on your first day. I'll let it pass this time. Normally I'd dock you two hundred fifty dollars for being late and arriving in a dirty uniform. Let this be a lesson for you, Shaffer," Pearl said.

"Y…y…yes, Ma'am."

"Do you have a locker?" she asked.

"Yes. It was assigned to me after my last training session."

"What happened to your leg?" she inquired as she looked down at my wound.

"Pearl," interjected Captain Morton, "Cinnamon banged her knee quite hard when she fell outside the building. It was very slippery."

"Thank you for the information, Captain." She turned to me. "Go get changed into a clean uniform and take the pantyhose off. The company doctor will need to look at that wound. If it's bad, he may put you on sick leave."

"Sick leave?"

"Yes. The doctor will explain it to you," Pearl said.

I limped to the locker room dragging my tiny suitcase behind me. The airline insisted that flight attendants pack for no more than three days in the small suitcase they call a crew kit, which is provided by Angel Air with its logo on one side. This included civilian clothing, makeup, and underwear. I was glad I decided to squeeze an extra uniform into that crew kit. I planned on leaving it in my locker for just such an emergency.

In the locker room, I changed out of my dirty, wet uniform. I took off my pantyhose being careful of my wound. Pain set in when I reached the dried blood on my knee that acted like glue.

"Ouch." I just sat on the bench in front of my locker and began to cry. The wound bled a little. All that work the night before ruined.

"Pearl must think I'm a bum," I said through my tears.

"Hey, are you all right?" came a female voice from across the aisle.

My eyes went to that voice. "No. Last night I'd spent most of my time getting ready for today. And for what? Because of the bad weather, it all just went down the drain. I fell and made a mess of my new uniform and banged my knee real good."

"Here, dry your eyes." She handed me a tissue.

"Thank you."

"By the way, I'm Jade Pinkerton."

"Cinnamon Shaffer."

"Is that Cinnamon as in the spice or green turnips?"

Her reference to green turnips made me laugh.

"As in spice. My dad was stationed in the Orient in the navy shortly after my birth, and he brought home all kinds of spices for my mom to try. That's where my name came from. Do green turnips really have cinnamon in them?"

"Not to my knowledge. It was my way to try to cheer you up."

"Thank you, Jade." She's an African-American and Miss America type of beautiful with a short and sassy Afro.

I finished changing, hobbled to the locker room door, and found Pearl waiting to escort me to the company doctor. *Is she doing this out of kindness?*

The medical office looked small to me. The doctor cleaned and dressed my wound located just under my left kneecap with a four-inch-square white gauze bandage. This stuck out like a sore thumb, although it was my knee that was injured, not my thumb.

"Doctor, could you please wrap an ACE bandage over the one you just put on my knee?" I asked.

"It's highly unusual, but why?"

"If you think about it, the color will look more natural under my pantyhose."

"That may be true, but I'd like you to stay off that leg for a few days. I'll put you on sick leave to give that wound a chance to heal."

"Please don't do that, Doctor. Today's my first day on the job. I need to be able to work."

"Just to remind you, Ms. Shaffer, serving passengers food and drinks requires you to be on your feet for most of the flight."

"Understood, Doc. Please? Let me work. Pretty please," I pleaded with my hands folded as if in prayer, "with sugar on top?"

"It's against my better judgment, but how can I resist such a charming and determined young lady? Let me give you a few pain pills along with some for infection. Take them as directed on the labels."

Upon my return to the employee lounge, Pearl was talking to Captain Morton and another pilot unknown to me. He had one less stripe on his shoulder boards, so maybe he's the junior pilot. In addition, there were two other flight attendants, who were also unknown to me.

"Is this a private party?" I asked upon approaching this group. "Or can anyone join?"

Pearl turned to me with a distracted look. "The wounded Angel has returned to the nest. What'd the doctor say?"

"I'm fit as a fiddle and raring to go."

"Yes, but what'd the doctor say?" Pearl asked again.

"What's the doctor got to do with anything?"

A little humor on my part never hurt anything, but you'd never have known it by the mean look on Pearl's face.

"Okay, okay. He told me I could fly."

She looked at my knee. "Your knee looks a little swollen."

"At my request, the doctor put an ACE bandage on so the white bandage won't stand out so much."

"Smart girl," Pearl said. "Let me introduce you to everyone. Captain Morton and Jade—you already know. And this handsome gentleman is Howard Duffy, our first officer. These flight attendants are Karyn Cayke and Marilyn Benoid, who will be on our flight. Everyone, this is Cinnamon Shaffer. She's our newest Angel."

After we all became acquainted, Pearl commanded Karyn and Jade to introduce me to all the other flight attendants in the room. I'd be working with some of them on future flights. Pearl, from what I've also learned, has been with Angel Air for more than twenty-eight years. She stands about an inch shorter than our first officer and is about two or three inches shorter than our captain. Karyn's hair is blond and done up in a bun. Marilyn's hair is red and straight. Karyn, Jade, and Marilyn are all about my height.

With all the other introductions over, Pearl made this announcement: "Ladies, our flight has been canceled. The airport is about to shut down due to the high winds and blowing snow on the runways."

Being the newbie, it behooved me to ask the stupid question. "Now what do we do?"

Pearl pointed to Jade. "Please take Cinnamon to the hotel."

On the way, Jade suggested we stop in the locker room to get our makeup. I accompanied her to the hotel, where we would spend the night. While we walked, we talked.

"Jade, are you related to that famous Pinkerton Detective Agency?"

"No. Sometimes I wish," she said. "If that had been the case, you wouldn't see me working here." She paused, then said, "Just for your information, Pearl is hard on new people until she feels confident in their work. However, away from the job, she's a wonderful person."

While we were walking, the pain in my knee began to work its way into my leg again, and Jade noticed my limping had gotten worse.

"I need to rest a bit and take some pain medicine. Please don't tell Pearl. The doctor told me to stay off my leg for a few days and wanted to put me on sick leave."

"Don't worry. Your secret is safe with me. There are a lot of medical things we don't tell Pearl about, just for that very reason."

"Why sick leave?"

"Because if we so much as get a paper cut on our fingers, Pearl won't let us fly."

"But, Jade, why would she do that for such a small wound?"

"Because we handle food." She pointed her index finger at me. "And I know what you're thinking. We could wear plastic gloves, but Pearl won't go for it."

"What about other more serious wounds?"

"It depends on if we're physically able to work. If we're sick, she'll put us on sick leave even if it's a minor cold."

"Speaking of cold, do we have to go outside again? It's freezing out there."

"No, Cinnamon. We'll take an elevator down one level and get into a cart like the ones that take passengers to their gates. From there, it's a short ride to our hotel, which is free, but we have to pay for our meals out of our own pockets."

"But aren't hotel meals expensive?"

"Relax, girl, the company gets us a reduced rate."

It seemed to me that Jade would make a fine friend. So far, she's been very kind to me. I remembered my mom's warning—don't trust a person you've just met until you know without a doubt that you can place your confidence in them.

The next morning, I woke to a loud, blaring noise that came from Jade's cell phone.

"Time to get up, sleepyhead," Jade chimed in a cheerful voice.

"Let me snooze for a while," I pleaded sleepily.

"Come on, Cinnamon. We have to shower, shine, do our makeup, and everything in between. Then we eat breakfast and must be ready for inspection before we begin work no later than eight a.m. sharp."

"But our flight doesn't leave until later in the day. What time is it?"

"Five thirty. The only time Pearl lets you sleep in is if you're on sick leave. The way you talked last night, you aren't. So let's go before Pearl comes looking for us."

"Okay, Jade. I'm up," I said even though my mind was still groggy.

"By the way, Cinnamon, how's your leg?"

"It still stings a little but feels better, thanks," I said.

The time is now 8:00 a.m. sharp. We had to toe the red line painted on a tiled floor near the back of our lounge. Pearl went down the line inspecting us with our uniform jackets open. At breakfast, Jade explained that this is because some of the flight attendants prefer to go braless, which won't be tolerated by the airline. Some of the others had minor gigs that Pearl pointed out. They were easily correctable. When Pearl stood in front of me, she looked me all over.

"Shaffer, how's your leg? And no snide remarks."

"It's better."

"Good," she extoled. "Are you sure you're able to work?"

"Yes, Ma'am" came my snappy reply.

If I didn't know any better, I'd say we just went through a military-style inspection.

"Oh! One more thing, Shaffer, do you have a valid passport and is it up to date? You'll need one if your flight goes overseas."

"Yes, Ma'am."

CHAPTER II

"Okay, ladies," Pearl announced, "it's time to go for our flight at gate thirty-three."

That meant a long walk almost to the end of the corridor. Our passengers would be boarding the plane shortly after we stowed our crew kits. Pearl made sure we knew each section so we could direct the passengers to their proper seats. We'd be flying on a 787 Dreamliner. As she talked to us, the pilot and first officer came aboard.

Captain Morton said, "Good morning, ladies. Cinnamon, how's the knee?"

The other flight attendants gave their greetings. I responded, "My knee is much better, Captain. Thank you for asking."

Within the next few minutes, our passengers began boarding for the flight.

"Here comes the rush hour," Karyn said.

The first person to enter happened to be a woman in a wheelchair pushed by one of the ramp agents. Pearl checked the lady's seat assignment, then showed it to me, and told the ramp agent to follow me into the first-class section. The woman looked to be about sixty and on the heavy side. She had an aisle seat in the first row. The ramp agent turned her wheelchair to face the seat. We then each took one side of the woman, lifted her up, and turned her around before lowering her into the seat. The ramp agent took the wheelchair and left while I helped this passenger with her seat belt. As I turned to leave, she grabbed my arm and wanted to talk.

"Thank you. You did that with perfection. You must be an old hand at helping people," she said.

"Not really, Ma'am. This is my first day as a flight attendant."

"Is that name tag correct? Your name is Cinnamon?"

"Yes, Ma'am."

She asked, "Will you be up here in first class to serve me, Cinnamon?"

"No, I'm sorry, Ma'am. Since I'm new, I've been assigned to work in the back of the plane."

"We'll see about that. Is your supervisor on this flight?"

"Why? Did I do something wrong?"

"No, Dear. You've been nothing but nice to me. Thank you."

"You're welcome, Ma'am."

"Would you be so kind as to tell your supervisor I'd like to speak with her when she has a minute?"

"Sure. In the meantime, if you'll please excuse me, I'm needed to help other passengers find their seats."

What's eating her? I wondered, heading back to the entryway.

When the door to the aircraft closed, I gave Pearl the message from the disabled lady in first class.

"Pearl, the handicap lady you asked me to help into her seat wants to speak with you."

"Did she say what she wanted?" Pearl asked.

"No. She didn't. Sorry."

"Okay. Thank you, Cinnamon. You may now go to the rear galley." Then she said to all of us within earshot, "Let's get to our stations for the public briefings so we can take off."

Pearl went to her station and picked up the in-cabin microphone. When she had everyone's attention, she proceeded to explain, as we flight attendants demonstrated, how to use the seat belt and the seat belt sign, the oxygen masks and how to use them in an emergency, and while over water how to find and use the life vest found under each seat. She also had us point out all of the emergency exits should they be needed and slides that can be used as floating devises. We'd be leaving this windy city momentarily for Hawaii.

A few minutes later, we were getting coffee and snacks ready when Pearl came storming back to our galley mad as a hornet.

"Shaffer, who do you think you are demanding to change work locations without prior authorization? Do you know who that woman in first class is that you asked me to speak to?" Pearl asked.

"How am I supposed to know who she is? This is my first day as a flight attendant."

"She's Melanie Willingham, one of the richest women in the world and a major stockholder of Angel Air Lines. She practically owns the company. We bend over backward to do whatever she wants to keep her happy."

"I'm sorry, Pearl. After helping her into her seat and with her seat belt, she asked me if I'd be working in first class. I explained that I'm new here, and I've been assigned to work in the rear. We never discussed anything about me working up front, honest Injin." I put my hand up like an Indian salute.

While we talked, Pearl began to calm down.

"I'm sorry, Cinnamon. I should have gotten all the facts before rushing to judgment."

"That's okay." I wanted to add, *Just don't let it happen again*, but decided against it.

Once our plane reached the mandated cruising altitude for our flight, the captain made this announcement. "Ladies and gentlemen, this is Captain Morton, along with First Officer Duffy. Welcome aboard Angel Air flight eight forty-one to Honolulu. We've reached our cruising altitude of thirty-five thousand feet, so I've turned off the seat belt sign. However, I'd like to suggest that you keep it fastened while you're seated. If there's anything any of the crew can do for you, please let us know. We hope you have an enjoyable flight. Thank you for choosing Angel Airlines, and we hope you'll think of us in your future air travel plans."

Now began our job as flight attendants to serve the passengers. The rear galley to galley phone buzzed. "This is Cinnamon," I announced into the phone.

Pearl came on the line. "Cinnamon, Ms. Willingham wants you to serve her. She won't let Karyn do her job."

"But—"

"No buts, get yours to first class and serve her ASAP," ordered Pearl.

"Okay." I hung up with a sigh. "Jade, I've been called to first class. I'll be back shortly."

"Let me guess, Ms. Rich Bitch?"

"That's right. How'd you know?"

"It's not the first time she's been on one of our flights."

Upon my arrival at Ms. Willingham's seat, my reasoning went over her head.

"Ms. Willingham, Karyn, is just as capable if not more so at serving you because she's worked here longer than me."

"You don't understand, my dear," she said sternly as she pointed her finger at me. "I want you to serve me, no one else."

Pearl's admonishment that we keep her happy ran through my mind. "Yes, Ma'am. Please excuse my confusion."

All right, I thought and went to the forward galley to get her refreshments. *I'll serve you on this flight, but hopefully, this'll be the only time. You're not as nice as the first impression you gave me.*

"I'm sorry, Karyn. I'm not trying to take your job. It's not right that I've been ordered to serve Ms. Rich Bitch."

"Don't let it get to you, Cinnamon. It happens every time she gets on one of our flights. The first person who is nice enough to help her get seated is the one she wants to serve her all through the flight. You just had the bad luck to draw the short straw this time."

After everyone had been served, Pearl came to the rear galley.

"Cinnamon, may I see you a moment?" Pearl asked.

We moved a few feet away from the other flight attendants.

"Cinnamon, thank you for serving Ms. Willingham. You'll have to continue to serve her until she leaves the plane."

"So I've heard, but I'd prefer not doing Karyn's job just to please Ms. Snob. It's not right."

"I'm glad you feel that way. If she wasn't so rich and in control of the company, I'd say you're right. Please remember when you serve her to be polite and smile."

"Yes, Ma'am." I sighed.

"By the way, you're doing a fantastic job so far. Keep up the good work."

"Thank you, Pearl."

With all the passengers and crew fed, we had a little time to relax after we collected trash, cups, napkins, and anything else the passengers wanted us to pick up.

"It feels good just to get off my feet for a few minutes, Jade. I didn't think this plane was so big."

"Did you see the passenger list, Cinnamon? If you include the entire crew along with the passengers, there are close to three hundred fifty people on this plane."

"No wonder I'm tired. Besides, my knee is starting to hurt again. Time for me to take another pain pill." I rose from my seat to get some water to take my pill, and all of a sudden, the plane shook violently. My thoughts were that we were in an earthquake. Then realization hit. Since we were in the air, it couldn't be an earthquake.

"What just happened?" I asked Jade.

She gave a one-word answer. "Turbulence."

I'd just taken my pill when turbulence again shook the plane. A few minutes later, there was more turbulence. That's when the captain turned on the seat belt sign, followed by Pearl's voice over the in-cabin intercom.

"The captain has turned on the seat belt sign. For those of you who are up and about, please return to your seats and buckle up."

When the turbulence continued, the captain came over the airwaves. "Ladies and gentlemen, we are experiencing some turbulence on this bumpy road. Therefore, I've requested air traffic control to descend to a lower altitude in hopes of smoothing out our planned route. We apologize for any inconvenience this may cause. Thank you for your patience."

When we arrived at our new altitude, it seemed to be raining cats and dogs. I decided to get some more trash bags ready for our last tour of the plane before landing when all of a sudden, a burst of lightning hit our plane and shook us to the core. *Have I gone deaf?* The sound of the jet engines disappeared. It also knocked out the electricity. Since it was daylight outside, it left the inside darker than usual. At least we could see what we were doing.

When the engines started up again, the electricity returned along with my hearing. That bolt of lightning felt like another earthquake to me. Since I'd been standing, the jolt knocked me to the floor. My head hit one of the cabinets quite hard. Jade unbuckled her harness and rushed over to me.

"Cinnamon, are you okay?"

I shook my head to clear my mind, then looked at Jade, and everything looked blurry. A few seconds later, my vision came into focus.

"I think so. Oh, my head. That bump gave me a headache."

Jade and Marilyn helped me to my seat and buckled me in.

"Thank you, ladies, for helping me up."

Jade then found some aspirin and a glass of water. Marilyn picked up the trash bags and put them back into the cabinet that I'd just taken them from. They both returned to their seats and buckled up.

"Thank you for the aspirin, Jade."

Relaxing made my head feel a little better. All of a sudden without warning, the plane fell. I'd been told jets went fast enough to get through air pockets. We were in a free fall for what felt like an eternity. In reality, the fall only lasted a few seconds.

"That was a whopper of a fall," Jade said to no one in particular.

"Does that come with fries or onion rings?" I asked.

"If you make it a combo." Marilyn laughed. "You'll also get a drink."

Pearl came to our galley. "Ladies," she said in a hushed whisper, "gather around. I've just come from the captain. We've got problems that he wants to keep quiet for as long as possible, but I'm afraid we may have to declare an emergency. Standby to put emergency procedures into place."

From what Pearl told us, our hearts started to beat a little faster, at least mine did. It also woke up my nerves. They began to get excited in the wrong way. Some of the passengers began to sense something was wrong and started to push their call buttons, then the captain came on the air to explain our circumstances to the passengers.

"Ladies and gentlemen, please make sure your seat belts are securely fastened. That lightning jolt we just felt caused some of our instruments to malfunction. Without them, we may not make it to our destination. I've tried to call the coast guard to track us just in case. If we have to ditch the plane, please follow the instructions of the flight attendants who are trained in emergency evacuation procedures. Thank you."

Pearl returned to the forward galley. After a few minutes of calm, I got up to get the trash bags again and glanced out the galley door window. It had stopped raining, but to my horror, we were not near the altitude we should be at.

"Hey, Jade. Aren't we supposed to be thirty-something thousand feet up in the air?"

"Yeah. Why?"

"Come here. It looks like we're maybe a hundred feet above the water. I can see marine life swimming down there."

"Yikes! Sharks," Jade shrieked as she looked out the window. She went to the galley phone and called Pearl, who said she'd get back to us. A few minutes later, Pearl hurried back to our galley.

She picked up the in-cabin microphone and said, "Ladies and gentlemen, as a reminder from the captain, please make sure your seat belts are securely fastened. Also please make sure your seats are in the upright position, and tray tables are up and locked." To us, she said, "All right, ladies, start collecting all trash and make it snappy."

Then she went forward to tell the other flight attendants to do the same while we went down our own aisles. One passenger on an aisle seat worked on his laptop computer, which sat on the opened tray table.

"Sir," I said to him, "would you please put your laptop away and return the tray table to its upright and locked position?"

"Okay," he grunted in a soft voice that was almost inaudible.

On my way back though, this same passenger still continued to work on his laptop.

"Sir, please put your computer away and return your tray table to its upright and locked position."

"This work has to be finished before we land," he said.

"Sir, you are finished as of now." With that, my right hand reached out and closed his laptop. With his right hand, he grabbed my wrist.

"Hands off, lady!"

My left hand dropped the trash bag, grabbed his right thumb, and bent it backward. He yelped in surprise.

"Some good advice, Sir, I wouldn't tangle with a black belt if I were you. This laptop is mine until we land, then you may have it back. Now please put your tray table up and lock it."

"You have no right to take my laptop," he sputtered.

"Sir, we may have to make an emergency landing. I'm only looking out for your safety."

"My safety? I'll have your job for this," he complained.

"That's fine with me. If you disagree with me, you can take your complaint to my boss or, better yet, take it to the Federal Aviation Agency. If we have to make an emergency landing, you'll need to brace. If that's the case, the tray table will cut you in half. Is that what you want?"

The nervous passenger next to him asked, "Are we going to crash and die?"

"No, Ma'am. The pilots will do everything they can to avoid anything bad happening. This is just a precaution."

After I'd taken the laptop and picked up the trash bag I'd dropped, I continued to collect trash with the minicomputer tucked under my arm. Then upon my return to the galley, I related to my colleagues the talk I'd had with the owner of this small computer.

Jade had a surprised look on her face. "You know karate, Cinnamon?"

"I've never taken a karate lesson in my life. It was just a hint to make him think he wanted to deal with someone who knows karate. What he doesn't know won't hurt him."

With the trash stored for landing, the plane hiccupped. This time, I'd held on to the cabinet. A moment later, the voice we heard was that of the captain.

"Ladies and gentlemen, it looks like we will have to ditch the plane. There's an island up ahead that I hope will keep us from sinking too deep. I'm sorry this is happening."

Pearl enhanced the captain's announcement over the in-cabin microphone.

"When the message comes from the captain, you need to brace yourself against the seat in front of you. Your tray table should be in the upright and locked position. Right now, make sure your seats are upright. Place your hands on top of the seat in front of you, bend at the waist so your head is almost touching your hands. Your arms should almost be touching the tray table. Once we land, follow the directions of the flight attendants. Do not, I repeat, do not open the overhead bins. Do not collect your belongings as you will not have time. You will need to evacuate the plane as fast as possible. Remember, calmly walk as quickly as possible to the nearest exit. Someone will be there to help you. At this time, please reach under your seat and retrieve your life vests, then put them on. Do not—I repeat—do not inflate them yet."

The next thing we heard from Pearl over the in-cabin intercom was "Brace, brace, brace!"

All of a sudden, we felt a terrible thrashing jolt, and then the plane stopped dead on the water.

"Everyone, now is the time to inflate your life vests" came Pearl's command. "Flight attendants, open the doors and activate the life rafts."

Each flight attendant opened a door and inflated a life raft nearest them. We'd landed in about three or four feet of water. When I looked out toward the front of the plane, the nose appeared to be on a sandy beach. Then we started directing passengers to our respective door and raft. We had to count how many passengers boarded our rafts so as not to overfill them, about thirty people each. We'd put almost all of the passengers in the rafts when Pearl called me to the first-class section. Ms. Snob refused to let anyone other than me help her.

"Ms. Willingham, I'm not strong enough to lift and carry you to the raft all by myself. You need to let someone else help."

The captain and first officer came by. Once I'd explained the problem, the captain got down on his hands and knees. "Cinnamon, help Howard put Ms. Willingham on my back. I'll carry her out like a fireman. Howard, after you do that, check to make sure all of the passengers are out of the plane."

"Yes, Sir."

"Captain, Pearl is in the process of doing that," I said.

"Okay. Cinnamon, please help Howard find some flares or something we can use to signal with."

"Yes, Sir."

The first officer looked around, spotted some signaling devices, and picked them up. He handed them to me so his hands would be free to pick up whatever first aid kits he could find.

Once we were all on shore, we, the crew, went around checking on passengers that had minor wounds from the crash. Some of the passengers were yelling for help while others were crying. The captain was with a man who had a small white shark wrapped around his leg. I went over to him as the captain pried the shark loose.

"Let me take a look at his wound, Captain."

He looked at me and said, "Do you think you're Nurse Nightingale or something, Cinnamon?"

"Yes, sir. I've got a nursing degree" came my reply.

"Then what're you doing as a flight attendant?"

"Captain, that's a long story for some other time. Why don't you take that shark, throw it back into the water, and tell its mother to feed it fish, not humans."

I went down on my knees and started to work on the passenger's leg. Just then, pain shot through my left knee and made me cry out. "Ow, my knee!"

"Are you all right, Cinnamon?"

"I'll be fine in a moment, Captain. It's just my bad knee."

While we were patching up his leg, the passenger said, "I'd like to hear that story. What's with your knee?"

Looking up at him, he turned out to be Mr. Laptop.

"I injured it in a fall yesterday. I'll be fine."

The captain then left to help someone else.

"I'm sorry for not listening to you about my laptop. It looks like I'll miss my deadline because of this plane wreck."

My curiosity got the best of me. "How'd you get that shark to attack you?"

"The water was only about three feet deep, so I decided to walk to shore and let someone else have my place in the raft. I'd taken just a few steps when my leg began to feel this pain. It turned out to be that baby shark."

"Cinnamon..., Cinnamon where are you?" Karyn called, her voice agitated.

"Over here!" I shouted, waving my hand in the air.

"Captain Morton wants you," she said as she came over to me. "Where is he?"

"He's over by the side of this big hill," she pointed.

"Okay. Karyn, can you finish with this patch?"

"Will do," she said.

For me to stand up wasn't as comfortable with my left leg, but I managed and went in the direction Karyn had indicated.

"Captain, what happened?"

He looked at me and said, "It's Pearl. She went around to the other side of this island, and something just exploded. We aren't sure what it was yet."

"We need to keep her warm. Have someone get some blankets and a pillow from the plane."

"Okay. Just let me pull this shrapnel out of her leg."

"Don't touch it, Captain. Leave it to the professionals. If that piece of metal has cut into her femoral artery, she could bleed to death in minutes."

"Then are you going to pull it out?" he asked.

"No. I'm not qualified. It needs a doctor who has studied more about medicine than a nurse. Do you know if there's a doctor on board?"

"Pearl should know. She keeps a list of passengers just for situations like this," he said.

"Where's the list?"

"Ask Pearl."

"I can't. She's in shock from too much pain."

Just then, Jade came past us. With one look at Pearl's wound, she turned away and vomited.

"Jade," I called, "do you know where the list of passengers is that Pearl keeps?"

When Jade turned back to me, her face looked as white as a ghost. "Why do you need the passenger list, Cinnamon?"

"Do you know if there is a doctor on board? Even a paramedic would be helpful," I said.

"There is a paramedic on the list, but he's helping others."

"Jade, please go find him. Pearl needs his help now. And see if you can find another boo-boo box."

"A what?" Jade asked. "What's a boo-boo box?"

"A boo-boo box is also known as a first aid kit."

"Oh, okay. I'll be back in a jiffy," she said and turned to find the paramedic and first aid box.

While we were treating the injured, loud explosions were occurring on the other side of this island's mountain and shaking it.

"What's happening, Captain?" I asked.

"Just before the lightning strike, I received a message that the Navy is conducting a military exercise in the area. I didn't want to alarm the passengers with that announcement. I'd hoped to ditch the plane a few miles beyond the training area."

"Does that mean they're using this island for target practice?"

Once I finished with treating the injured, I made up my mind to climb this mountain and see what caused the explosions on the other side. This so-called mountain, which was about one hundred feet high, looked like climbing it would be rather easy.

Everything about the climb gave me problems, like handholds. The rocks appeared to be reliable and stable, but when I'd step on them or put my hands on them to pull myself up, some of them broke loose. I'd taken a white sheet, a flare gun, and an American flag with me. All these items were in the emergency kit that thankfully made it to shore. Near the top, an explosion hit near my right hand as I found a handhold.

"Ow!" I cried out in pain.

It sent me flying down almost to the bottom, being violently tossed head over heels and sideways. And I didn't even have any wings. My head swam with dizziness, and my whole body ached with bumps and bruises. *So much for a clean uniform. Sorry, Pearl.* My right hand was not only in pain but bleeding as well. The paramedic came over to me and bandaged it.

"No more climbing for you, young lady," he said. "Do you have any other bleeding wounds?"

"I'm not sure. My head feels like it's swimming in dizziness, and my body aches like someone had a field day punching me all over. Other than that, I'm just peachy."

"Lie there after I've finished with your hand."

"That's what I thought. You just want to hold my hand. Typical male."

This lighthearted humor made him smile. "You can't be hurt too bad if you can joke like that," said the paramedic. "Rest here for a while before you try to get up." Then he left to check on another injured passenger.

"Cinnamon, are you okay?" asked the captain, rushing up to me, followed by Jade.

"It only hurts when I laugh, Captain."

"Then don't laugh, Cinnamon," he remarked.

"Ah, she's all right, Captain. Cinnamon's tough as nails," Jade told him with a smile and turned to walk away. She then turned back to make sure.

"Just let me rest a few minutes, Captain."

Later, I ignored the paramedic's warning, got up, and went back to climbing this monster of a hill. Even though my hand throbbed,

I finally made it to the top. I'd just stood up when another explosion hit and jarred the mountain, making me fight to stay upright. After regaining my balance, I took the flare gun and fired it into the air, then waved the white piece of cloth. Next came the American flag. It'd been in my pocket, and when unfurled, it just happened to be upside down.

At that point, an explosion close by me, hit so violently that it knocked me out.

CHAPTER III

I'VE NO MEMORY of anything that happened after the explosion until I woke up sometime later. My eyes scanned the room. In a chair on the right side of the bed sat my boss reading a magazine.

"Pearl?" My voice sounded weak, and the left side of my face felt numb.

"Cinnamon," she said with tears about to overflow. "We've been worried about you." She got up a little clumsily from the chair, put crutches under her arms, and came to the bed to give me a gentle hug.

"Where am I?"

"You're in the Kona Community Hospital in Hawaii."

"I'm sorry about messing up my uniform."

"Don't worry about it, Cinnamon. After what you did, I'm sure the company will give you a brand-new uniform. The one you messed up was beyond repair."

Just then a Navy Commander walked into the room.

"There's my Cini-Mini," he said, smiling.

"Daddy?" This surprised me to tears. "Daddy, can you just hold me?"

He gave me a kiss on my right cheek and tried to get next to me to hold me, but it seemed next to impossible. Every muscle I moved produced pain.

"Calm down, Honey. Everything's going to be okay. Just relax." To Pearl, he said, "I'm Tom Shaffer, Cinnamon's father."

She replied, "Pearl Bacon, I'm Cinnamon's supervisor."

"Daddy, where's Mom?"

"She's a little under the weather and couldn't make it. I'll call and let her know how you're doing."

"You're one tough cookie, Cinnamon," Jade said as she walked into the room.

After I introduced Jade to my dad, she asked, "How're you doing, Cinnamon?"

"I'm alive and kicking. Well, maybe not kicking yet, but at least, I'm alive."

A few weeks later, the hospital let me go home. I missed a lot of work. When I walked into the Angel Airline terminal, every employee welcomed me back and congratulated me. *What's with all the congratulations?* In my mind, *just going to work does not require anything special. It's not my birthday, and I'm not married. So what's the big deal?* If that wasn't bad enough, when I went into the employee lounge, all of the flight attendants, even the ones whose names I'd forgotten, came over to congratulate and hug me, which added to my confusion. Captain Morton came over.

"Cinnamon, let me hug Angel Air's newest Angel."

"Please be gentle, Captain. I'm still a little sore."

After his gentle hug, he asked me to go with him to a table in a far corner of the lounge.

"Please have a seat, Cinnamon. Is there anything you'd like to drink? Coffee? Tea? Juice?"

"No, thank you, Captain."

He sat opposite me at the table.

"Cinnamon," he began, "next week, there's going to be a party with all the big shots, and you are invited."

"I'm sorry, Sir, but I'm not the partying kind. If you don't mind, I'd prefer to stay home and relax."

"Let me rephrase that. You are required to attend, and you need to be in a clean uniform. That's an order from the CEO himself."

"Why? What's happening?"

"It's mandatory, Cinnamon. You have to go. I'm not at liberty to say anything more."

"Don't I have a say in this matter?"

"Cinnamon, if you don't want to go for yourself, will you please go for me? I guarantee you'll be glad you did."

"Is that a money-back guarantee?"

"Yes, Ma'am," he said with a huge smile.

"Okay." I sighed.

Before he stood up, his right hand patted my left hand and said, "Good girl."

I'm still in a fog as to why everyone is being so friendly to me. *Is it because I'm back to work after spending time in a hospital? Do they believe that a hospital in Hawaii is like living in paradise? Are they jealous?*

At that moment, getting up from a chair, any chair, isn't as easy for me as it was before. Once on my feet, Pearl came over to me. She now used a cane to help her walk. Without any warning, she gave me a gentle hug, which is something I'd expect from my mother, not my boss.

"What's with the hug, Pearl?"

"It's a thank-you for what you did on that island. Now I've got some news, Cinnamon." Pearl spoke firmly. "You won't be flying for a few more days. It's just to give your injuries a little more time to heal."

"So what do you want me to do in the meantime?"

"I've also been put on the no-fly list for a while. Since I'll be on the ground, I'll have to work behind a desk, which I'm not too happy about."

"Well, at least you have something to do," I said.

"I've persuaded my boss to let you work with me," Pearl said. "Only until you can get back to flying."

"How long will that be? I'd much rather be in the air than pushing a pencil."

"If everything goes okay, maybe we can work something out after the big party?"

"What about you? Will you be stuck behind a desk permanently?"

"I've got to prove to the big shots that I'm able to walk without this cane before they'll consider letting me back up in the air. How much longer that will be only God knows."

The doorbell to my apartment rang. It didn't just ring. Whoever was at the door kept pushing the bell again and again.

"Okay, okay, keep your shirt on!" I shouted.

Opening the door, the first words out of my mouth were "Whoever you are, I don't want…" Then I realized the people standing at my door were my coworkers "…any." The last word came out in a whisper. "Oh, hi, guys. What are you doing here?"

Jade pushed her way in, followed by Karyn and Marilyn—all three in their uniforms. Jade said, "Pearl told us you don't like parties, so she sent us to make sure you get to the party in your uniform."

"But Captain Morton talked me into going."

"We're here for insurance, Cinnamon," Marilyn commented.

"At least, you guys could let me get dressed. I've just stepped out of the shower, and I'm naked under this robe."

"We'll wait," Karyn said. "Just don't take all day."

After I'd gotten dressed and put on my makeup, we arrived at the party to be greeted by Pearl, who showed us to our table.

"Let's go, ladies, right this way," Pearl commanded, grabbing my left hand and pulling me along. "You're almost late. Our table happens to be up in front of the stage."

Tonight was the first time I'd seen her without her cane, just a limp, and she could move fast when need be. At a glance, the decorations of crepe paper in the Angel Airlines colors and the Angel Air logo were everywhere. They served us a holiday meal of turkey with all the trimmings. When we'd finished our meal, we sat drinking. Some had alcohol while I had coffee. I'd never had the stomach for liquor.

A few minutes later, the CEO of Angel Air went to the microphone on the ministage to get everyone's attention.

"Ladies and gentlemen," said Mr. Stickler, "tonight is a special occasion to honor a special person. We have with us Ms. Melanie

Willingham, one of the major stockholders in the company who would like say a few words."

A friend pushed her wheelchair to the center of the stage, and she received the mic as the audience stood and applauded.

"Thank you, Mr. Chairman," said Ms. Willingham. "I recently took a trip to Hawaii and had the pleasure of meeting a young lady who claimed it was her first day as a flight attendant."

My heart started to pound as I realized she was talking about me and decided to stand up when Pearl grabbed my arm and commanded in a whisper, "Cinnamon, sit down!" She then put a finger to her lips in a motion for me to be quiet.

Ms. Willingham continued. "The trip turned into a disaster as our plane crash-landed on the edge of an island. The lady we honor tonight saved the day. I'd like to turn this microphone over to Captain Morton for the details."

He went to the stage with applause and thanked Ms. Willingham as she handed him the mic.

"Ladies and gentlemen, I'd like to continue the story that Ms. Willingham started. Because of a lightning storm, some of our instruments were damaged and would not work. Then we hit a large air pocket. Usually, we go fast enough to get through them, but not this one. I'd tried to contact the Coast Guard or Navy for assistance but, no one answered our distress call. Later, I learned that the lightning storm knocked out our communications. We could call out but not receive anything in return. Anyway, I managed to land the plane in shallow water on the beach of a small island. In the middle of this island was a mountain roughly one hundred feet high. When we were all safe on the island, our newest flight attendant said she had a nursing degree and helped a paramedic who happened to be on board…"

My heart rate ratcheted up a notch, and my nerves started to run wild as though running from a ghost.

"Our chief flight attendant, Pearl Bacon, went around the other side of this island and came back wounded. We heard loud booms that violently shook the island. Our newbie attended to Pearl's wounds, then all of a sudden, took off, and climbed up our side of the mountain. When she reached the top, a big boom hit, and she fell almost to the ground. The paramedic bandaged her bloody right hand, and when he turned away, she went back up the mountain in spite of his warning not to do so. This time, she made it to the top and stood up…"

My nerves must have been in an earthquake because they were vibrating at hyper speed, and my heartbeat sounded to me like it was at the Indianapolis 500 speedway racing for the checkered flag.

"We could see she unfolded the American flag. Then there was another loud explosion. From the ground, we couldn't tell what happened. After a while, the US Navy came and picked us up. In talking to the Navy captain, he told us that when he saw the American flag, he ordered a ceasefire. He also mentioned the island was supposed to be deserted. But one round had already been fired before the order came to stop. This young lady saved a few hundred lives at the risk of her own.

"At this time, I'd like to have Pearl Bacon come up and bring Angel Airline's newest hero, Cinnamon Shaffer, with her."

Just then, Pearl grabbed my arm and practically dragged me out of my chair as the audience stood and cheered. Once we were both on stage, the CEO had Pearl stand beside me as he placed a ribbon around my neck while Captain Morton read the citation.

"Angel Air Lines is proud to present this Medal of Valor to flight attendant Cinnamon Shaffer for going above and beyond the call of duty in saving close to three hundred fifty lives. She provided medical treatment to those in need, and she single-handedly stopped the Navy from further damage to the island they were using for target practice until we were evacuated."

When the captain finished reading, Pearl turned me to face her, with tears in her eyes, gave me a hug and whispered, "Thank you, Cinnamon, and congratulations."

Her tears ran down her face as she pulled away from the hug. It made me cry as the audience stood and cheered. The CEO, Mr. Stickler, gave me a tissue with one hand and a microphone in the other.

"Cinnamon," he said, "after you dry your eyes, would you like to say a few words?"

Shaking from the shock of this honor, I wiped my eyes once and stammered as my tears continued, "P-P-Pearl's wound was similar to wounds I've seen at the Navy rehab center. Yes, I'm a Navy brat."

The audience cheered. My tears overflowed again, and dabbing my eyes, I continued. "My training as a nurse just kicked in even though I tried to put that behind me. I'd have preferred to do something different with my life. Don't get me wrong. Nursing is a great profession, but it just wasn't for me. It helped me in this situation. When I'd meant to raise the flag upright to show we were Americans, it happened to be upside down. I'm sorry. I did not mean to offend anyone."

"No offence taken!" came a shout from the back of the room. It sounded like my father. "You were in distress."

The audience cheered as a few more tears escaped from my eyes.

"I just wanted to do the right thing…Mr. Stickler, Ms. Willingham, and everyone who made this award possible, I humbly thank you with all my heart for this great honor."

Then all the flight attendants in the room mobbed me as the contestants do for the new Miss America. They hugged me and congratulated me one after another. Then the grateful passengers did the same with some of them lavishing kisses on one or the other of my cheeks. Even Mr. Laptop was there to congratulate me. My family came last. I'd never felt so much love from a room-full of people, most of whom were strangers.

CHAPTER IV

THE NEXT DAY at work, some of the employees who were not at the party stopped to congratulate me, shake my hand, or give me a hug. Some did both. When Pearl saw me, she came over and said, "Cinnamon, I'd like to talk to you over here." She pointed to a table in a far corner of the lounge. When we sat, several flight attendants had gathered around.

"Scatter," Pearl commanded. "This conversation is between Cinnamon and me only." She waited for the crowd to dissipate.

"Did I do something wrong, Pearl?"

"Cinnamon, thank you for what you did on that island. In the hospital, the doctor told me you were right about not taking that piece of metal out of my leg like the captain wanted to do. You saved my life." There were tears behind her eyes.

"You're welcome, Pearl. My training as a nurse just kicked in."

"Why'd you give up nursing to come work here?"

I took a deep breath and exhaled. "Growing up, my dream was to help people as a nurse, but in reality, it wasn't what I'd thought it would be. Being a flight attendant is a lot less stressful and more fun. Don't get me wrong, I'm willing to help with my medical knowledge when the need arises."

"That's good to know. By the way, Cinnamon, where's your medal?"

"Medal? Oh that. It's in my apartment. Why?"

"You are required to wear it on your uniform every time you're on duty. No exceptions."

"But, Pearl, I'm no hero like the company says. To me, it's just a medal."

"Cinnamon, you were given that medal for a reason. You saved hundreds of lives. That means the company wants everyone to know that we consider you a hero. I'm only going to say this once. You go get that medal right now and put it on your uniform, or you're fired. Do I make myself clear?"

"But, Pearl…"

"No buts, Cinnamon. That's what ashtrays are for," Pearl said exasperated. "Look, Cinnamon, I can understand your reluctance to wear it. You don't feel like you've done anything special but tell that to the people whose lives you saved. What would've happened if you hadn't stopped the navy from firing on that hillside?"

Pearl paused to let her words sink in.

"When you signed up to come work for Angel Air, part of your training included abiding by company policy. If you disagree with it, then you need to go through proper channels to change what you don't like. Then your ideas may or may not make a difference. That'll be up to the top brass to decide, not you."

"I'm not happy with what you just told me, Pearl," I said, pouting.

"Maybe, just maybe the big shots might listen to you since you received that medal. I can't say they will for sure, but you may have a better chance of making a change than any of the rest of us. Just don't get your hopes up." Pearl patted my hand with a smile on her face. In my mind, she might be my boss, but, she seems to be fair. This turned my pout into a smile.

CHAPTER V

This time, we would be on a Boeing 767 headed for San Antonio. It's not quite as luxurious as the Dreamliner, but it's comfortable and holds just under three hundred passengers and crew, which included Karyn and Marilyn. Also with us was a new flight attendant. She's a Native American and very attractive. I'm told she took my place during my stay in the hospital. Jade introduced us.

"Where are you from, Cheyenne?" I asked.

"Hannawa Falls, New York," she responded.

"Never heard of it."

"It's a small town about five miles south of Potsdam. My dad moved us there to get away from city life. It's very peaceful there."

"So what brings you to the big city?"

"Boredom," Cheyenne answered. "There's not much to do in Hannawa. The only jobs available are the ones owned by the local Mom-N-Pop stores, and most of the time, they aren't hiring."

"Being a flight attendant can be anything but boring," Jade told her. "Just ask Cinnamon if you don't believe me. She spent more time in the hospital than on the job," she said with a playful chuckle.

"You don't say," Cheyenne mused. "I heard you were in the hospital, but it never occurred to me you're the one whose place I'd taken."

"Unfortunately, Jade's right. On my first day, I fell into a slush puddle and scraped my knee. The next day, our plane crashed, and the navy almost blew me up."

"Our navy?" Cheyenne asked. "You mean they were aiming at you, Cinnamon?"

"No. They were using that island for target practice, not realizing we crashed on the other side."

"Cinnamon got the navy to stop firing on that island, and we were rescued because of her actions," Jade interjected.

"Now it makes sense to me why people are calling you a hero. Is that what that ribbon on your uniform is for?" Cheyenne asked.

"Yes, unfortunately. In my eyes, I'm not a hero."

Pearl came over to our gathering with another flight attendant. This one I didn't know.

"Ladies, this is Jaylene Thomas. She'll take my place for the flight to San Antonio. Please show her the same respect as you do for me."

With the introductions made, Pearl left, and Jaylene made this statement. "Ladies, I'm here to take Pearl's place temporally. I do hope we can work together for the good of the company. If any of you have questions for me, I'll be happy to answer them, and by the same token, if you see me doing something different from what you're used to, please let me know."

We'd just finished serving refreshments and were cleaning up when a passenger came back seeking assistance.

"Excuse me. Could one of you ladies please help? I think my wife's about to have a baby. She's not due for another month or two."

"Which seat is she in? Marilyn asked.

"Sixty-three D."

"Sir, can your wife walk? We have a bed in the back she can use," Jade told him.

"I'm not sure," he responded.

"Jade," I commanded, "get the bed ready. Marilyn, call Jaylene to come back here and have her find out if we have a doctor or paramedic on board. Cheyenne, come with me. By the way, what's your name, Sir?"

"Billings, Hank Billings."

"Mr. Billings, please take us to your wife, and what's her name?"

"Flo."

We got Flo onto the bed, and I asked, "Flo, when is your due date?"

"I'm not due for another five weeks," she responded with worry.

"Did your doctor agree with this trip?" Cheyenne asked her.

"Yes. This is my first baby. I don't want to have it on the plane."

"You may not have a choice," Marilyn told her as Jaylene arrived.

"What's going on, Cinnamon?" she asked.

"Mrs. Billings may be going into premature labor," Cheyenne said.

"Have any of you ladies ever delivered a baby before?" Jaylene asked after she'd asked the passengers if a medical professional was on board.

"No, but Cinnamon has a nursing degree," Karyn mentioned.

"Thanks a lot, Karyn," I said and threw her a pretend dirty look.

"You're welcome, Cinnamon." She giggled.

"Okay, Cinnamon, you're it," Jaylene said. "I'll inform the captain."

A few minutes later, the captain came. "How long before she delivers?" he asked.

"I'd estimate maybe fifteen minutes. Give or take," I said to the captain.

"We'll start our descent in about five minutes," he said, looking at his watch.

"I'm sorry, Captain. We can't land until Mrs. Billings has her baby. You'll have to tell the passengers about this."

"Okay, I'll alert the tower and have an ambulance standing by."

The captain left, and we asked Mr. Billings to wait in his assigned seat while his wife fretted.

"Don't worry, Mrs. Billings," Marilyn said. "Cinnamon is a nurse. You're in good hands."

After Mrs. Billings delivered a healthy baby boy, I sent Marilyn to get Mr. Billings. Then Jaylene called the captain to make the announcement.

"Ladies and gentlemen, I've just been informed that Mrs. Billings delivered a healthy baby boy. He's about nineteen inches long, and she gave him the name Tex. Now we can land."

The passengers applauded at the announcement. Once we were on the ground, an ambulance and a truck with stairs chased us to the other end of the runway.

We had a layover until the next day. At our hotel we, Cheyenne, Jade, and I decided to go to the famous San Antonio River Walk. Marilyn and Jaylene opted to stay at the hotel and watch TV. We walked around for a while and found a quaint little cafe to have supper. Then we went shopping at some of the small shops along the River Walk with the hope that we could find bargains galore. It was not to be. This area was for tourists. We did pick up some items, like the T-shirt with a picture of the Alamo that Jade bought and the postcards that Cheyenne purchased of the Alamo to send home. I paid for a Western-style bolero jacket with fringe around the edge.

After the boat ride, which we all enjoyed along the River Walk, we went over to the Alamo a short distance away.

The room where Jim Bowie died seemed small to me. No one knows for sure exactly what happened to Davy Crockett. Some say he died at the Alamo, while others claim Santa Ana's Army captured, tortured, and then murdered him. What interested me is where Colonel William B. Travis, the commander in charge of the Alamo, drew the line in the sand. How did the historians know where it was drawn? Did they just guess, or did they find out for sure?

By the time we returned to the hotel, we were exhausted.

CHAPTER VI

Jade's alarm went off the next morning.

"Wake up, Sunshine," Jade said in a commanding voice. "It's five thirty."

"Already?" I asked. "We just got to bed a few minutes ago."

"Your few minutes ago happened to be seven and a half hours ago."

"Okay, I'm up." My brain told me to sleep some more and made me yawn. "Jade, what time is our flight today?"

"If memory serves me right, it's ten fifteen this morning."

"Are you kidding me?"

"Come on, Cinnamon, hero or not, go take your shower. We still have to get to work on time and don't forget your passport."

"Yes, *mien* führer," I muttered.

It was a long walk to the end of a long row of gates. When we arrived at the entrance to our plane, it was filled with many flight attendants. Jaylene introduced all of us. We were assigned to the Airbus 380, which could accommodate 853 passengers with a crew of 22. That meant two separate crews for the long flight to Paris, France. One team would start the trip, and the other would take over for the second half. Jaylene, our supervisor, would stay with our group of nine flight attendants while Francine Murphy would supervise the other nine. At the beginning of our flight, we all worked together. Once we were airborne, the other crew had the chance to relax and sleep while our group worked. About halfway into the flight, both groups switched places. Near the time for landing, both groups came together to finish the flight.

While walking through the terminal, I glanced out the windows and saw a funny-looking plane and mentioned this to Jade.

"Oh," she said, "that's a Beluga."

"A what?"

"A Beluga. It's named after that type of whale."

"Do we have a Beluga in our fleet, Jade?"

"No. It's used for cargo only. It's big enough to carry the fuselage of an Airbus three eighty like the one we just came over here on. They're only used by airlines here in Europe."

"Maybe Angel Air should purchase one," I commented.

"What would we do with a Beluga, Cinnamon?"

"Dah! We'd use it the same way they do here in Europe."

"We don't have that much cargo to move around the USA like they do over here. It'd be a waste of money."

"It was just a thought."

"They also have one that's a little bit smaller called a Guppy. Its nose is a little bit longer."

"A little bit like Pinocchio?"

"Ha ha, very funny, Cinnamon."

Once we cleared customs and immigration, we found our rooms for the rest of the day. Jade wanted to take me sightseeing. I'd have preferred to take a nap since we'd have an early morning flight back to New York but decided to go with her. On our first stop, we visited Notre-Dame Cathedral. Before we got off the bus, Jade warned me.

"Cinnamon, there are pickpockets in this area. Keep your purse close to your body and don't show anyone how much money you have."

Near the entrance, a man was passing out what looked like maps of Paris.

"Thank you," I said and started to walk away. That's when he asked for money.

"Five euros, Mademoiselle."

It turns out that he wanted to sell these maps, not give them out for free. I returned the map and followed Jade inside the cathedral.

"Jade, how much money is five euros in American money?"

"At the current exchange rate, I think it's about six dollars and some change."

Our next landmark took us past the Arc de Triomphe and then the Eiffel Tower, where we had lunch in a restaurant high above the city.

"The views are fantastic from up here," I said to Jade.

The Louvre came next where we spent about an hour in the museum. It had a lot of art objects to include the *Venus de Milo* and the famous *Mona Lisa*.

The trip to the Palace of Versailles is about ten miles southwest of Paris and sits on 2,014 acres of land. Built on what at that time was a swamp, which took 30 years to drain. Then it took another 40 years to build. Completed on May 6, 1682, it became abandoned after King Lewis XIV died in the year 1715. It features 700 rooms, 67 staircases, and can accommodate 20,000 people at one time. The hall of mirrors were lit with 20,000 candles proudly standing in the massive chandeliers. There are 40 European gardens on 19 acres. Because of currency exchange rates, it's estimated to be worth between two and three billion dollars in today's money.

"Wow! It must be nice to be rich even for a king. In my case it, would be queen," I said to Jade.

We returned to Paris in time to take the dinner cruise down the Seine, the river that runs through Paris. For me, that was the best part of the tour. We had three tour guides who translated all of the landmarks and sights of interest along the way in five different languages (English, Spanish, Italian, German, and French).

CHAPTER VII

Back home, Jade walked with me from the locker room to the doors of the terminal until she spotted her boyfriend, Willie. "See you later, Cinnamon," she said.

"Until next time" came my reply.

Outside the airport terminal, I looked around to find an airport shuttle to take me to my apartment.

"Cinnamon"—a female voice called—"Cinnamon Shaffer."

Looking around, a good friend of my parents came up to me. "Hi, Mrs. Glade, how are you?"

"Would you like to share a ride home with me, Cinnamon? Your place is just a couple of blocks from mine."

"That's very kind of you, Mrs. Glade. I'd love to. Thank you." My smile competed with the Grand Canyon.

"You look tired, Dear. Are you all right?" she asked.

"I'm fine. It's just that in addition to work, I tried to play tourist in between flights, and it's taken a lot out of me. It's good to be home again just to relax and take it easy for the next couple of days."

We continued to talk as we walked to her car.

"So what brings you to the airport, Mrs. Glade?"

"Sitting home alone with nothing to do just wasn't for me. Since my loving husband, bless his heart, passed, life has become boring for me. Then an idea came to me to contact my travel agent. We planned this wonderful trip that I'm now returning home from."

In the car on the ride home, my eyes drooped to the point that to keep them open just wasn't possible. When we arrived at my apartment building, Mrs. Glade woke me up. I started to apologize when she interrupted me.

"That's okay, Dear. You were tired. How about after you've had a chance to take a hot bath that you come over to my place to relax, and I'll make us a wonderful dinner?"

"Thank you, Mrs. Glade, but I don't want to impose on you."

"Nonsense, Dear. I'd love to. Besides, you'll be good company for me."

"Okay"—my answer came out in a yawn—"is there anything special you want me to wear for the occasion?

"You can wear jeans and a turtleneck if you want. Just come in whatever makes you feel comfortable."

"About what time would you like me to come, and do you want me to bring anything?"

"If it's all right with you, would six o'clock be okay? And no, you don't have to bring anything but yourself."

"Okay, see you at six," I said, getting out of the car and closing the door.

Home sweet home went through my mind as I entered my apartment. My hand went to the light switch, and that's when all hell broke loose. Pain slammed into to me in the form of an intruder. He punched me and threw things at me without giving me a chance to react to the situation. Then he punched me in the left eye, slapped my face with his other hand, punched me in the stomach, and gave me a left hook to the chin. If that wasn't enough, he picked all 115 pounds of me up and threw me like a rag doll across the room onto some furniture he'd overturned and broken. The pain upon landing from all this made me lose consciousness.

When my eyes opened, the pain seemed to intensify. Also, my surroundings were different! This wasn't my apartment. I'm in an open field in the middle of nowhere. There were some bushes and small trees near me, and wheatgrass covered most of the ground. Horses approached. The men upon them were something out of King Arthur's time.

"Where is this place?"

"Cover thy self, wench," commanded the lead horseman. He tapped my thigh with some long pole.

"Hey, watch it with that pointy thing," I demanded.

Looking down, my skirt had risen to midthigh. Embarrassed, I quickly pulled the hem down.

"This pointy thing you refer to is a lance. Its main use is in tournaments. It's useful in rounding up vagrants like you. Now move to the castle, wench."

He pointed me in the direction of a castle a few hundred yards from our location and made me walk in front of him to the entrance. All the way there, he kept prodding me with that lance and insisting that I cover my legs. My skirt only went down to my knees, and my explanations went in one ear and out the other.

At the castle entrance, he dismounted, grabbed my arm, and escorted me inside.

"Take your cruddy hands off me. You're hurting my arm," I commanded.

He ignored me, and we continued into the castle. He stopped in front of a table where several people were eating. The gentleman in the middle wore a crown.

"Your Majesty," the horseman said. "We caught this wench out in the field half naked. She needs to be put to death for blatantly exposing herself in public."

My head turned to him. "I'm not naked."

"Now, Sir Barkly, let's give this woman a chance to explain."

The king turned to me and asked, "Who are you? And from whence does thou come?"

"My name, Your Majesty, is Cinnamon Shaffer. I'm from a city far from here that's called the Windy City. I'm sure you've never heard of this kingdom, and I'm not naked. This is the way women dress where I'm from. Some women wear much shorter skirts. What I'm wearing is a uniform for my work."

"What type of work do you do, Cinnamon Shaffer?"

"I'm a flight attendant. I don't expect you to understand that line of work."

"What kind of work is that?" asked the king.

"My customers get served drinks and snacks in the air."

"Oh, you're a barmaid."

"No, Sir!" My voice came out louder than it should have.

"I'm not a barmaid. I'm a server of food and beverages like the people who serve you at this table. My question is, where am I, and what am I doing here?"

"This is Camelot. As for what you're doing here, you need to explain."

"My mind went blank before waking up, and your knight in shining armor here found me."

"Why is your clothing so dirty? Do you always go out like this?"

"No, Sir. I'm sorry. I'd like to remember, but at this point, I can't."

"What's with all the blood on your face, Cinnamon Shaffer? Did you fight with your mate?"

"Your Majesty, I'm not married. Again, my memory can't recall anything."

"Your Majesty, enough with this charade," said Sir Barkly. "Let's put her to death and be done with it."

"Your Majesty, are you going to listen to this fool?"

He turned to look at me as my left arm and hand went toward his face. My hand landed on his chin right where a boxer would strike for a knockout. Down he went, out cold.

"Oh. I'm sorry, Sir Barky," I apologized and bent down to tap lightly on his face in an attempt to revive him. Then more to myself, "It was an accident." In my mind, *Yeah right! Accidently on purpose.*

Sir Barkly came to, and we both got to our feet.

"Your honor…I mean, Your Majesty. The gentleman you call Sir Barky…"

He interrupted, "That's Sir *Barkly*."

"Sir Barkly insulted me by calling me a wench and inferring that I'm naked."

"She is, Your Majesty," Sir Barkly barked.

"Not by the standards of dress where I'm from. Why don't you mind your own beeswax, Barky? Sir…"

"That's Sir *Barkly*!" he said to me with a mean look. "And that's Sire to you, wench," Sir Barky interrupted and pointed to the king.

"Stop calling me wench. My name is Cinnamon," I told him.

"All right you two, that's enough," the king said. "By the laws of Camelot, anyone who has been insulted has the right to do mortal combat with the one who issued the insult, but since you're a woman, you aren't allowed to fight. Therefore, you may choose a champion to fight for you."

"Sire, if it's all right with you, my knowledge of how to fight is superior to most women back home. If I'm given a choice of weapons, I'd prefer to use a bow and arrow at one hundred paces."

"Please be aware young lady, that Sir Barkly is an expert marksman with a bow and arrow," the king warned.

"I'll take my chances, Your Majesty," I smiled.

Outside, the task was given to one guard to explain to me what we were to do. He had Sir Barky stand with his back to mine and gave us each a bow and one arrow.

"On my count, you each will walk fifty paces, turn, and shoot your arrow."

He started counting. At fifty paces, we both turned. Sir Barky said, "I'll even give you the first shot."

My arrow went high and to my right, his left. This was done on purpose since I didn't want to kill him.

"You missed!" he shouted, laughing.

"That's because I forgot to allow for the wind." My shout to him sounded louder to me. "Maybe it's because of the distance between us."

"Now it's my turn," he responded.

"Take your best shot, sonny boy," I remarked.

His arrow came right at my heart. My left hand went out to catch the arrow and stop it within an inch of hitting its mark. Everyone who witnessed this feat was stunned. Even the king couldn't believe what he'd just seen.

The young lady who sat at the table to the king's left came over to me to escort me back inside.

"My name's Charmaine, the kings' daughter. You may call me Charm."

"That's not right. You should not be called Charm. You should be called Princess Charm."

"It's not a request. It's a command," she stated.

"Yes, ma'am…Charm it is, and at the same time, I'd prefer that you only use my first name, Cinnamon."

"You've got a deal, Cinnamon." The princess turned to shake my hand.

Inside, Charm had some of the servants clean my wounds and take measurements for clothing that would be more suitable for this time and place. With my wounds cleaned and patched, the dressmaker came to give me a dress she'd already made. While I removed my uniform to try on this new dress, the princess stood in shock at my underwear.

"What kind of undergarments are those?"

"The top is called a brassiere, or bra for short, and the bottoms are called panties. That's what most women wear under everything back where I'm from."

This new dress fit perfectly. As my body still ached from the trauma I'd received that my memory would not let me recall, I asked to be taken to a bed to lie down and rest for a while. I'd have preferred to take some aspirin, but knew in the days of kings in merry old England, they had no such medicine. The princess led me to what she called my quarters and let me lie on the bed.

"I'll send someone to call you for supper."

"If I'm not able to come, I'll send that person to tell you I'd prefer to sleep."

The next morning, the knock at my door woke me up.

"Come in."

"Good morning, Cinnamon," said the princess, opening the door to come into my room.

"Morning, Your Highness," I said, and she frowned. "I'm sorry. Good morning, Charm."

"That's better. How are you feeling today, Cinnamon?"

"I'm still sore, but there is not as much pain as yesterday."

"Are you ready for breakfast?"

"Just give me a few minutes to wash my face and put my makeup on."

"Makeup?" the princess questioned. "What's that?"

"Ah, forget I said that. You wouldn't understand."

"Try me. Please explain what you mean about this makeup. What is it?"

"Charm, the easiest way to explain what makeup is, it's to paint your face."

"Paint your face? I don't understand. Why would anyone want to paint their face?"

"Women don't physically paint their face like you'd paint a wall. They apply what's called makeup to make their face look prettier. It's more like putting a type of cream on their face, then touch up their eyelashes and eyebrows with a special type of pencil, and put on lipstick. Sometimes they use powder to soften their look."

"How do you use this makeup, Cinnamon?"

"It's easy to apply. Let me show you."

"What if I don't like it? Then what?" asked Charm.

"Then you wash your face."

"Let me try some."

"First of all, I'm not sure there is any makeup in my possession."

"What about in that funny-looking bag you brought with you?" asked Charm.

"What bag are you referring to?"

Charm went over to the only chair in the room and brought over what looked like a backpack.

"That's my bag. I don't remember bringing it with me. Maybe I'll get lucky and find some makeup in there, then I'll be able to show you. Some women think they aren't pretty enough, so they use makeup."

I did find my makeup, and Charm had me apply some to her face.

"Now go look in a mirror, and you'll see the difference, Charm."

She did and couldn't get over how much it had improved her looks.

"Now all I need is my morning coffee."

"What's morning coffee? Is that in the bag also?" asked the princess.

"I'm not sure. Let me look." With the bag open, my hand searched and found a small Glad bag with some coffee grounds. "Well, what do you know? There is coffee in my bag."

"That's coffee?" the princess asked.

"Not exactly. These are coffee grounds. Now all we need is some boiling water. Once the grounds have had a chance to steep, which takes a few minutes, then the coffee is ready to drink.

"What do you mean *steep*?"

"It's the process of making ground coffee beans into a liquid to drink."

In the kitchen, servants were making breakfast. Charm called one servant who had brown skin over to help with the coffee.

"Jade?" I questioned.

"Who's Jade? Cinnamon, her name is Sukura," the princess said.

"She looks like a friend of mine. We work together."

"Sukura has been here for a long time and knows nothing but work in the kitchen. She came from Africa." Charm turned to this girl. "Sukura, please help Cinnamon make her coffee."

"Sukura, please get a small pot with about this much water." I showed her with my fingers about six inches apart. "Then put it on the stove to boil. When it boils, empty the contents of this bag of coffee grounds to the water and let it boil until the grounds sink to the bottom."

She nodded her understanding and went to work. A few minutes later, Sukura poured our coffee into mugs.

I warned Charm the coffee would be hot and to sip it slowly. She did and loved it. "Let's give some to the king," she said.

Since this is a huge castle with many rooms and hallways that look alike, finding anything without getting lost seemed next to impossible. My idea would be to hire a tour guide. I'm sure the princess would question that.

"Charm, would you please direct me to the outhouse?"

"The what? What's an outhouse?" She looked confused.

Feeling a little embarrassed about explaining it, I whispered in her ear.

"Oh, you mean the garderobes?"

"Huh? The what? I've never heard it called by that name before."

She explained how to get there. That night, my bladder told me to go. I decided to take my chances of going in the right direction. It all looked different at night than it did during the day. While trying to decide which hallway to take, a hand grabbed my arm from out of nowhere. It belonged to Sir Barky. He turned me to face him and shoved me up against the cold wall with his other hand pressing my neck in a choke hold.

"I do not appreciate being made a fool of in front of the king or anyone else. If you know what's good for you, you'll get your things and leave this kingdom tomorrow. Do you understand?"

With my nerves shaking, I tried to nod and said the first thing that came to my mind. "I've got just one question." It came out as a squeak. "Where's the outhouse?"

"The what?" he asked.

"The outhouse. Ah, the garderobes?"

This just made him angry. "Be gone by tomorrow!" he commanded. "The garderobes are that way." He pointed and stalked off.

"Thank you," I called after him. "Nice talking to you." It came out in a whisper.

My main concern right now was to find the outhouse. I'd talk to Charm tomorrow about Sir Barky. Finally, the smell told me I'd taken the right direction, and sure enough, what served as the outhouse came into my view.

The next day after breakfast, Charm went with me back to my quarters where some guards were waiting for me.

"What are you doing here?" the princess asked.

"Your Highness," one of the guards answered, "the servants who were cleaning your guests quarters found two small swords they said were mixed in with her clothing. We think she was sent here to kill your father." He handed one to Charm, who turned to me. Her smile turned to anger.

"Cinnamon, are you here to kill my father?"

"No, Charm. Like I've said before, I don't know how or why I'm here. Please believe me. As for the swords, they are part of my ninja uniform."

Does that mean I'm a Ninja in King Arthur's court? went through my mind.

"Ninja uniform? Explain before I have these guards throw you into the dungeon."

"Ninjas were basically used for spies in the early days. In more modern times, they learned how to fight. The swords the guard refers to are part of the training. I'm not here to harm your father or his government. Please believe me."

"Your swords are no match for the ones the guards have. They are way too small and flimsy."

"Don't dismiss those swords as ineffective. In the right hands, they can be deadly."

It seemed that the more I talked about my Ninja uniform and Ninja swords, the deeper trouble I was getting into.

"So you are a spy!" she shouted.

"No! Your Highness. I'm not a spy."

"Then you're an assassin?" she asked with a frown.

"No. I've done nothing wrong. Please believe me."

"Take her to the dungeon!" the princess commanded the guards.

"No. Please, Charm, I'm not a bad person. You've got to believe me," I pleaded as the guards dragged me off to the hoosegow.

My eyes opened. "What is this place?" The room was all white. "It's a funny-looking dungeon."

"Hi, sleepyhead," said Jade.

"Where am I?"

"You're in the Roseland Community Hospital. I'd say you were having a bad dream, something about a dungeon?" she asked.

"Try nightmare, Jade. Where are my parents?"

"They just went to the cafeteria to get a bite to eat and asked me to stay with you until they return."

"How long have I been here?"

"About a week," Jade said.

"My dream started with me waking up in some kind of field and a guy in a funny-looking dress who called himself Sir Barkly, I called him Sir Barky,…" Jade laughed at my mispronunciation of his name. "Anyway, he told me to cover my nakedness. The hem of my uniform had inched up my leg to about midthigh, and my hand pulled it down swiftly. He still considered me half-naked, then took me to the castle.

"When we arrived in front of King Arthur, Sir Barky insisted the king put me to death for exposing my naked legs in public. In my defense, I lashed out at this Barky guy and happened to knock him out. When he came to, the king decided we had to fight each other. He had a problem in that women were not allowed to fight. Finally, the king accepted my explanation about women who fight where I'm from. He also gave me a choice of weapons, where I chose the bow and arrow at one hundred paces. The king warned me that Barky was an expert marksman with bows and arrows.

"Outside, a guard counted fifty paces, we turned, and Sir Barky let me go first. My shot went high and over his left shoulder. I didn't want to kill him. His shot went straight for my heart, and at the last second, with my left hand, I grabbed the arrow just like Mr. Miyagi did in the *Next Karate Kid* movie. All were stunned, which angered Sir Barky, who left in a huff." I continued to tell Jade all about my dream.

"We went inside, and the king's daughter had one of her servants get a proper dress for me that went all the way to the floor. Anyway, the next day, I found some coffee grounds in my backpack. How it got into my dream, I'll never know. We went to the kitchen to make this coffee, and there you were."

"You included me in your dream, Cinnamon?" Jade asked.

"Yes, only your name was Sukura, and you were from Africa. The princess had you make the coffee per my instructions. Then one of the guards found my Ninja suit with two small swords, and after my explanation of the suit, the princess decided that I'd come to harm her father. Then she told the guard to put me in the dungeon. That's when I woke up."

"So I had to serve you?" Jade asked.

"I'm sorry, Jade. It was just a dream. Please don't get mad at me."

Her face turned into a pout. "I'll think about it, Cinnamon." Then she laughed. "I've thought about it. I'll forgive you this time. By the way, Cinnamon, I thought you said you'd never taken a karate lesson in your life."

"I've never taken a lesson, so how it got into my dream, I'll never know."

My mom then came into the room and hung over my bed with tears in her eyes.

"Hi, Sweetheart," she said with a concerned smile. "We've been so worried about you. You've been in a coma since your accident."

"Mom, please hold me."

She very gently put her arms around my shoulders.

A few minutes later, one of the nurses came in. "I'm sorry, Mrs. Shaffer, you and your friends will have to leave. Sleeping Beauty here needs her rest."

"As Arnold Schwarzenegger once said, 'I'll be back', and I'll bring your father." Mom winked. "He went to the men's room."

"Mom, Arnold didn't add 'and I'll bring your father.'"

We all laughed. She knew my meaning.

After Mom and Jade left, the nurse said to me. "We've got to move you to a different room. This room is for sick people."

"You mean I'm not sick?"

"No, Cinnamon, you're injured. There's a difference."

"And if I was sick, would you say this room is for injured people?"

"You're beginning to catch on. Right now, you're in the maternity ward. We didn't have enough rooms when you first came in. Now we do, and we need to move you to your own room."

The nurse smiled. "By the way, a local police sergeant wants to talk to you."

"Why? What'd I do?" My heart started to pound, and my nerves began to vibrate.

"He wants to ask you about your accident. His name is Fatter… Fudder…no, Pudder…Puddergast. Sergeant Puddergast. That's his name."

CHAPTER VIII

AFTER THE NURSES moved me to my new room, my parents, along with a strange man, entered.

"I'm Sergeant Puddergast, a detective with…"

"The nurse in the maternity ward told me you wanted to see me," I interrupted.

"Can you tell me in your own words what happened in your apartment, Ms. Shaffer?"

"When I entered my apartment and turned on the lights, some guy slammed into me. He punched me in the left eye and, with his other hand, slapped me very hard on the cheek. That slap belonged to a very big hand."

"Can you tell me how big?"

"Did you see that *Star Trek* movie when Captain Kirk was young? The doctor gave him an injection and later the antidote. He had a bad reaction, and his hands swelled up like huge cartoon hands."

"Please go on."

"His next punch hit me in my stomach, and then another one landed on my chin. Instead of punching me again, he picked me up and threw me like a piece of paper across the room onto some broken furniture. He was big and powerful. Because of the intense pain, when I landed, everything went black."

"Can you describe what he looked like? His height or weight, his build, any distinguishing scars or marks?"

"I'd say he had to be over six feet tall. He made me think of the Incredible Hulk—only he wasn't green. If my memory serves me right, he had a stocking over his head, but all I'm sure of is that his face was distorted. It wouldn't surprise me if he'd grabbed one of my stockings and pulled it over his head. It all happened so fast."

"Do you know of anyone who might want to hurt you or maybe has a grudge against you, for any reason, Ms. Shaffer?"

"Not offhand. On my maiden trip as a flight attendant, I took a laptop computer away from a passenger who refused to put it away when I'd him asked to. After we crashed, I gave him first aid for a leg wound, and he apologized for not listening to me. No one else comes to mind."

"Do you remember this passenger's name?"

"I'm sorry, Sergeant, but the answer is no."

"Could he have been your intruder?"

"I'd be surprised if that were the case because my intruder towered over me. I'm talking about a giant. The laptop passenger stood about my height, maybe an inch or two taller."

"Okay. I'll leave my card here in case you think of anything else."

The sergeant turned to leave and then turned back. "Oh, one more thing, Ms. Shaffer. Do you have any idea what this person was searching for in your apartment?"

Shades of Lieutenant Columbo.

"No."

After the sergeant left, I'd been dying to ask my parents who found me and brought me to the hospital.

"Mom, who found me?"

"Mrs. Glade," Mom said, "she called nine-one-one and then called us."

Mrs. Glade walked in at that moment.

"Speak of the devil," my father mentioned.

"That's why my ears were burning." Mrs. Glade marveled. "How are you doing, Cinnamon?" She came over to the bed to give me a gentle hug and had flowers for me.

"I'm still sore, but I'll be okay. Mom told me you're the one who found me. Can you tell me what happened?"

"It's not like you to be late for supper and not call. When seven o'clock came, I decided to check on you. The door to your place was ajar, and the furniture looked like a tornado came through your apartment. Then I looked around and saw you lying on the floor in an unnatural shape. That's when I backed out the door and started shaking. I called nine-one-one and told the operator to send the police and the paramedics. The uniform officer who responded asked me what happened. After my explanation, your landlord appeared and wanted to go inside to inspect the damage. The police refused to let him in until the paramedics brought you out. Then they told him he could go in but not to touch anything. When your super came out, he had a furious look on his face, and he said, 'She'll pay for this, or I'll sue her. That furniture will cost me a fortune to replace.' Then he left."

"He wants me to pay for the damage?" I sat up abruptly, ignoring the pain.

"That's what he said, Cinnamon. I'm sorry."

"The nerve of that guy. It's not my fault someone attacked me and ruined my apartment. I'm the victim here!" My voice rose in anger.

"Calm down, Honey," Mom admonished.

"Anyway," Mrs. Glade continued, "the officer told me some detectives would come and ask more questions. At this point, he noticed my shaking and asked if I'd like to sit down and had one of your neighbors get a chair for me. By now, several of them came out to see what had happened."

Tears came to my eyes.

"Mrs. Glade, could you please hug me?" I asked. "You're my hero. Thank you."

The moment Mrs. Glade hugged me, she felt more like family than just a friend of my parents.

"You're welcome, Cinnamon," she said.

"Honey," my father said, "let me investigate this matter. When all is said and done, your landlord will be the one who will pay, not you."

A few hours later, Pearl and Jade came to see me, both with flowers, and Pearl asked how I was doing.

"I'll be okay," I responded.

Pearl gave me the news from work.

"I've been kicked upstairs," she said. "Someone else will have to take my place as your supervisor."

"Who might that be?"

"Marilyn got a promotion to supervisor," Jade said. "But we don't know if she'll be over us or someone else. In the meantime, hurry up and get well. We miss you, Cinnamon."

"That's ditto for me," Pearl mused.

My fellow employees' compassion made tears come out of my eyes. "Thank you."

CHAPTER IX

My left arm had been in a sling for almost three weeks when the hospital released me. My parents were insistent that I not return to my apartment alone for fear of more problems from someone wanting to hurt me or trouble with my landlord. Mrs. Glade wanted me to stay with her until this mess with the super could be worked out.

When my dad went with me to my apartment, we found a note tacked to the door that said No Trespassing. I put my key in the lock, but it wouldn't turn. My personal property was still in there, so we went down to apartment number 100, where my landlord, Mr. Dobbins, lives, and knocked on his door.

"What'd ya want?" he asked when he opened the door and saw us.

"My apartment key doesn't work."

"That's because the lock has been changed to keep you out."

"All I want, Mr. Dobbins, are my personal things. You can come with us to make sure."

"When you pay your bill for the expenses of replacing all the furniture and repairs to that apartment, then I'll let you in, not before."

Fuming, my dad told Mr. Dobbins, "My daughter only wants what belongs to her, nothing more. And by the way, since she was attacked without a chance to defend herself, we intend to sue you for her medical expenses. The safety of your tenants is your responsibility."

"She should've kept her door locked," my super said.

"Sir, I'd been out of town and had just came home when this incident happened. I made sure the door was locked before I left. Now please let me go into that apartment. I'll just get my things and be out of your hair in no time."

Funny, I should mention hair. Mr. Dobbins is bald. He makes me think of Uncle Fester on the Addams family and looks like him. The resemblance is remarkable.

Another week went by, and my sling is a thing of the past. Since my parents refused to let me live in an apartment that they weren't sure was secure, they agreed with Mrs. Glade to have me stay with her. My feeling was that I'd be imposing on her. She was lonely and said I'd be good company for her. The only reason I agreed to stay with her was because she's my hero. If it hadn't been for her, I might have died in the break-in of my old apartment.

My doctor just told me that I'm well enough to go back to work. Upon my arrival the mood is somber. Most of the flight attendants are talking about the possibility of a strike.

"I'm almost afraid to ask, Jade. What's this about a strike?"

"The union flight attendants are talking about going on strike," Jade confirmed. "Our current contract will expire in a few days. We want better benefits and pay."

"Call me dumb or naïve, but what will we do if there is a strike?"

"We'll walk the picket line until an agreement is reached. When that happens, then we vote on it. If we approve, then we go back to work. If not, we continue to strike, and the negotiators go back to the bargaining table."

"In the meantime, we don't get paid" was my observation.

"That's right. Will you join us, Cinnamon?"

"I'm not sure."

"If we do go on strike and you cross the picket line, you can consider our friendship terminated."

"Why?"

"You will be what we call a scab. You'll be consorting with the enemy or, if you prefer, management."

"I don't understand."

"Cinnamon, let me explain it this way. Do you remember studying about Benedict Arnold in school?"

"Yes, but what's he got to do with a strike?"

"What did Benedict Arnold do? He was a traitor. Now do you understand?"

"Oh, call me dumb. I've never been around any business where a strike could occur."

"Does that mean you're with us?"

"I guess. My question is, what do we do for pay if we're on strike?"

"I'm not sure at this point, Cinnamon. Some unions pay their members a portion of their wage for supporting the strike, and some do not. We'll find out at the next union meeting."

A few days later, Jade's prediction came true. We went on strike.

"Cinnamon," Jade warned me, "if you're going to walk the picket line, you need to wear some comfortable loafers. Maybe something like tennis shoes?"

While walking the picket line, I happened to see Marilyn cross and go inside.

"Jade, how come Marilyn crossed our picket line?"

"Don't you remember, Cinnamon? She became a supervisor, which means she's the enemy now."

"But…I thought we were friends."

"We were while she was one of us. That changed when she became management."

"I'm going to miss her friendship."

"Yeah, me too," Jade sighed.

"How long do you think this strike will last?"

"Who knows, it could last a few days, or it might last for several weeks or months. It depends on how far apart the union and company negotiators are and how much each side is willing to give. Just be glad it's happening now and not in the winter."

"I see your point, Jade. But this slow walking is starting to get to my legs."

"Well," Jade said, glancing at her watch, "our two hours of walking the line are almost up for today. Then we can sit and relax. If I'm right, I'd say, this is your first time picketing."

"How'd you ever guess?" My smile became very wide.

"You'd better get used to it, Cinnamon, because I'm sure we'll be walking for more than just today.

Once we finished our picket duty, Jade and I went to a small cafe off the airport grounds to have a snack and some coffee.

"It feels good just to sit down after all that walking."

"You said it, Cinnamon," Karyn said, sighing as she came over to our table. "Do you guys mind some company?"

"Feel free, Karyn," Jade said.

"Hey, have either of you heard from Cheyenne lately?"

We both answered, "No."

Jade said, "The last time she showed her face around us, she wasn't too happy. From what I heard, she had to take the least desirable routes. Each time she'd find a route, she wanted someone else with more seniority would grab it away from her. It won't surprise me if she is about to quit, if she hasn't already."

"By the way," Karyn asked, "how's that fight with your landlord going, Cinnamon?"

"We haven't gone to court yet. The lawyers are still arguing about how much we should sue for. They will hopefully decide in the next few days."

With the court date set, our attorney gave us an option. Either he could represent us or we could represent ourselves like litigants do on *Judge Judy*. He, of course, would charge us a fee if he went with us. If we went on our own, it would be less expensive. Our lawyer also explained that because of the amount of money we wanted to sue for, we'd have to go to a district court. The Judge Judy type of court was for small claims, where we could only sue for ten thousand dollars or less. We decided on district court, and so did my landlord.

Our judge went by the name of Jim Beam—no relation to the whiskey company.

"I've read your complaints," said the judge. "Mr. Dobbins, you're suing the defendant for twenty thousand dollars for damages to one of your apartments?"

"Yes, your honor," he said.

"And, Ms. Shaffer, you're countersuing for one hundred thousand dollars for hospital bills, missed wages, and pain and suffering. Is that correct?" asked the judge.

"Yes, your honor," I replied.

"I'll start with you, Mr. Dobbins. Tell me what happened," the judge said.

"On the day in question, I'd been minding my own business in my own apartment when all of a sudden, police cars with sirens and flashing lights stopped in front of my building. They ran upstairs to apartment two-oh-seven. That's the apartment the defendant had been renting from me."

"Had been?" asked the judge.

"Yes, your honor. I intend to evict her because of the major damages she's done to that apartment," he replied.

"That's a lie, Mr. Dobbins!" The judge made a face at me and put his finger to his lips motioning me to be quiet.

"Continue, Mr. Dobbins."

"Outside the apartment, the lady who is sitting next to the defendant talked to a police officer. Another police officer barred me from going into the apartment to inspect the damage until they brought the defendant out on a stretcher."

The judge turned to Mrs. Glade.

"Ma'am, would you please step up, give us your name, and explain your relationship to the defendant?" Judge Beam asked.

Mrs. Glade stepped up next to me.

"My name is Alma Glade. I'm a friend of Ms. Shaffer's parents."

"And how are you involved in this case?" the judge asked.

"Ms. Shaffer and I just happened to be at the airport at the same time. I offered her a ride back to her apartment, which isn't far from my home. Since she looked tired, I offered to cook dinner for both of us. When she was more than an hour late without calling, I figured something must be wrong and went to investigate. Upon my arrival, her apartment door happened to be open, maybe two or three inches."

"Wait a minute. Back up if you will, please. How'd you gain entry into the apartment building?" the judge inquired.

"That door wasn't locked. I just turned the doorknob and walked in."

"Mr. Dobbins," said Judge Beam, "why wasn't the door to the apartment building locked?"

"It was locked, your honor. On occasion, we've had trouble with that door. Sometimes it doesn't shut completely tight like it should," he replied.

"Ms. Shaffer, did you find the door shut tight or not when you went into the building?"

"Your honor, I'm sure it was. After punching in my code to get in, the door opened with ease as usual. It shut tight for me. By the way, your honor, awhile back, some of my coworkers came to get me for a party my employer was having, and they came right to my apartment door. It did not enter my mind at the time how they got into the building."

"Mrs. Glade," the judge asked, "did you enter Ms. Shaffer's apartment?"

"Yes, your honor."

"Do you make it a habit to just walk into someone else's apartment?" the judge asked.

"No, your honor. The door was already open, and I'd begun to nervously look around at the mess, and that's when I saw Ms. Shaffer lying on top of some broken furniture. I've seen enough detective shows on TV to know enough not to touch anything and left the apartment to wait in the hall while I called nine-one-one."

"Mr. Dobbins, according to Ms. Shaffer's complaint, you went and changed the lock on her apartment without telling her. Is that true?"

"Yes, it was to keep her from doing any more damage to that apartment."

"I did not damage that apartment, Mr. Dobbins!"

The judge banged his gavel. "Ms. Shaffer, you can respond when it's your turn. At that time, you will address your remarks to me, not the plaintiff. Do you understand?"

"But…"

"Do you understand, Ms. Shaffer?" the judge asked a little more forcefully.

"Yes, your honor."

"Continue, Mr. Dobbins."

"The defendant came to me demanding to be let her into that apartment, and she had a big guy with her who claimed to be her father, and he threatened me."

"That's a lie, Mr. Dobbins! My father just wanted to tell you that we were going to sue you. That's all." My words came out rather strong.

The judge banged his gavel again. "Ms. Shaffer, you will address your remarks to me, not the plaintive. One more outburst like that again, and I'll award this case to the plaintiff."

"But your honor, he's lying…"

"Ms. Shaffer, I'm not going to tell you again. Be quiet until it's your turn."

"Yes, sir."

"How did the defendant's father threaten you, Mr. Dobbins?" Judge Beam asked.

"Well, ah…ah, he said in a harassing way that he was going to sue me. He said it with a mean look on his face, and I felt threatened."

"Ms. Shaffer, did Mr. Dobbins eventually let you get all your personal items?"

"Yes, your honor. He went with us to make sure we did not take anything that belonged to him. He still hadn't cleaned up that mess."

"Mr. Dobbins, do you have any pictures of the apartment in question concerning your claim?"

"Yes, your honor." Mr. Dobbins fumbled around in a folder for some pictures and handed them to the bailiff to take them to the judge. After looking at them, the judge had the bailiff hand them to me.

"Ms. Shaffer, are those pictures of your apartment?"

"Yes, your honor. That's exactly how I found the apartment when I walked in. Then the intruder beat me up."

"Ms. Shaffer, do you have a habit of leaving your apartment door unlocked?" Judge Beam asked.

"No, Sir. My dad taught me as a little girl to always lock everything up. The door to my apartment is always locked when I'm out and even when I'm in."

"Then how did this intruder, as you say, get into your apartment?" The judge wanted an explanation.

"I've no idea, your honor, unless Mr. Dobbins gave him a key."

"Mr. Dobbins, did you give this intruder a key to Ms. Shaffer's apartment?"

"No, your honor. She's making that up."

"Has anyone fixed the entrance door to the building and the lock on it?"

"Most of the small repairs like the door and lock I do myself. It cuts down on cost."

"Do you own the apartment building in question, Mr. Dobbins?"

"Yes, your honor."

"Mr. Dobbins, as the owner of the building in question, it is your responsibility to keep all your tenants safe at all times when they are in your building. Since you were negligent with that outside lock, your complaint is dismissed. I suggest that in the future you hire a reputable locksmith. Judgment for the defendant in the amount of fifty thousand dollars." Judge Beam banged his gavel.

"But, your honor…"

"Cinnamon, be grateful for what the judge gave you," Mrs. Glade said.

CHAPTER X

Back on the picket line, Jade and Karyn wanted to know all about my court case.

"We won, but the judge only gave me half the amount I'd asked for. He claimed it was all I should get because the rest of it should come from the health insurance for my hospital stay. Now I've got to contact the company about the health insurance they have for employees."

"Don't do it, Cinnamon," begged Karyn. "If you cross the picket line, the company could fire you for any flimsy reason they want, and nobody on our side will lift a finger to help you."

"But..."

"There's a better way, Cinnamon," Jade explained. "You can call the health insurance company directly and not even involve our enemy. I'll look up the information after we finish our picket duty."

Jade found the insurance company info and told me to call their 800-number. The robot that answered said, "Press or say one for policy rates. Press or say two for claims. Press or say three to make changes in your policy, and so on." After all that came music that played over and over interspersed with commercials for all my insurance needs. I'd been on the line for about fifteen minutes. It seemed like an eternity when finally someone answered. I told the agent who answered my name and that I'm a flight attendant for Angel Airlines.

"I'd like to file a claim for my hospital stay," I said.

The agent took down all my information and agreed to file the claim. She explained it would be reviewed and that I'd be notified when they made their decision.

Karyn had been on her phone conversing with someone else while I'd been talking to the insurance company. She hung up with a happy tone in her voice.

"Guess what, guys? The union and company have reached a tentative agreement. We vote on it tomorrow at the union hall."

"What do we get?" Jade asked.

"We'll find out when we go to vote. That's all I've been told."

Suffice it to say we ratified the new contract and went back to work.

"I'm glad to be working again, Jade," I smiled happily. "The amount the union paid us to walk the picket line wasn't enough to shake a stick at."

"I'm with you, Cinnamon," Jade replied. "But at least, it helped in some small way with the bills."

"Hey, guys," Karyn greeted us. "I'm going on the Miami run. I'll get to see the Dolphins."

"Why go to Miami to see the dolphins?" I questioned. "You could go to any sea adventure park or the ocean to look at the dolphins."

"Cinnamon, sometimes I think you're from another planet. I'm talking about the football team, not some fish. They're from my hometown."

"So you're saying that at other times you think I'm from planet Earth?"

"I'm sorry, Cinnamon. That was stupid of me to say. Please forgive me."

"Well, since we're still friends, I'll forgive you. It's just that I'm not a sports fan."

"Okay, now that we've got that settled, Cinnamon and I are headed for Quebec via Ottawa," Jade interjected. "Got your passport, Cinnamon?" Jade asked.

"It's in my pocket."

Karyn looked at her watch. "I've got to go, guys. My flight leaves in about thirty-five minutes."

"We'd better go also, Cinnamon. I've heard a rumor that we're getting a new supervisor for this trip."

"Any idea what her name is?"

"If I'm not mistaken, her name is Felicity Lamoure. She speaks French. It'd be a good idea to get to know her before we start our flight."

"Is she someone new? I've never heard of her."

"Pearl said she came from another airline. Which one, she did not say, but she said this Felicity Lamoure has about nineteen years of service."

By the time we got to our plane, Felicity was already on board. She had strawberry-blond hair to her shoulders, hazel eyes, and a dimple at the end of her nose. We introduced ourselves.

"I'm looking for one more flight attendant to arrive shortly," she told us.

Just then, a gentleman appeared.

"I'm looking for Felicity Lamoure," he said, smiling.

"You're looking at her," Felicity said.

"My name's Josh Lamberg, the new flight attendant."

Felicity introduced us, and then we went to our respective galleys to check on the food we would be serving.

"Jade, this doesn't seem to be enough food and beverage for our flight."

"Maybe it's because this is what I call a minibus. This plane is smaller than the ones we've been on lately," she replied. "This seven thirty-seven holds a little under two hundred passengers. Anyway, we need to get back up front to greet the passengers when they come aboard."

When we were all together, Felicity explained what she wanted from us and what we could expect from her. She finished her mini-speech just before the passengers began to arrive.

Josh towered over all of us. I'd guess his height to be about six feet three inches. Felicity's height closely matched ours. Josh had black hair and blue eyes and was a handsome devil. Well, maybe *devil* isn't the right word, but…

Once we were back at home base and were about ready to go home for the day, Josh asked me if I'd like to go out with him.

"Me? I'm…I'm…" It came out as a stammer. The word *flabbergasted* came to mind after I'd shut my mouth.

Jade saw me trying to decide and said, "Cinnamon, come on, say yes. You two can double-date with Willie and me."

Jade had become a good friend and saying no to her, in my opinion, might hurt her feelings.

"Josh, would a double date be okay with you?" I smiled up at him.

"Sure."

"Okay, just let me call my roommate and tell her not to expect me for supper."

When Josh heard me say roommate, he gave me a look like he might have fun with not only me but another girl just about my same age.

"Josh, my roommate is a friend of my parents. She's about their age and is letting me stay with her until I can find a secure apartment."

All he said was "Oh."

Willie took us to the Olive Garden, which is one of my favorite restaurants. My only problem with eating here is that I overeat. When the waitress took our orders for drinks, Willie ordered a Manhattan. Josh wanted a rum and Coke, and Jade decided on a strawberry daiquiri. My order was coffee.

After the waitress left, Jade said, "Cinnamon, we're not on duty now. You can have whatever you want to drink."

"Any alcoholic drink no matter what kind it is, is not in my vocabulary, Jade. I've never touched the stuff and never will."

"A drink now and then never hurt anyone," Willie said.

"If you guys want to drink, that's up to you. I've seen what can happen to people who drink too much and want no part of it." The last part of that sentence came out a little too forceful.

"Calm down, Cinnamon," Jade responded. "No one's putting a gun to your head and telling you to drink or else."

"I'm sorry, guys. It just seems like every time someone wants to drink, they want me to drink also. It makes me feel left out."

"So you're going to be our designated driver, Cinnamon?" asked Jade.

"I hadn't thought of it that way, but yeah, I don't want you guys getting into an accident because you've had too much to drink. You're all my friends."

By the time we'd finished eating, our waitress asked if we wanted dessert. I decided to have some tiramisu. Nobody else wanted any.

"Why don't we share my tiramisu? I'll divide it into four pieces. It'll be a small piece for each, and you don't have to eat that much to enjoy it."

CHAPTER XI

THE AIRCRAFT FOR this trip would be the Dreamliner. Even though it's big, there's more room for us in the galleys. This time, we're headed to Korea. The captain told me that our route would take us toward Alaska and down the coast of Russia and China well away from the two-hundred-mile coastline.

Our shift would get to relax at the start of the flight and then work for the second half. Also we would be working with Marilyn for the first time since she became a supervisor.

Roughly one-half hour before we began our descent into Kimpo International Airport, Jade and I were working out of the forward galley. She'd gone to the back of the first-class section for one final walk-through for trash.

All of a sudden, a large arm came from behind me and went around my neck. I dropped the tray I'd been carrying and reached to pull his arm from my throat.

"You call the captain and tell him we're going to go to Fiji," the big man said as his left arm tightened around my throat.

"You're choking me. I can't breathe!" I raised my voice in the hope that someone would help me.

"Do what you're told, bitch!" he commanded.

"I need to breathe if you want me to help you."

He shoved me into the forward galley. "Get on the horn to the captain now!" he shouted.

"I'm not permitted to, Sir. Only the supervisor can contact the captain." My nerves were shaking like a 10.9 earthquake.

"Do you want another punch in the gut like in your apartment?"

"N-n-no, please don't hurt me."

"Then make that call!" he demanded.

My hands were shaking so bad that I almost dropped the phone. "C-c-captain, this is Cinnamon. I've got a man out here with a g-g-gun. H-h-he says he w-w-wants to go to Fiji."

"Cinnamon, please let me talk to this man," the captain told me.

"The c-c-captain wants t-t-to talk to you."

He grabbed the phone out of my hand. "Yeah?" he bellowed. Then he listened a few seconds. "What do you mean you don't have enough gas to go to Fiji?" Silence again. "Fourteen hours from here? How long before we get to Korea?" More silence. "Okay, here's what's going to happen. We land in Korea, get fuel, then we go to Fiji. Nobody gets on or off this plane. Understand?" He listened again. "In the meantime, I've got your girl. Anything goes wrong, she dies."

He hung up.

"Leave the lady alone." A male voice came from out of nowhere.

The bad guy turned to him. "Stay away!" he shouted. "Or I'll kill her!"

It was then he raised a gun and put it to my head. I glanced sideways and saw it briefly before I felt the point of it against my scalp. The gun reminded me of one of those computer paper printouts because it was so small. It only has the capability of one shot. Suddenly, my memory went back to the intruder in my apartment. *WAIT! This is the same guy. I'll never forget that huge hand.*

"H-h-how'd you get that g-g-gun past security?" I struggled breathlessly to ask.

"Simple. When my TSA friend asked me about it. I told him it was origami, and he turned a blind eye when it went through the x-ray machine."

"Put the gun down," Jade ordered him. She'd just come back with trash. That distraction gave me a chance to try to slam my right elbow into his ribs. This movement made him move the gun away from my head. It went off right into Jade's stomach. The force of the bullet shoved her hard, knocking her head against the edge of the shell that surrounds one of the seats in the herringbone design in first class.

Three or four American military men traveling to Korea then rushed to the terrorist and subdued him.

"J-J-Jade!" I cried, still shaking, and fell on my knees next to her, tears streaming down my face. Marilyn and Sun Hi (Sunny to most of us—she's one of the Korean flight attendants) came running to the forward galley. Marilyn looked at Jade and went quickly to the in-cabin intercom.

"Is there a doctor or paramedic on board? If so, please come to the front of the first-class section immediately." She then called the pilot.

"Captain, Jade has been shot, and thanks to some military personnel, they've subdued the shooter. We need an ambulance to take Jade to the hospital."

When Marilyn finished talking to the pilot, she came over and knelt down to see what she could do. Just then, an Army sergeant came forward.

"Ma'am, I'm a medic. I'll do what I can for this young lady, but I'm not a doctor."

"Sergeant, Cinnamon is a nurse. She's the one crying," Marilyn said.

"Ma'am," he asked me, "are you just going to cry, or are you going to help?"

I continued to cry.

"If you're just going to sit there and cry, then please move."

Marilyn gently took hold of my arm while Sunny took my other arm and lifted me to my feet.

"Come on, Cinnamon," Sunny pleaded. "You need to stay out of the way if you aren't going to help."

They strapped me into the seat that I use for takeoffs and landings. I could feel their nerves shaking like mine. Marilyn returned to the Army sergeant.

"Ma'am, do you have a first aid kit on board?"

"Sunny, please get it for the sergeant. I need to make an announcement." Marilyn went to the in-cabin intercom. "Ladies and gentlemen, the captain has turned on the seat belt sign. For those passengers who may be up and about, please return to your seat, bring your seat back up and your tray table to the upright and locked position. Because of an incident on board, the captain has alerted the tower to our emergency condition. Once we've landed, please remain in your seat until the police have cleared you to leave. There will be a bus to take you to the terminal at that point. Once the police come on board and ask you what happened, please tell them and be as brief as possible. There are a lot of people on this plane. Thank you, and please don't let this one incident keep you from flying with Angel Airlines in the future."

Marilyn went back to the Army medic to help.

"Sunny will go with the injured flight attendant. We have a couple of other flight attendants who speak Korean to assist the police in translation."

With everyone strapped in their seats for the landing, the pilots made it smooth. As soon as the wheels touched the ground, we heard sirens following the plane. The captain took us to a remote place away from where other aircraft had to land. It took forever for someone to get the door open. Then the police and paramedics rushed in. Two policemen escorted the shooter off the plane.

Next Sunny directed the paramedics to Jade. They were Korean. She interpreted as to what happened and the first aid that the sergeant had given her. Once Jade was strapped into the gurney, they took her off the plane.

I said to Marilyn, "I need to go with Jade," and I left with Sunny and the paramedics.

At the hospital, the paramedics and Sunny gave the doctors in the emergency room an update as to what happened and how long Jade had been in this condition. Then Sunny was told to take me into the waiting room and stay there. By this time, I'd managed to stop crying.

"Sunny, what am I going to do? It's my fault. If I'd reacted differently, maybe Jade wouldn't have gotten shot."

"Cinnamon, you didn't know what would happen. It's not your fault. Stop blaming yourself. Think positive. Jade's going to be all right. Korea has some excellent doctors."

"But..."

"No buts, Cinnamon. If you really want to help Jade, why don't you pray for her?" I did. After that, time just dragged. An hour went by, and we heard nothing from the doctors. At the end of the second hour, still nothing. Marilyn entered along with Chae (our name for her was Jaye, another Korean flight attendant), the captain, and two police officers. They wanted to ask us questions about the shooting. Between Jaye and Sunny, they interpreted as I didn't speak Korean. The police took Sunny and me to a secluded place to talk to us. Tears again wet my face during my explanation of what happened. I'd been told that the Korean police do know some English, but my speech at this point was almost incoherent. My mind went to Jade and I prayed she would survive.

Back in the waiting room, hour 3 had long since passed with nothing yet.

Another half hour passed before one of the doctors whom we'd seen when we first arrived came in along with another doctor. Sunny and Jaye talked to both doctors in Korean. The rest of us joined them even though we didn't understand.

Sunny was the first to explain in English. "Jade lost a lot of blood." Her expression became a frown. "However, she's been stabilized."

"Does that mean she's on the mend?" asked the captain.

"Not necessarily," Jaye said. "Remember she hit her head when she fell. The other doctor is a neurosurgeon. He expressed concern for Jade's memory. She may have amnesia."

"And it's my fault!" The tears in my eyes took their cue to run down my face again.

"Stop beating yourself up, Cinnamon," declared Marilyn. "There was nothing you could have done." Then to Jaye, she asked, "Please ask the doctor when we can see her."

"The doctor said only one of us could see her and for no more than five minutes," Sunny mentioned. "Also he said no crying around Jade."

"Please let me go," I begged.

"Cinnamon, that is not a good idea since you've been crying most of the time," the captain said.

"I'll stop if you let me go. I promise."

"Jaye, go with Cinnamon. If it looks like she is about to cry, yank her out of Jade's room," the captain commanded.

"Yes, Sir," Jaye acknowledged.

Just outside the door to Jade's room, Jaye stopped me.

"Remember, if you start to cry, I'll come in, pull out, and you won't be able to see her. Do you understand, Cinnamon?"

"Yes."

The door opened like a pocket door and Jaye stayed near the door while I went to Jade's bedside. Her eyes were closed.

"Jade"—my shaky voice almost a whisper—"if you can hear me, I'm so s-s-sorry for w-w-what's happened. Please don't get mad at me. I'll do anything you say when you get out of here. This whole mess is my fault. Please get better. I'll pray for you." Nothing else came into my mind. "I'm so sorry, Jade."

I turned to the door as Niagara Falls erupted again, and true to her word, Jaye came in and pulled me out of the room.

When we arrived at our hotel, I had a verbal disagreement with the captain concerning staying in Korea with Jade.

"The answer's no, Cinnamon."

"But, Captain, it's my fault that Jade's here in the hospital."

"Cinnamon, I've been told it wasn't your fault. It just happened," the captain explained. "Regardless of the facts, you're not permitted to stay here in Korea. If you want to come back to Korea another time, that's up to you, but right now, you're required to return home with us."

Back home, it fell to me to give Willie the bad news of what happened to Jade. He could see my puffy red eyes.

"Hi, Cinnamon." When he saw my sadness, he asked, "Are you okay?"

"Not now."

"Did Jade get stuck with something that will take her a little longer?"

"Willie, I need to talk to you. How about we go to that café across the street all of us flight attendants like."

"I wanna wait for Jade if you don't mind, Cinnamon," Willie said.

"Jade's not coming. That's what we need to talk about."

"Why, did something bad happen to her?" This put worry on his mind.

"Please, Willie, not here."

Once we were seated at a table in the cafe and had our coffee and pastry, I explained everything but not without my waterworks going into overtime.

"I'm sorry, Willie." I'd never seen such a stunned look on his face; after all, the love of his life was in a hospital thousands of miles away.

"Where's that guy? I'll kill him!" Willie's face turned to anger.

I put my hand on his arm. "He's in a Korean jail. Since this incident happened on an American airplane, the US government will have to extradite him back to this country. If it helps any, he turns out to be the one who attacked me in my apartment. So I'm just as angry as you are at him. If it hadn't been for some of our Army guys, he might have gotten away."

"I'm going to Korea," Willie declared.

"Willie, even if you apply for a passport tomorrow, it will take a few weeks to get one. By that time, Jade may be on her way home."

"But, Cinnamon, to sit here and do nothing is a no go."

"That reminds me, I need to renew my current passport."

"At least, I'll have one if she isn't home by then."

"That's why starting tomorrow, I'll try to get any route they give me changed to Korea."

On my day off, I decided to go find Marilyn to talk to her about me leaving for Korea to see Jade.

Karyn saw me and came over to talk.

"Hi, Cinnamon. What are you doing here? Aren't you supposed to have the day off?"

"I'm here to find Marilyn. Have you seen her?"

"She left about an hour ago on a flight to Vancouver."

"Is there another supervisor I can talk to?"

"Why don't you talk to Pearl? She's still here."

"Good idea, Karyn. Thanks."

Finding Pearl's office took some doing. When she'd worked in an office before, it was on the ground floor. Now her office was on the third floor. I'd never been near any executive office. I found it and knocked on the door.

"Come in," Pearl said.

I went in smiling. "Hi, Pearl."

"Cinnamon?" She got up from her desk and came around to greet me. "How are you? It's been ages since we worked together. What brings you here?"

"I'd like to talk to you for a few minutes if that's okay?"

"Sure. Have a seat." She gestured at a chair as she turned back to her desk.

"It's about Jade."

"Yes, I've heard. I'm sorry. Do you know if she'll be okay?"

"No, that's why I'm here. I want to go back to Korea to see her. Someone else is scheduled to work on that flight, and I'd like to change with her."

"I'm sorry, Cinnamon. Company policy states that the more senior people have priority. If the person you want to change with doesn't want to change, then you're out of luck."

"You once told me that maybe I could get upper management to change policy."

"Changing policy and changing shifts with another flight attendant with more seniority are as different as night and day. I'm sorry, Cinnamon. That's not going to happen."

"But…"

"I understand you want to see Jade and help her but not on company time. If you want to see her, you'll have to do it on your own time."

CHAPTER XII

I'D BEEN TRYING to get a flight attendant to change with me to get me back to Korea for a little over two months with no luck. At the same time, just in case, I applied to renew my passport so I could travel during my vacation. It still took a few more weeks before it came in the mail.

I'd rather have taken my vacation at a later date. Flight attendants with more seniority took all the good vacation times. Since my passport came at the same time as my vacation, it meant that now I could go to Korea.

Willie coordinated with me so we could go at the same time. When we arrived, we went directly to the hotel we flight attendants stayed at before. After checking in, we had a front desk employee write down the address for the hospital in Korean to show the taxi driver. On the reverse side of this small sheet of paper, we had this person put the address of the hotel.

Upon our arrival at the hospital, we went directly to the room Jade occupied. I remember Jaye writing Jade's name in English next to her name in Korean. The patient's name on the wall next to the room door had been changed.

"What's going on, Cinnamon?" Willie asked. "You led me to believe this is Jade's room."

"When we were here before, it was her room. I'm at a loss with the change. Let's go to the front desk and find out where they moved Jade to."

Wouldn't you know it? Nobody at the front desk spoke English. Stupid me. I should've known that might happen. Then an idea came to me.

"Willie, do you have a picture of Jade?"

"Yes."

He fished in his wallet and found a picture, which he showed to the desk clerk. She recognized Jade and tried to explain to us but in Korean. She shook her head no. Because of the language barrier, we weren't sure what the clerk meant.

"Maybe somebody at the American Embassy might be able to help," Willie suggested.

"Let's go. Maybe they'll have someone who can translate," I said.

We went back to the hotel to get directions to the embassy in Korean. We found an employee by the name of Jin Hee.

"I'll be glad to help," she told us.

We returned to the hospital where Jin Hee asked in Korean the front desk clerk about Jade. The clerk looked in her computer and told Jin Hee her findings.

"This clerk," said Jin Hee, "told me Jade just walked out of the hospital without authorization and left everything she owned behind. Hospital personnel notified the police, but no one's seen Jade."

"Jin Hee," I confided, "did they tell you where Jade went? Her husband is looking for her."

"Didn't anyone see her walk out?" Willie asked.

"Apparently not, and her doctor made a big stink about Jade leaving unnoticed like that."

Maybe if they thought Willie was her husband, the hospital would tell us more. So since the hospital had no idea if they were married or not, Jin Hee asked. They did give us Jade's crew kit. After looking inside, we knew it belonged to Jade. But where could she have gone?

Jin Hee took us to a place where we could have Willie's picture of Jade enlarged to put on a missing persons poster.

An hour later, we had a thousand pages that we began giving to anyone who would take one. This poster offered $1,000, which translates into ₩1,129,835 (₩ = won—Korean money).

At the end of the week, we were no closer to finding Jade than when we started. I had to return home and to work. Willie said he'd stay longer. My heart sank faster than the *Titanic* at not finding Jade. Most of my waking hours on the plane home were blurry because of my tears.

Jade, where are you?

Mrs. Glade, who was my landlord and roommate, gave me comfort and did her best to cheer me up.

"Cinnamon, we can't always have everything we want. I know you became friends with this Jade."

"She's another Angel Air flight attendant. She came to my aid when I had problems on my first day at work."

"Cinnamon, you can't let her disappearance ruin your life." She gave me a warm hug. "Life goes on even in the worst of times."

"But it still hurts. It's my fault she was shot and went to the hospital."

"You could not have known what would happen in that situation. I've got an idea. Come on, Cinnamon, let's go bowling. I'll bet I can beat the pants off you."

"Are you saying you want me to take off my pants in public, Mrs. Glade?" My face turned red with embarrassment at the thought, but this just put a smile on her face.

"No, I'm not saying that. I'm just saying I'm a better bowler than you. If you think you can beat me, then prove it. Let's go bowling and find out for sure."

"But…"

"No buts, Cinnamon. To make it interesting, let's say the winner has to win two out of three games. The loser buys dinner for the winner. The exercise will do you good, and it'll help take your mind off Jade."

An hour later at the bowling alley, the first game was a total disaster on my part. My ball went into the gutter more than in the strike zone. Mrs. Glade wouldn't let up. She kept cheering me on. She'd say something like "Come on, Cinnamon, you can do better than that" or "Okay, let's see a strike this time" or "Keep your eye on where you want the ball to go, concentrate."

It seemed to me in our second game that she would purposely make mistakes to let me win. I did but not by much. In our third game, my confidence improved, and she made me work hard to try to win. She proved to be the better bowler by winning this game.

"Cinnamon, did you work up an appetite like me? I'm hungry. Let's leave and find a restaurant."

"Mrs. Glade, you're too much. First, you want to take me bowling, and now you want to take me to a restaurant. At least, let me pay for the meal."

"That's exactly what I'm going to do. You lost, therefore you pay. That was our agreement."

"Mrs. Glade, where do you get all your energy?"

"From you, Cinnamon. It's a joy just to be with you."

CHAPTER XIII

It's been a year since Jade disappeared in Korea with no word from the American Embassy or Willie. I've put more effort into my work at Angel Air than ever before to take my mind off Jade.

During this time, Josh Lamberg has taken me out on fun dates. There have been some flights where we worked together and other flights where we seemed to be in different worlds. That's right, we were an item, and all along, I thought we were humans. One night, we decided to eat supper at a fast-food restaurant and had just sat at a table overlooking the play area when we spotted Willie in line waiting to order. Once he received his order, he went looking for a table.

I hollered, "Hey, Willie. Come join us."

He smiled and came to our table. Josh stood and shook hands with Willie while Willie hugged me.

"It's been a while. When did you get back in town?" I asked.

"Last night." He didn't look too happy.

Josh asked, "Did you manage to find Jade?"

"Unfortunately no" was his sad response.

"You mean you've been in Korea all this time and still can't find her?" My eyes became moist.

"That embassy lady, Jin Hee, told me she thinks Jade may have stumbled onto a country family with no way of getting any news. They may be helping her in her recovery. I've looked everywhere I possibly can think of and covered every lead to no avail. I just can't stay there forever." Willie looked almost like he might cry.

"Come on, Willie, eat. It'll help take your mind off Jade for a few minutes," Josh said. He turned to look at me. "You too, Cinnamon. Then we can talk about things that are more pleasant."

Once we'd finished our meal, we invited Willie to go home with us. I'd moved out of Mrs. Glade's house when I started dating Josh. She wasn't too happy about that because she said the house felt empty without me, and she did not approve of me moving in with a man before marriage. My father wasn't happy either for that same reason.

Since I'm of legal age, I'm in the right. Don't get me wrong, the love of my parents and Mrs. Glade still makes me happy but, it was my choice.

Upon entering our apartment, Willie took his shoes off.

"You don't have to take your shoes off, Willie," Josh remarked.

"I'm just used to it. In Korea, it's the custom to take your shoes off as you enter someone's home."

"Make yourself at home, Willie." My arm gestured toward the couch. "If you'd like a drink, Josh will get it for you. As for me, I'll make some coffee. You're welcome to have coffee if you prefer."

"I suppose you don't have any soju?" Willie asked.

"What's that?" Josh asked.

"It's a popular alcoholic drink in Korea."

"You won't find something like that here, Willie," I responded. "How about a soft drink?"

"Okay, what about Cheon Yeon Cider?" he asked. "Its taste is similar to our 7UP but, in my opinion, has a much better flavor."

"Sorry, fresh out. It's either my coffee or Josh's drink, whatever that is."

"Cinnamon, if that coffee is decaf, I'll have that."

"Fine, Willie. What about you, Josh?"

"You talked me into it, Cinnamon."

While we were in the living room drinking coffee, we began to reminisce about old times. Eventually, the talk turned to Jade.

"I remember my first day at work. I'd fallen in the wet slush outside the terminal and not only did my overcoat get wet, but my uniform did also. I'd banged my knee and had to change in the locker room. My pantyhose stuck to my injured knee, and at this point, everything seemed hopeless to me as my tears began to fall. Jade came over to me and offered a tissue to dry my eyes. Then she tried to cheer me up." The tears in the back of my eyes came forward, ready to spill over the dam.

"That sounds like, Jade. We met at a party where she'd been carrying a tray of drinks for several of her friends. You know, like cocktail servers do. With the other hand, she tapped me on the shoulder and said something that I didn't quite catch. I turned to ask her what she said, and my shoulder hit the tray spilling all the drinks."

We laughed at Willie's story.

"My apology was loud enough for almost everyone around us to hear. She looked like she wanted to kill me. After I helped her pick up everything, she thanked me, and you know the old saying. It was love at first sight. She didn't think so at first until I asked her to go out with me. Then she agreed to go out again. Then we dated most weekends after that. We'd been going together for almost a year when you took that trip to Korea."

"That's nice, Willie." Josh beamed.

"The sad part is that when you guys came back from Korea, I'd planned to surprise her with an engagement ring. You can see how I felt that day, Cinnamon, when you told me about Jade not coming home."

"Excuse me," I said as I got up from the couch, ran into the bedroom, and flung myself on the bed crying. The memories of Jade being shot came back to me, and it hurt. That's when I heard the front door open and Willie saying goodbye. Then Josh came into the bedroom to comfort me.

"Why the tears, Cinnamon?"

"Willie brought back that terrible day when Jade… It was my fault that Jade got shot, Josh. My fault!"

"From what I've been told about that incident, you couldn't have known what would happen. So stop beating yourself up."

"But it still hurts." Tears continued to stream down my face.

When I entered the locker room at Angel Air the next morning, Karyn greeted me and noticed my puffy eyes.

"Cinnamon, what's the matter? Have you been crying? Did Josh do something bad to you?"

"No. We ran into Willie and were talking about Jade. When he mentioned that he wanted to give her an engagement ring, it brought back the memory of Jade and what happened on that plane." My emotions made it hard to speak. "Please don't talk about it anymore. I'm afraid I'll start to cry all over again."

A few days later, Karyn met me in the lounge as I arrived at work.

"Cinnamon, are you going to Pearl's retirement party?"

"As I've mentioned before, I'm not the partying kind. I'm sorry, Karyn."

"But, Cinnamon, it's been thirty years for her. Stop and think about it. She was your first supervisor. I'm not saying you have to spend the whole evening at the party, just make an appearance."

"I'd rather not, Karyn."

"Why? Has she been mean to you?"

"Well, she refused to help me get back to Korea to find Jade."

"Are you going to hold that against her?" Karyn questioned. "Come on, Cinnamon, has she done anything to make you mad at her other than that?"

"No, but…"

"Then you owe it to her to attend even if it's for only a few minutes. Do you know what I overheard her say to one of the other supervisors? She said, 'I hope Cinnamon attends the party. She holds a special place in my heart for saving my life.'"

"You're just making that up to get me to go."

"No, she's not, Cinnamon." Marilyn joined our conversation. "That supervisor happened to be me."

"Well, do we need to wear our uniforms?"

"This is a retirement party. You do not need your uniform. It would be nice if you wore an everyday dress," Marilyn mentioned.

"Can Josh come?"

"He'd better. He's part of this company as well," Karyn said.

At Pearl's retirement party, we had German Chocolate cake with vanilla ice cream and cherry-flavored fruit punch. Well…there goes my diet. Speeches were made, and presents opened. Josh and I decided to give Pearl some money. Near the end of the party, we all lined up to say goodbye and good luck.

Then my turn came. "I've mentioned many times before about not attending parties. You were my first supervisor, but that's not the reason for me being here. Remember when I was in the hospital in Hawaii?"

"Cinnamon, how could I forget? Your medical advice saved my life, and for that, I'll be forever grateful."

"It was you, Pearl."

"Me?"

"You stayed by my bed when my dad wasn't there. It's like you kind of stood in place for my mother since she could not be there. That's why I'm here."

We hugged each other.

"We'll miss you, Pearl. Any idea what you're going to do in the days to come?"

"No, I've been too busy cleaning out my desk and saying goodbye to several friends. I want to thank you for everything, Cinnamon. You've been not only a good employee but a good friend as well."

CHAPTER XIV

On our day off, Karyn went with me to the mall. After shopping for a few hours, she spotted Willie. He'd just come out of a men's clothing store and met up with a beautiful pregnant African American woman.

"Willie," Karyn called. He turned to see us.

"Oh, hi, ladies." He then introduced us to his lady friend. "Cinnamon and Karyn, this is my wife, Laura."

"Wife?" we asked in unison as we looked at each other. It's not that we were against Willie getting married. It had been some time since we'd seen him and didn't know about Laura.

"Willie, you got married and didn't invite us?" Karyn asked.

"Shame on you, Willie," I said. "No reflection on you, Laura. The last we knew Jade was Willie's girlfriend."

"Laura, you remember me telling you about Jade?" Willie mentioned to his wife. "Karyn and Cinnamon were her coworkers."

"Does that mean you just gave up on finding Jade?" Karyn wanted to know.

"Well…my efforts to find her were futile. I couldn't wait forever. I'm not getting any younger."

"Don't say that, Willie, because it means we're all getting older," I said.

Karyn changed the subject. "Is it going to be a boy or girl?" she asked Laura.

Before Laura could answer, I remarked, "Willie, don't say we hope so!"

"Ha ha, Cinnamon, very funny," quipped Willie.

Laura smiled and said, "It's a boy."

"Have you picked out a name for your son?" Karyn questioned.

Laura responded, "Not yet. We just found out a few hours ago and haven't decided."

After we said goodbye to Willie and his new wife, we went on our way.

"Well, now we know why we haven't seen Willie for a while," Karyn mused.

The next day at work, Marilyn introduced me to Suki. She was a petite Japanese American with cute brown eyes and a beautiful smile.

"Suki will be with us for the San Francisco run," Marilyn said.

"It's nice to meet you, Cinnamon." Suki smiled and extended her hand for me to shake.

"The pleasure's mine" was my response and reciprocated with my own hand.

Karyn came over to join the party. "Where are you headed, Karyn?" Suki asked.

"I'm going to New York City," she answered.

"Want to trade places, Karyn?" Suki asked. "New York City is my hometown."

"You two know each other?" I inquired.

"We met a little while ago," Karyn answered. "Sorry, Suki, I've always wanted to see the Radio City Rockettes. Maybe next time."

According to my watch, we had to go to our plane. Karyn still had about an hour and a half before her flight left.

As we walked to our gate, Suki asked me, "Cinnamon, have you ever been to San Francisco's Chinatown?"

"I've never been to San Francisco, let alone their Chinatown."

"How about you, Marilyn?" Suki asked.

"No. Chinatown has been on my list of things to do, but I have been to San Francisco."

"If you two would like, maybe we can go to the Japanese version of Chinatown. It's a little different but still enjoyable. I'd be happy to show you around."

"Sounds like fun. What do you say, Marilyn?" I asked.

"First, we have to get there. Then we can talk about it," Marilyn quipped.

This aircraft happened to be a 737, so Marilyn took first class, and we had the aft galley.

"One thing about this type of aircraft that I'm not happy about is the small galley in the rear."

"Look at it this way, Cinnamon," said Suki. "At least, we have a job. It's better than nothing."

"You're right, but that doesn't mean I have to like the small galley."

After we made preparations for takeoff, we went forward to greet the arriving passengers. Everything went smoothly on takeoff. Once we reached our cruising altitude, the flight became a little bumpy.

"Ladies and gentlemen, this is Captain Green. I'm here with First Officer Jenkins. We are experiencing a little turbulence and hope to ride out of it soon. Until then, I'd like to ask you to refrain from any unnecessary moving about the cabin and please keep your seat belt on. On the lighter side, we hope you will enjoy your flight with us and keep Angel Airlines in your future travel plans. Thank you."

"Suki, the captain must have decided to take the city streets. This is a bumpy road."

"Yeah, he should've taken the highway," she said. "Maybe it was too crowded."

Shortly before we started our descent, Marilyn came to our galley to make sure we were okay and had put everything away. Then she returned to first class. Just as the front tires hit the runway, we heard a loud boom. That gave the pilots a hard time steering the aircraft. It wanted to slide first one way, then the other until we came to a complete stop with the nose of the aircraft off to the side of the runway. At least, the landing gear remained in its locked position, but we were facing the opposite direction from the taxiway that would lead us to the terminal. Then we heard sirens coming behind us.

"Ladies and gentlemen," Marilyn said into the in-cabin intercom, "please remain in your seats until it is deemed safe to get up. I repeat please remain in your seats."

Shortly after, a fireman came on board. He took the in-cabin intercom for this announcement. "Ladies and gentlemen, the reason we're here is that the aircraft blew a tire. We've called for buses to take you to the terminal. As soon as they get here, you can get your belongings and then deplane. Until then, please remain seated. Thank you."

Suffice it to say that my nerves, as well as I'm sure almost everyone else's on this flight, were vibrating like Mexican jumping beans, even though we were well North of the Mexican border. My heart was also running like my feet were on the ground and wanted to get away from a wind-driven raging forest fire. By the time all of our passengers had left the plane, my heart rate had calmed down. My nerves had also slowed their rate of jumping but continued to gyrate.

Once we were in our hotel room and had changed into civilian clothing, we let Suki be our tour guide.

The first thing she said was "In Japan, when anyone says someone's name, they add *san*. For example, Cinnamon San or Marilyn San. It's rude not to say san after someone's name. I need to remember that as I'm going to Japan tomorrow instead of back with you guys."

"So you're saying your name would be Suki San?" I asked.

"That's correct, Cinnamon. Please don't get mad at me if you hear me add *san* to your names. It will be good practice as I'm going to visit my grandparents in Tokyo."

"Marilyn, if Suki San isn't going back with us, who is?" I asked.

"I've already contacted a supervisor here. Suki's replacement will be a new flight attendant called Heidi. It will be her maiden flight," Marilyn said.

"Does that mean I'll have to train her?" I asked.

"No, Cinnamon. That's my job. You'll be on your own in first class."

The taxi driver left us at the curb in front of what looked to be a Japanese version of San Francisco's Chinatown. We agreed to split up and meet back here in two hours. It resembled a flea market to me but in Japanese fashion. The route I took had a few small restaurants. They were literally not much bigger than a hole in the wall with jewelry stores and Japanese fashions along with American styles made in Japan. There were also some small Japanese tables like what we'd call coffee tables. In Japan, these are used as family dining tables where everyone would sit on the floor to eat.

I'd purchased a beautiful Japanese kimono as well as a beautiful jewelry box with inlaid mother of pearl on the corners. Near the time I'd decided to head back to the curb, the urge to use a restroom became too great to wait until we returned to the hotel.

The signs for the restrooms left no doubt about where they were, but they were secluded away from the shopping area. I made my deposit, washed my hands, and headed toward the curb when a strong hand abruptly grabbed me from behind. The brute of a man who looked like he might be homeless pulled me toward him and began to lift my skirt.

He wanted to rape me right there. I began to scream. "Fire, fire, fire!" He had me on the ground in seconds and began to grab for my underwear. His pants were already around his ankles. In my hysterics, somehow my leg came up to my chest and kicked him hard in between his legs. Just as he screamed in pain, a female police officer told him to freeze. (*Is that chilling or what?*) As he moved, she used her Taser on him. Her partner put him in hand-cuffs and hauled him off me. Then she came over to comfort me. I was upset and crying. She helped me to my feet, gathered up my purchases, and led me to a bench with a table and sat with me until I calmed down.

"What's your name, Honey?" this officer asked me.

"Cinnamon Shaffer."

"I'm Elizabeth Bentley. You can call me Liz…Now, Cinnamon, do you have any identification on you?"

"Yes, it's in my purse." Tears were still running down my face.

After I'd given Officer Bentley my identification, she asked, "Cinnamon, is this your current address?"

"Yes."

"What are you doing here?"

"I came here with a couple of my coworkers."

"What kind of work do you do?"

"I'm a flight attendant for Angel Airlines."

"What were you doing near the restrooms?"

"I'd finished using the facility and came out to go meet my friends when that guy attacked me."

"Cinnamon!" someone shouted. "Cinnamon, what happened?" Marilyn asked as she and Suki came closer.

"Who are you?" asked Liz.

"I'm Marilyn Benoid, Cinnamon's supervisor, and this is Suki, another Angel Airline flight attendant."

"We've been looking all over for you, Cinnamon," Suki said.

"I'm Officer Bentley. Your friend has been mugged and was nearly raped."

"Oh, my..." said Suki, covering her mouth with her hand. "I'm so sorry, Cinnamon. If I'd known something like this would happen, I'd never have brought you here."

"It's not your fault, Suki." It came out almost as a whisper between my shaking nerves.

"Come on, Cinnamon," Marilyn said, "let's get you back to the hotel."

"She can't go just yet," Officer Bentley intoned. "We need to take her to the station and get a statement from her. Then she'll be free to go."

At the station, I gave my statement about the attack on me and then asked how the police were able to respond so fast.

Officer Bentley replied, "We've had trouble in that part of town before. So we'd been assigned to patrol the area a little more frequently near where you were, Cinnamon. That's why we were able to arrive so quickly."

On the way to the hotel, Marilyn asked the taxi driver to stop at a drugstore to get some medicine to help me relax. She got out of the cab and went inside while Suki put her arm around my shoulders and tried to comfort me.

Once we were in our hotel room, both of them tried to help me with a warm, relaxing bath and then helped me get into bed. The next thing I knew, we were waking up to a new day.

CHAPTER XV

AFTER BREAKFAST, WE went to the Angel Airlines lounge. Marilyn went over to a telephone to make some calls while Suki saw a friend from her flight training. I grabbed a cup of coffee and decided to sit at a table by myself and wait for our flight.

Suki came back to me to tell me she had to go. Her flight would be leaving in about an hour. After a goodbye hug, she said, "I hope everything works out for the better for you, Cinnamon."

"Thank you, Suki. Have a safe and wonderful trip to Japan."

"Thank you, Cinnamon."

Just then, Marilyn came over.

"Cinnamon, I've arranged for another flight attendant to take your place. She'll be here shortly."

"Take my place? But why, I'm able to work."

"Cinnamon, it's my opinion that you are in no shape to do your job. You'll ride back home as a passenger, not as a flight attendant."

"But, Marilyn, please let me work."

"I understand what you're saying, but it's my call as a supervisor. You were in a traumatic situation last night. It takes time for something like that to heal. I'm sure that if Pearl were here instead of me, she'd say the same thing."

"But, Marilyn…"

"No buts, Cinnamon. If you disagree with me, take it up with upper management."

I kept thinking of almost getting raped all the way back to our base of operations, and it kept my nerves vibrating on a small scale compared to the incident itself. Maybe Marilyn was right.

I'd been looking forward to Josh putting his comforting arms around me for protection. The moment my key unlocked the door and it opened, my eyes saw a huge monster. The next thing I knew, paramedics were attending to me on the sofa.

"Wh-wh-what happened?"

"You collapsed." Josh pointed out, still in a Halloween costume minus the headpiece.

"Do you remember what happened, Cinnamon?" asked the paramedic. He'd gotten my name from Josh before I regained consciousness and sat up.

"When I opened the door and saw a monster, my thought was that another intruder wanted to harm me and everything went black."

After the paramedics left, Josh said, "Cinnamon, what you saw was me in my Halloween costume. I'd just put it on when you came in." He had a smile on his face. "Do you like it?"

"That's not funny, Josh. You need to leave. Get out, and don't ever come back. I don't ever want to see you again!"

"What?" His face showed surprise. "What do you mean you don't ever want to see me again?"

"Josh, I was mugged and almost raped in San Francisco and came home to find you dressed in a frightening costume without you giving me advanced notice."

"But, Cinnamon…"

"No buts, Josh. Just get out of my sight!" My voice rose with every word.

"Fine," he said, disgusted, "I'll be back later after you've calmed down." He grabbed his jacket and left.

My eyes created twin rivers that flew down my face. I'd been molested and came home to what appeared to me to be another home invasion. I had to get out of here. After I packed a bag and changed into civilian clothing, I called Mrs. Glade and asked her if it would be okay for me to stay with her for a while.

It took some time for me to maneuver through traffic to arrive at her home. Somehow without thinking, I managed to go during rush-hour traffic.

She must have sensed my hurt feelings because she rushed out her door to meet me. Her warm hug made me feel comfortable.

"Whatever's wrong, Cinnamon, we'll work it out," she said as she led me inside and had me sit next to her on the sofa.

"Thank you, Mrs. Glade. I'm grateful for your help. If my parents didn't live so far away, I'd have called them."

"Now tell me, what's your problem?"

"My boss assigned me to go to San Francisco with her and another flight attendant by the name of Suki. She's a Japanese American, and she wanted to go to Tokyo to visit her grandparents. She asked Marilyn and me if we wanted to visit the Japanese version of San Francisco's Chinatown. We agreed, and once we were at the entrance, we decided to split up and meet back at the curb in two hours' time.

"At about the two-hour mark, I decided to use the public restroom. I'd just emerged from the ladies' room when a big brute of a guy grabbed me and tried to molest me."

"Oh no!" exclaimed Mrs. Glade.

"He had me on the ground." I'd begun to get emotional. "I started to yell fire when some police officers just happened to come along. If it hadn't been for them...," by now my tears were in a free fall—"he would have raped me."

Mrs. Glade handed me a tissue to stem my Niagara Falls.

"You poor thing," she said as she put her arm around me.

"Then to top it all off, when I walked into my apartment with Josh, he had on a scary Halloween costume that made me think he was another bad guy who wanted to hurt me. After what I'd been through, it caused me to black out. While I was unconscious, the paramedics had been called. The whole incident made me so angry at him that I kicked him out and called you."

"Did you tell him about what happened in San Francisco, Cinnamon?"

"Yes."

"What'd he say?"

"Not much. Other than he'd be back after I calmed down."

"Did you give him a chance to tell you he was sorry for scaring you?" Mrs. Glade asked.

"No."

"Did you even leave a note for him?"

"Yes, it just said I'm done with him and not to contact me ever again."

"Cinnamon, it seems to me that at least you owe it to him to let him tell his side of the story and maybe apologize."

"Why?" My tears continued. "It's like everything bad is happening to me all at once. Why? Why me?"

Mrs. Glade hugged me even tighter and let me cry into her shoulder. When my tears began to dry up, she gently laid me down on the sofa, put my feet up, and took my shoes off. Then she covered me with a blanket and told me to sleep. It had been a long flight home. I admitted to being tired and slept knowing nothing bad would happen to me here.

I woke up to see Mrs. Glade reading the newspaper in a chair opposite the sofa. When she heard me stir, she put the paper down.

"How are you feeling, Cinnamon? she asked.

"A little better."

"How about some supper? You must be hungry."

"Thank you, Mrs. Glade. I'm sorry to put you to so much trouble. You shouldn't have to wait on me."

"Cinnamon, who else am I going to make a fuss over? I'm all by myself except when you're here. You make good company for me. In that light, I should thank you."

"Mrs. Glade, you're too kind."

She got up from her chair and came to me. "Come on, Cinnamon, supper is ready. You'll feel better after you've eaten."

Mrs. Glade was right. She made a supper of breaded veal cutlets, Duchess potatoes, and buttered broccoli with homemade rolls. Dessert consisted of spice cake and ice cream. There goes my diet. I ate everything she set in front of me and more. My stomach was so stuffed it wanted to explode. When we were cleaning up the table, I told Mrs. Glade I'd do the dishes since she went to all that trouble to fix such an excellent meal.

After I finished the dishes and before returning to the living room, Mrs. Glade asked, "Cinnamon, how about an ice cream float?"

"No, thank you. I'd love one, but my stomach says no. It's too stuffed. Maybe I'd better rename it Stuffy?"

This provoked a laugh from both of us. We adjourned to the living room to let all the food digest when a knock came at the door. We both went. Before Mrs. Glade opened the door, there was a side window to peek through.

"It's Josh. I don't want to see him. Tell him I'm sleeping, please, Mrs. Glade." I then headed for the bedroom I'd used before when my apartment had been vandalized. Then Mrs. Glade opened the door.

"Are you Mrs. Glade?" Josh asked. "I'm Josh Lamberg, Cinnamon's roommate. Her parents said she might be here. I'd like to see her."

"I'm sorry, Mr. Lamberg," Mrs. Glade answered. "Cinnamon is very stressed out and has gone to bed."

"Oh! Would you please give her a message for me?"

"If it'll hurt her in any way, the answer's no."

"It's nothing like that. Please tell her I'm sorry for all the problems I've caused her. I love her and want to marry her if she'll have me."

"I'll let her know, Mr. Lamberg. Goodbye."

Mrs. Glade shut the door and turned around to see me standing just a few feet away.

"You heard?" she asked.

"Mrs. Glade, you don't understand."

"Oh, I understand a lot better than you think. You came home with the idea that Josh would welcome you with open arms and comfort you after your ordeal in San Francisco. Instead, he scared you half to death, and you didn't like that reception."

"But..."

"Cinnamon, you can stay here tonight, but you should try to patch things up with Josh tomorrow," Mrs. Glade said lovingly. She put her arm around me and led me back to the bedroom. "Why don't you try to get some sleep, and we'll sort this out in the morning."

But of course, sleep evaded me most of the night.

"Cinnamon, are you awake?" Mrs. Glade asked. "Wake up, sleepyhead." Her tone was soft and gentle.

My eyes didn't want to open.

"Good morning, Cinnamon," Mrs. Glade said.

"Already?" came my sleepy response. *Maybe some coffee might help.*

Mrs. Glade then led me to the kitchen table, poured two cups of coffee, and brought them over to the table to sit with me.

"From the looks of you, I'd say you should call in sick so you can get some sleep. Are you all right other than sleep-deprived, Cinnamon?"

"My stomach kept me from sleep. Other than that, I think I'm okay." My yawn tried to compete with the Grand Canyon.

The next day started out to be great. Great that is, until I saw Josh in the Angel Air lounge. No matter where I went, he followed me everywhere except the ladies room. Karyn had seen me go into the restroom and also came in to use the facilities.

"Cinnamon, what happened between you and Josh?" she asked.

Just after I finished my explanation to Karyn about us, Jaylene Thomas came out from one of the stalls.

As she washed her hands, she said, "Cinnamon, you can't let a little spat keep you from doing your job. You've been assigned to go to Anchorage along with Josh."

"No, please change my assignment, Jaylene."

"I'm sorry, but the assignments are set in stone. You need to get that kind of approval at least twenty-four hours in advance. Your flight leaves in about two hours."

"But, Jaylene…"

"No buts, Cinnamon. Either you go as scheduled or turn in your uniforms."

"Can't you make an exception in Cinnamon's case, Jaylene?" asked Karyn.

"If I allow it, I'll be making changes for everyone who wanted to change. It would create a mess for all concerned, Karyn. I'm sorry," she said.

CHAPTER XVI

The trip to Anchorage made Josh happy since he would be with me on the same flight. I, on the other hand, felt miserable that we had to work together. I'd be pleasant to him for the sake of the passengers, but when we were alone in the galley, my tone changed. Jaylene noticed and again took me aside to admonish me. I was glad when we turned around and headed back to home base.

On our arrival, I went to the ladies' locker room while Jaylene went someplace different. I'd just changed out of my uniform when Jaylene found me.

"Cinnamon, Marilyn wants to see you. It's time for your yearly evaluation."

My "okay" came out as a sigh. "Where is she?"

"She's in her cubicle."

Her cubicle happened to be on the other side of the lounge from the ladies' locker room.

"You wanted to see me, Marilyn?" I asked and entered the little cubicle she occupied.

"Yes, Cinnamon," she said. "Please sit." She motioned me to a chair opposite her desk. "It's come to my attention that you are slacking off on your duties. I've seen you do better, and I'm worried that you are not doing your best. Your performance has to improve if you want to continue working here."

"You used to be friendly with me. Now it's almost like you've become my enemy."

"Cinnamon, since I've become management, I see things differently. I'm not out to hurt you, but you've got to understand that it's part of my job to make sure you do your job to the best of your ability. Whatever is causing you to go lax has got to stop. If it's your personal life, then you need to straighten it out."

I related my problem with Josh in the hope it would make a difference. It didn't.

"My advice to you is work out your differences with Josh. The sooner, the better," Marilyn said. "I've listed your evaluation as a little less than satisfactory. If you can convince me in the next day or two that you've made the changes I've mentioned, I'll upgrade this evaluation."

Mrs. Glade picked me up at the airport and took me to her home. When we arrived, Josh was there waiting for me.

"Mrs. Glade, what's he doing here?"

"He wants to talk to you, Dear."

"Well, I don't want to talk to him."

"Cinnamon, you can't let this go on forever. You're going to have to talk to him sooner or later. It may as well be now."

"But…"

"No buts, Dear. Talk to him. Listen to what he has to say. If he wants to apologize, let him."

Josh came over to the car and opened the door for me.

"Cinnamon, please listen to me. I'm not sure why you are refusing to see or talk to me, but I'm sorry for whatever the reason and want an explanation. Then if you still don't want to talk to me, I'll leave you alone."

"Okay. When I came back from San Francisco, I just wanted you to hold and comfort me. Instead, you had that horrible Halloween costume on, and that frightened me. My thought was that you were an intruder intent on hurting me like that bad guy from my first apartment. My nerves just couldn't take it anymore."

"I'd just gotten that costume and tried it on just as you opened the door. I'm sorry, Cinnamon. I didn't mean to hurt you in any way. Can you ever forgive me?"

"Why?" My questioning look stared him in the face.

"I'll promise to never do that again if you'll forgive me. At this point, my only thought is that I'm in love with you and want to marry you."

Surprise showed in my eyes. I'd forgotten that he mentioned to Mrs. Glade about wanting to marry me.

"I'll have to think about it."

"What's there to think about, Cinnamon?"

"I'll give you an answer in a couple of days. I've got a lot on my mind right now that has nothing to do with you."

A few days and several flights later without Josh, Marilyn came to me.

"Cinnamon, I've noticed that your work has improved."

"Thank you."

"I've scheduled you and Karyn tomorrow for Atlanta and Washington, D.C. I'll be with you on the first leg, and Suki will join you in Washington."

"It'll be nice to see Suki San again." I smiled. "Not to change the subject, Marilyn, but what are the chances of me going to Korea? I want to try to search for Jade again."

"That would be like looking for a needle in a haystack, Cinnamon," said Marilyn. "Do you know that Seoul alone is one of the largest cities in the world? It's possible you could go right past Jade and not even see her."

"I'd still like to try."

"Let me see what I can do, but I'll make no promises."

"Thanks, Marilyn."

"Don't thank me yet. I'll let you know if or when that request can be arranged."

"Hi, Cinnamon," Karyn said as she came over to me. Marilyn had just left.

"Hey, Karyn, have you heard? Suki will be joining us in Washington."

"Wonder how her vacation went," Karyn mused. "Guess we'll find out tomorrow. Come on, Cinnamon, I'll walk you to the curb."

We talked as we walked.

"How's it going with you and Josh?" Karyn wanted to know. "Have you forgiven him yet?"

"I'm still thinking about it and leaning toward maybe forgiving him."

"Just maybe? Come on, Cinnamon. Wake up. He's madly in love with you. You can't keep stringing him along forever."

"I know. It's just that I'm not one hundred percent sure right now."

Karyn's ride appeared as we approached the curb. Mrs. Glade hadn't yet arrived. Just then, my cell phone rang.

"Hello," I said.

"Is this Cinnamon Shaffer?" asked the female voice on the other end.

"Who wants to know?"

"This is Liz Bentley of the San Francisco police department. I'm the one who came to your aid in that mugging in the Japanese portion of Chinatown."

"Oh yes, I'm grateful you were there to help me. Thank you."

"You're welcome, Cinnamon. How are you?"

"I'm okay."

"I'm calling in reference to the summons for you to appear in court concerning your case."

"So far I've not received any summons. It may have just come in the mail today. I just got off work and haven't arrived home yet. Oh, I see my ride just arrived. Can I call you back in about an hour?"

"Call me back at this number." She gave it to me even though it appeared on my phone.

When we arrived at Mrs. Glade's home, Josh was waiting for me. "What are you doing here?"

"This just came for you from the San Francisco Court. What'd you do, Cinnamon, rob a bank?"

"Don't you remember me telling you about being mugged and almost raped? The bad guy is in jail, and they want me to testify to keep him there." Opening the letter confirmed what I just told Josh, and my hands began to shake. At the same time, my knees turned to jelly. Josh caught me and picked me up.

Mrs. Glade had put the car in the garage and came over to us.

"Let's get her into the house," she said.

Josh carried me inside and deposited me on the couch.

"What happened to Cinnamon?" Mrs. Glade asked.

"She collapsed after she read this summons," Josh answered. "Apparently, she has to go back to San Francisco to testify in a court case."

"Did you know before you opened the summons?" Mrs. Glade directed her question to me.

"The lady cop who helped me after the incident called me just before you arrived to pick me up, Mrs. Glade. I've got to call my boss and tell her."

"Are you all right, Cinnamon?" Mrs. Glade looked worried.

"I'll be fine after a minute. I've never had anything to do with testifying before in a courtroom against a bad guy."

"Cinnamon, you rest, and I'll start supper. Josh, you'll stay, won't you?" Mrs. Glade asked.

He looked at me, and I nodded.

"I'd be delighted, Mrs. Glade."

A few minutes later, my nerves calmed down, and I called Marilyn. She answered almost right away.

"Marilyn, this is Cinnamon."

"Just the person I need to talk to. I thought about calling you but decided to wait until tomorrow. I've been able to schedule you for that flight to Korea that you've been asking about."

"Bad timing, Marilyn. The bad news is that I've been summoned to go to San Francisco to testify in a court case involving me. I need to be there tomorrow."

"How long will you be there?"

"The summons says I should be available for court for at least a week."

"Okay," Marilyn sighed. "I'll make the necessary changes."

CHAPTER XVII

Given the time of day that my flight to San Francisco would have me arrive an hour late for my court appearance had me arriving at ten the night before.

I packed a regular suitcase instead of my crew kit since I knew I'd be there longer than overnight. That meant I'd have to go to baggage claim, something that normally I'd be able to avoid.

A skycap helped me retrieve my bag from the luggage carousel and earned a tip from me.

"Thank you, Ms. Angel," he said. I'd traveled in my Angel Airline uniform.

Liz told me she'd meet me in front of the Angel Airlines baggage claim at the curb, but the ladies' room called me first. It seemed to be a long walk from where I picked up my bag. By the time I'd gotten to the curb, most passengers had dispersed. One lone unkempt man walked up to me and grabbed my free arm in an iron grip.

"Ow, you're hurting me," I yelped.

"I'll kill you if you testify against my brother. I know where you'll be and how to find you." He angrily spat.

The threat frightened me because of the harsh tone of his voice, and his tight grip on my arm hurt. It made my nerves vibrate at hyperspeed.

"Let go, you're hurting me!" I yelled and noticed a tattoo on his arm.

Just then, he let go, ran inside, and disappeared. At that moment, Liz pulled up in her police cruiser.

She got out and asked, "Who was that guy you were talking to?"

"He…he threatened me," I stammered. "He…he had a tattoo on his…a…arm. It said MS Thirteen."

Liz then helped me into the car and put my bag in the back seat.

"Are you all right, Cinnamon?" she asked.

"With you around, I'm okay," I replied, rubbing my arm.

"Lock the door," she told me. "I'll be right back." She then went into the terminal looking for my would-be attacker. She came back out about five minutes later alone and got into the car.

"He disappeared," she said. "I found a skycap and asked him to check the men's room. When he came out, he told me it was empty."

My nerves were still vibrating but at a much slower speed.

"We'll continue to look for this guy tomorrow morning. In the meantime, it might be safer if you stay at my house. My husband also works for the SFPD. He's a detective. Since we both work on the force, he installed an alarm system on all the windows and doors that work with electricity and on battery. Also, he installed bulletproof windows for the safety of our three children."

"How old are your children?"

"Five, eight, and eleven. You'll adore them." She smiled.

When we entered her home, she greeted her husband warmly and introduced me to him. His name is Rick and is built like Mr. Universe. His gray eyes and warm smile made him look appealing to almost any female. As he was tall, he made me look like a shrimp in size.

While on the ride to her house, Liz asked me to give Mr. Universe a detailed description of the bad guy from the airport.

"I'll see what I can do," Rick promised.

The next morning, I took a quick shower and dressed in civilian clothing. When Liz saw me enter the kitchen, she introduced me to her three children. Jasmine, the oldest, looked a lot like her mother. Ryan had red hair like his father, and Andrea, the youngest, reminded me of a girl I'd known from first grade. Gee, that seemed to be a long time ago.

"Kids," Liz said, "this is Ms. Shaffer. She'll be staying with us for a few days. Please say hi to her."

They did, and I responded in kind.

"I'll take the kids to school today," Rick said, beaming, "since you and Cinnamon have a court date."

After the kids and Rick left, Liz asked, "Cinnamon, would you like a cup of coffee?"

"I'd love some" came my response. "Maybe it'll calm my nerves. At this point, I'm not sure that I'll be able to testify."

"Why, Cinnamon?"

"I've heard about those MS Thirteen guys—how they threaten, rape, and murder women. I-I-I'm afraid." My nerves started to vibrate.

"Cinnamon, you have to testify to put him in jail where he belongs. If you tell what happened, then maybe others will tell their stories. You can put him in jail for only eight years. If others testify, he'll stay in prison longer. You've got to be the first. Otherwise, he'll be back out on the streets hurting other women."

"You're right, Liz. I understand what you're saying, but I'm scared. What happens after I'm finished on the witness stand, and this guy comes after me?"

"We can protect you."

"I've heard that story before, and the witness ends up dead." My nerves were picking up speed, and my eyes were close to overflowing.

"That's because the witness did something stupid that they were told not to." Liz then came around to my side of the kitchen table after she picked up a tissue from somewhere in the kitchen.

"Cinnamon, I won't let that happen to you. I'll protect you with my life. Triple your money-back guarantee."

That last remark put a smile on my face.

"Thank you, Liz."

In the courtroom, Liz had me sit right behind the District Attorney in the front row. The session started with each attorney giving a brief opening statement. Then the D. A. began to call each witness. He started with me. Once I'd been sworn in, my testimony started. The D. A. asked me several questions related to my attack.

"Ms. Shaffer, is the person who attacked you in this courtroom?" asked the D. A.

"Yes," I replied.

"Would you please point to that person?" he asked.

I pointed to the defendant. "That's him at the defense table."

When the defense attorney cross-examined me, he tried to get me to change my story. He fired questions so fast that my mind became confused. Liz told me before we went to court that the defense attorney might try to trick me, and boy, did he ever. This had me in tears like Niagara Falls. The defense attorney finally gave up. Then the judge told me to step down, and I returned to my seat. The D. A. next called Liz. After her testimony, Liz took me outside to try to calm me down. She had me sit on a bench and went to get a glass of water for me.

"You're dead meat, Shaffer," spat that voice who warned me not to testify.

"You harm, Cinnamon, in any way," said Liz as she came up behind us, "and I'll find a big enough hole to bury you so deep you'll think you're in China."

"Why, Officer, are you threatening me?" this bum asked.

"No! That's a promise from me to you," she told him.

With that, he left.

"What? No money-back guarantee?" I asked with a smile.

From that point on, Liz stuck to me like conjoined twins. She wouldn't let me out of her sight for any reason until we arrived at her home and went inside. She had me lay down on her sofa and began to tell me her life story about how she became a police officer and how she met her husband. Then she asked me about my life and what made me decide to become a flight attendant. All this talk made me feel better. We spent most of the rest of the day talking about our hopes and dreams.

"I'd like to go to Disneyland with my whole family," Liz mused. "But with three kids, it's hard to save that kind of money."

"My fantasy is to go back to Korea to find Jade, one of my fellow flight attendants," I said to Liz. "My boss had made arrangements for me to go just after you told me I'd have to come here to court." I then had to explain why Jade was lost in Korea.

We put those thoughts aside when her children came home from school. When it came time for supper, Liz fixed rice and chili with mixed vegetables on the side and milk for the kids. The adults had coffee. She also put out a bottle of Tabasco sauce for anyone who wanted it. I put a lot of Tabasco sauce on my chili, but Rick put even more on his. After supper, I helped Liz clean up and do the dishes. With the kids in their respective rooms, Rick told us about his day at work.

He related the call he received about a shootout with the police at a pawnshop. The uniform police shot and killed a robber who had killed two people in this store—a customer and an employee. He took a picture out of a folder and showed it to me.

"Is this the guy who threatened you, Cinnamon?"

This was a mug shot that looked like him.

"Yes, that's him." My nerves began to vibrate with excitement at knowing he would no longer be able to harm me in any way.

CHAPTER XVIII

It felt good to come home. Upon entering the apartment Josh shared with me, I found a note he'd left. It told me he'd be home the next day. *That's okay.* I'd decided to forgive him. *About marriage, that's something I'm still not sure about. I'll see what happens when he returns.*

The house phone rang. "Hello," I answered.

"Cinnamon?" Marilyn asked. "I thought you'd still be in San Francisco."

"No. My part of the trial is over with. I'm surprised they let me come home early. I'll be available for work tomorrow."

"The reason for my call is that Josh went to Boston two days ago and was supposed to come home yesterday. In the meantime, I'll put you back on the fly list."

"He left me a note saying he'd be home tomorrow."

"Cinnamon, he must have left that note the day before yesterday. What's the date on the note?"

"It says the ninth. Then his note meant yesterday?"

"That's correct. The plane he flew to Boston on developed engine trouble, and the company had to fly in another aircraft. In that case, he'd have to wait an extra day in Boston. That's when a bad snowstorm hit the area. I tried to contact my counterpart there, but the power is out. I've been unable to find out anything and wondered if he's okay. Please keep me informed if he shows up."

"You've got it, Marilyn."

After I'd hung up and unpacked, I made myself a bologna sandwich with a glass of milk to wash it down. Then I turned on the TV just in time for the ten o'clock news. Their lead story was about the massive snowstorm that blanketed the northeast part of the country. Marilyn hit the nail on the head about the bad storm. And she didn't even have a hammer. They got hit with several feet of snow. There were several accidents, and the storm knocked out their power. It made me wonder if cell phone service had also been affected. I tried Josh's cell number, but no answer—no nothing. Maybe I'd misdialed and tried again. Still nothing. After the news, there wasn't anything else to do but go to bed. Maybe the power would be restored in the morning. To my surprise, I'd fallen asleep almost instantly.

"Hey, Josh," I said upon opening the door to our apartment. "What happened to you?"

His face was all bloody as he entered the room and collapsed. He came directly from an airplane crash instead of the hospital. Immediately I placed a call to 911, and they responded quickly. In the hospital, the doctor came and told me Josh died.

"No!" I cried. "No, no, this isn't supposed to happen."

That's when I found myself sitting up in bed crying. *Oh, thank Heaven.* It was only a dream. Looking at the clock on the nightstand told me it was almost time to get up. *What a nightmare!*

"Welcome back, Cinnamon," Karyn said on my arrival in the Angel Airlines lounge and gave me a hug. "How'd your court case go?"

"I'd rather not talk about it right now. Maybe in a few more days. I'm more concerned about Josh because he was supposed to be back two days ago according to Marilyn."

"Did you try to call him?"

"Yes. Twice last night, before I went to bed and again early this morning. The power is still down in Boston. I'm just glad my nightmare about Josh wasn't real."

"What happened in your nightmare?"

"Josh came home straight from a plane crash with a bloody face. I'd gotten him to the hospital where the doctor told me he died. That's when I woke up."

"Whoa. What a dream! Let's hope that dream doesn't turn into reality. Do you think you can work okay, Cinnamon?"

"That's what I'm counting on. As long as I'm too busy to think about that dream, I'll be okay."

"That's good to hear," Marilyn said as she approached. "Cinnamon, you're on the Albuquerque run and straight back here."

"Any news about Josh yet, Marilyn?" I asked.

"Not yet. Maybe there'll be something by the time you return."

Twenty-four hours later, I heard that Josh's plane had returned and searched the entire lounge. He had not yet shown his face.

"Where is that big bruit?" I said in a loud voice to no one in particular. I'd been looking near the restrooms and had my back to them.

"That big bruit is right behind you," Josh mocked as I turned to face him. He just stood there, and then I punched him in the stomach.

He halfway doubled over and said, "Call nine-one-one."

"Do you need to go to the emergency room?"

"Yes," he said.

"Why? I didn't hit you that hard."

He straightened up and began to laugh. "Just kidding," he said.

"What? Just kidding?" My voice was angry. "Are you out of your mind? It's not funny, Josh."

"Don't take it so seriously, Cinnamon."

"Where have you been? I've been worried about you. Why didn't you call?"

"Communications were down along with the power. So no one could call or get any type of message out. We couldn't even use the internet."

"You're just using that as an excuse."

"At least, it's a viable excuse," Josh said.

"Let me ask you something, Josh. Are you thrilled being a flight attendant?"

"No. I just took this job to get my foot in the door. I want to be a pilot."

"Why couldn't you just apply for one of the pilot vacancies? You do know we have several positions available."

"Yes, I know, and took their test. The test they gave me seemed easy enough, but they told me I flunked. When I joined the Air Force, the test was very hard for me. It took several tries to make the grade. Studying just doesn't come easy for me. Flying is my joy in life. I figured that by becoming a flight attendant, it would give me the experience of more than just being a pilot and would give me time to study in between flights. So far, it hasn't worked out. On the other hand, I met the girl of my dreams here."

"And just who is this girl?" I demanded to know.

"Her name is Cinnamon Shaffer," he said.

"Very funny, Josh."

"No. I'm serious, Cinnamon. You're the one I want to marry."

"I've forgiven you for that nasty Halloween costume, but I'm not yet ready to make a marriage commitment.

"Why?" he asked.

"Tell you what I'll do. If you're serious about becoming a pilot, I'll help you study so you can pass your pilot's test, on two conditions. One, I'll think about your marriage proposal after you pass, repeat, think about it. And two, you have to help me raise money for my friend Liz Bentley in San Francisco."

"Why do you have two conditions to my one, and who is Liz Bentley?"

"I'm the girl, and I'm the one making the deal. Liz Bentley is the police officer who helped me when that bad guy attacked me in San Francisco."

"And just what did you have in mind to help this friend?" Josh asked.

"She wants to take her whole family to Disneyland, but with three children, she's having a hard time saving enough money for such a trip."

"Cinnamon, you're...for the lack of a better word, a skillful negotiator."

"So what's it to be, Josh?"

"Agreed," he said as he gave me a bear hug. "Thank you, Cinnamon. You're an Angel."

"Aren't all flight attendants for Angel Airlines Angels?" I smiled and returned his hug, although mine wasn't as strong.

The next day at work, I asked Marilyn about getting me that route to Korea.

"By the way, Marilyn, I'd appreciate it if it were not on that Dreamliner."

In the meantime, she booked me on the Los Angeles, San Diego, and Houston run. This would be on one of our new 737 MAX 8s. We boarded this aircraft a little early to get a feel for our new surroundings. Just as we gathered to start boarding passengers, the captain made an announcement over the in-cabin intercom that we were all to go straight to the employee lounge, no questions asked. Angel Airlines had purchased ten of these new planes. The employees scheduled to go on these planes had gathered to hear an announcement from the CEO, Mr. Stickler.

"Ladies and gentlemen," he said, "you may have heard that a couple of seven thirty seven max eight aircraft have crashed, and most other countries have grounded them. I've just received an announcement from the president of the United States. He has grounded our entire fleet of new seven thirty seven max eights for the safety of our passengers. Until we can make other aircraft available to replace our new planes, you will all be sent home with pay. Are there any questions?"

With this unexpected time off, I placed a call to Disneyland for the cost of a five-day, four-night stay for two adults and three children. My next call went to Angel Air for airfare for five passengers from San Francisco to Los Angeles round trip.

Someone called my name as we dispersed at the curb. It was Ms. Willingham.

"Cinnamon, it's been a while since we've flown together. How are you?"

"Ms. Willingham, I'm fine. Thank you. How about you?"

"Couldn't be better, my dear. Well…maybe I could if it weren't for this wheelchair."

"What brings you here, Ms. Willingham?"

"I'm on my way to Europe. I'm dying to travel on one of our new airplanes."

"Are you referring to one of those new seven thirty seven max eights?"

"Yes. Have you flown on one yet, Cinnamon?"

"No. Today was supposed to be my first time. We've just been told that all our new planes are temporarily grounded. Have you heard about the two accidents involving those types of aircraft?"

"Yes," she responded. "If that's the case, how'll I get to Europe?"

"Right now, even our CEO isn't sure how we'll be able to tend to our passengers' needs. He's scrambling to find enough of our older aircraft to be put back into service. Some have already been put in mothballs or are in the process of being sold to other companies."

"I'll have to talk to Mr. Stickler about that. By the way, Cinnamon, how's that friend of yours? What's her name, the black girl with the short Afro?"

"You mean Jade?"

"Ah yes, that's the one."

"Jade hasn't been seen since we went to Korea together on the Dreamliner." Just remembering her made me fight back tears.

"Why are you becoming emotional, Cinnamon?"

"We were friends, and I miss her so much."

"Did she quit?"

"No. On a flight to Korea, she was shot by a bad guy who somehow smuggled one of those computer-generated printable guns on board. He claimed it was origami. Anyway, he shot Jade, and she fell against the edge of the shell that surrounds one of the seats in the herringbone design in first class. Upon landing, we took her to a hospital. We couldn't stay, and by the time I'd been able to go back, she'd walked out of the hospital unseen by anyone and disappeared," I said this with tears running down my face. Ms. Willingham handed me a tissue.

"Thank you. Her boyfriend went to Korea and searched for a whole year before he gave up. Now he's married to someone else."

"I'm sorry, Cinnamon. If I can be of any help, please let me know."

"Thank you, Ms. Willingham." Just then a thought came to my mind. "Ah, Ms. Willingham, maybe you can help me. I've been trying to get back to Korea to look for Jade. My supervisor had made arrangements for me to go to Korea at a time when I had to go to court in San Francisco. Since then, she's been unable or unwilling to help me."

"Let me talk to Mr. Stickler, Cinnamon."

"There's just one thing. It has to be on an aircraft other than a Dreamliner."

"Why that particular stipulation?"

"Jade was shot on that type of aircraft. I'm not sure I'd be able to do my job on that plane."

"Are there any other stipulations, Cinnamon?" she asked.

"No, Ma'am. I'm sorry to put you through all that trouble just to satisfy my wishes."

"Don't worry about it. I can't make any promises, Cinnamon, but I'll try."

"Understood. Ms. Willingham, thank you."

CHAPTER XIX

I'd just returned from my flight to Korea and my unsuccessful search for Jade with my mood down in the dumps. That's not all that awaited me.

"Hi, Cinnamon," Josh smiled in good spirits as I walked into the apartment.

"Hey, Josh, how's the studying going?" came my sad reply.

"Okay...must be you couldn't find Jade?"

"That's right. But what do you mean by just okay?"

"Well...to tell you the truth, I've been slacking off studying until you returned. It's not the same without your help."

"Josh, I'm not always going to be here to help. You need to do this on your own. Let me give you a simple test to see what you've learned so far."

"Fair enough, Cinnamon."

"Question number one: If the wind blows in one direction and then changes direction by one hundred eighty degrees, what direction is the wind now blowing? Is it; (A) the same direction, (B) the opposite direction, (C) it's blowing either left or right, (D) all of the above, or (E) none of the above?"

"It's going around in circles?"

"Josh, the answer is B, the opposite direction. No wonder you had problems getting your pilot's training in the military."

"No one's perfect, Cinnamon."

"Do you have dyslexia, Josh?"

"No."

"Let me ask you this. If the wind did an about-face in the military, which direction would it be going?"

"The opposite way."

"Bingo. You hit the nail on the head." His answer made me smile.

"But I didn't have a hammer," he countered.

"Josh, are you naturally stupid or what?" My frustration wanted to knock some sense into his head.

"I'm just joking with you, Cinnamon." He laughed.

"This is no joking matter. If you want to become a pilot, you need help beyond what I'm able to give you."

"Any suggestions? I'm headed to Georgia tomorrow. Where are you going?"

"According to the schedule, I'm on track for London. I'm not sure, but I think Captain Morton is scheduled to be on your flight. I'll ask him for his advice on getting you the help you need to become a pilot."

"But, Cinnamon, I've always had a problem with book learning, and you promised to help me."

"Josh, when I'm not here, you don't take studying seriously. You think your joking around like this is no big deal. If you really want to become a pilot, you must be dead serious about studying."

"How can I study if I'm dead?"

"That wasn't the meaning I'd been going for, Josh" came my exasperated reply. "The term *dead serious* is a metaphor, meaning, 'you have to be determined enough' to want to become a pilot, which means you have to study hard for your pilot's license. With that in mind after I talk to Captain Morton, I'll move in with Mrs. Glade so you won't have any distractions."

"But, Cinnamon…"

"No buts, Josh. If you really do want me, that's the way it's got to be."

"Cinnamon, how can you be so mean?"

"I'm not being mean, Josh. You passed your test in the military without me. Why can't you do the same here? You already have the basic knowledge of flying."

"That was different."

"Why? What was so different?"

"Well…I'm not sure. It's just different is all."

"Do you really love me like you say you do?"

"Yes, of course, with all my heart."

"If what you said is true, then you have a choice. Let me put it this way. When it comes to studying, it's either me or the highway. No in between."

I talked to Captain Morton, and he told me he'd be glad to help Josh. Once I'd relayed this information to Josh, I kept my promise and moved in with Mrs. Glade, who welcomed me with open arms. I'd begun to think of her as a second mom.

During the day between shifts and work, when we were able to get together, I'd help reinforce what Josh had learned from his tutor, Captain Morton. My biggest problem stemmed from not getting enough sleep. One evening after supper, Mrs. Glade noticed my eyes drooping.

"Cinnamon, why don't you go to bed? You look exhausted."

"I am, Mrs. Glade." She helped me up from the couch and pointed me to the bedroom.

As soon as my head hit the pillow, my eyelids shut. After what seemed like two minutes, the alarm went off.

"Is it time to get up already? Where's the snooze button?" My eyes located the alarm clock, which told me it was eight thirty. "Eight thirty!" The volume of my voice rose. "I'm late for work."

I'm not sure, but I might have broken a record for getting ready for work.

When Mrs. Glade saw me rush across the living room, she said, "Cinnamon, where are you going in such a hurry?"

"I'm late for work, Mrs. Glade."

"Isn't this your day off?"

Her question stopped me dead in my tracks. *My day off?* The more that phrase played over and over in my mind, the more I realized Mrs. Glade was right. *This is my day off.*

"How about some breakfast, Cinnamon?"

"I'd love some. I'll change right after."

"Do you have any plans for today, Cinnamon?"

"Maybe the mall? You're welcome to come with me, Mrs. Glade."

"I'd like that."

Mrs. Glade took me to the mall. Before we split up, we agreed to meet at the food court for lunch at eleven. About half an hour later, with my purchases in my hand, my mind wondered aimlessly upon entering the walkway to the next store.

Am I hallucinating? Just coming out of a men's store was a man who looked like Sir Barky, but it couldn't be. He came up to me with a smile on his face.

"Good day, Cinnamon Shaffer. You're fired."

"Huh, what are you talking about?"

"I just bought your company and fired everyone. You're the first one I've told in person." He gloated. "Isn't that right, Honey?"

The lady he referred to stepped out from behind him and took his arm.

"That's right, Darling," she said, looking at him.

"J-J-Jade?" My stutter reflected my nerves coming unglued.

"Her name's Sukura, and she's agreed to become my wife," Barky extoled.

"No. You can't mean that, Jade." My voice became shaky.

"Oh, I most certainly do, and there's nothing you can do about it, you bad girl. How'd you get out of that dungeon anyway? You should still be there for plotting to kill the king," she smiled.

"No, this isn't right. How can you do this to me, Jade? We're supposed to be good friends."

"We were until you had me shot," she said, smiling.

"I didn't have you shot. It happened by accident."

"So you say." She smirked.

"No, no. Please believe me. I'm innocent."

Then a distant voice kept calling my name. It came closer and closer.

"Cinnamon, Cinnamon, wake up," Mrs. Glade called to me.

My eyes opened, and there was Mrs. Glade sitting on the bed next to me.

"What are we doing here? We were at the mall."

"No, Cinnamon. You were having a nightmare."

"But it was so real."

"You're right," Mrs. Glade said. "Your subconscious can play tricks on you or make you think a dream is real."

"Are we home?"

"Yes, Cinnamon."

CHAPTER XX

Days turned into weeks, and weeks turned into months. Finally, there was enough money for me to go to Disneyland to purchase the vacation package I'd been looking at.

I asked the clerk to put all the tickets and other information about Disneyland into an envelope. That way, my fingerprints wouldn't be on the gift. Next, I'd gone to the person I'd been talking to at Angel Airlines for round-trip airfare from San Francisco to Los Angeles for a family of five. Again, I asked that this person put everything into an envelope.

Josh asked me if my trip was successful. "Of course. Now I need your help."

"Okay. What do you want me to do?"

"Take these two envelopes and find a bigger one to put the contents in. Then make a label with the Bentleys' address on it, but do not—I repeat—DO NOT put a return address on it."

"But why, Cinnamon?" he asked.

"I don't want Liz to know it came from here, and without my fingerprints on it, she can't prove it came from me. After that, get the postage and let me take it to San Francisco to mail it at one of their post offices. I'll use some white gloves at that point."

"Why not mail it from here, Cinnamon?"

"Because police officers aren't supposed to receive gifts from grateful people they've helped. This way, it can remain anonymous, and they can't return it."

"Won't they be suspicious with the airline tickets from our airline?"

"I hope not" came my reply. "By the way, Josh, when's the test for your pilot's license?"

"Tomorrow, wish me luck."

"That I'll do, and I'll even pray for you."

The next day, Josh left early to take his test. I proceeded to try to find a route to San Francisco. Later in the week, we learned that Josh had passed his written test with flying colors, but he came home with a sad look on his face.

"What's the matter, Josh?"

"I got the promotion, but as a copilot, not as a pilot."

"Josh, you have to start at the bottom. Think of it this way, you are the backup pilot if need be. In that sense, you can be the pilot."

"The problem I'm dealing with now is that I've got to go into a flight simulator for more testing."

"At least, it's not book learning. That shouldn't stop us from getting married."

This put a smile on his face. "Did I hear you right? You want to get married?"

"Of course, you big lug. I'm not planning on being a spinster the rest of my life."

While Josh went to the simulators, I found a route to San Francisco. At the airport, I'd asked an Angel Airline employee to locate a post office for me to mail a package. I mailed it and returned to the airport for my flight home.

Over the next six months, Josh trained in several of the flight simulators. Once he finished his training, we started to plan our wedding as I promised.

Josh had three brothers and one sister. My side of the family consisted of my sister, Veronica, who would be my maid of honor. I'd also asked Karyn to be a bridesmaid along with Josh's sister. My father had the honor of walking me down the aisle.

When the preacher asked, "Who gives this woman to be married to this man?"

My father said, "Her mother and I do."

I'm not sure, but I believe there was a sadness in my father's voice. Later at the reception, we found a moment to be alone, and he confessed to his sadness. He knew this day would come but really hadn't prepared for it. I'd be leaving the nest. This would happen again in the future when my sister found the man she wanted to spend the rest of her life with.

Josh suggested we go to Hawaii for our honeymoon. That was also my choice. A two-week honeymoon under the sun and fun turned out to be way too short. Now if it'd been a month, that would have been great. Not all wishful dreams come true.

Getting used to my new last name wasn't easy. Almost every time, I'd give my name as Cinnamon Shaffer instead of Cinnamon Lamberg. Back at work, everyone wanted to know all the details of our honeymoon.

When I talked to Marilyn about me being on the same flight as Josh, she told me the company frowned on husband and wife working together. With the possible exception of an emergency, schedules would not be worked out for the same flight. Anyway, Josh was happy to be flying in the cockpit while he learned more of Angel Air procedures.

One evening, when we arrived home after an exhausting day, a phone call came for Cinnamon Shaffer on my cell phone. Since we were tired and wanted to sleep, Josh answered and said, "Hello." After a short pause, he said, "There's no one here by that name. May I ask who's calling please?"

He listened for a moment and said, "I'm sorry. You've got the wrong number."

"Who called?" I asked.

"Someone by the name of Liz...I forgot her last name already," he said with a yawn. "I'm tired. Let's go to bed." "That Liz wasn't Liz Bentley by any chance?"

"Maybe. Yeah, now that you mention it, it might have been her. Josh, I'll bet she wanted to ask if we were the ones who sent that vacation package to her and her family."

The phone rang again. The same number appeared again.

Josh said, "It's still the wrong number and hung up."

The third time, he let it go to voice mail, and we went to bed.

In the morning, we checked the voice mail, and it was Liz. She wanted to know why I refused to answer the phone. It's simple. If I'd answered the phone, she'd know without a doubt that, one, I'd sent her the vacation package, and two, that she might return it to me. The Angel in me was my way of thanking her for helping me. Somehow she knew it came from me, but since my fingerprints were not on any part of that package, how could she prove it?

Anyway, after breakfast, we got ready for work and had a few minutes before we had to leave. For the first time, I'd really taken notice of my new husband in his uniform.

"Hey, handsome, you're looking sharp today."

"Thank you and you look like an angel," he replied.

"Aren't all Angel Air's flight attendants supposed to be angels?"

"I meant the prettiest Angel in the fleet. Period."

"Thank you, Honey."

Then we departed for work.

My five-year service anniversary with Angel Air was only a few days away when I unexpectedly ran into Pearl, my old boss at Angel Air.

"Pearl, is that you?"

"Cinnamon Shaffer? It's good to see you again. How are you?"

"I'm fine, Pearl, but my name isn't Shaffer any more. I'm married to Josh Lamberg. Do you remember him?"

"Yes, isn't he the only male flight attendant?"

"Sometime after you retired, he took his test to become a pilot. He wasn't too happy when they made him a first officer. A few months later, he made captain."

"Wonderful. How about you? Are you still a flight attendant for Angel Air?"

"Yes, my five-year anniversary is almost here."

"I'd have thought you'd have become management by now."

"No. I'm happy just being a flight attendant. By the way, we haven't seen you since you retired."

"That's because I moved to the suburbs and pretty much have stayed home. Occasionally, I'll come back to the city."

"Pearl, would you like a cup of coffee? I'm buying."

"For me, it would be a sacrilege not to accept your offer. I'd love a cup, Cinnamon. Thank you."

We sat at a table for two after we'd gotten our coffee at a local coffee shop.

"So how's the old gang, Karyn, Marilyn, and Jade?"

"Karyn and Marilyn are fine. We never did find Jade." My answer made me sad. "Willie, her boyfriend, searched for over a year and couldn't find her. He then decided to marry someone else."

"If I remember right," said Pearl, "you and Jade were good friends."

"Yes, on my first day with Angel Air, I'd just finished changing out of my dirty uniform and began to cry wondering if it'd been worth all the trouble I'd gone through the night before. Jade came over to me with a tissue and tried to cheer me up. It's something I'll never forget."

"Losing a friend is never easy," Pearl commented.

"What makes me so sad about Jade is that it's my fault she got shot."

"That's not what I heard, Cinnamon. You couldn't have known what would happen in that situation."

"But it still makes me sad."

Pearl could see the sadness take over my mood. She began to stare at me.

"What are you doing, Pearl?"

"Cinnamon, are you pregnant?"

"What? What makes you think I'm pregnant?"

"I've always had the ability to know when a woman is pregnant. Don't ask me how. I'm not sure I'd be able to answer that question."

"Can you tell if it's a boy or girl?"

"No, just if you're pregnant."

"I'd been to the doctor a couple of days ago complaining about being tired and nauseous. That's when he told me I was pregnant."

"Does Josh know?" she asked.

"No. He's been overseas and hasn't come home yet. He'll be home tomorrow," I replied.

"That's great, Cinnamon. Congratulations."

"Thank you… Ah, Pearl, what will happen to my job? Can I still work?"

"Unless the rules have changed since my retirement, you can work up until you start showing. Then you'll have to take maternity leave. At the time of your leave, it'll be up to you to decide if you want to return to work or be a stay-at-home mom. Some women return to work as soon as they can make arrangements for someone to care for their new baby while they're at work."

"What would you recommend?"

"It's not up to me, Cinnamon. It depends on your financial need at the time. Do you need to work, or would you be more comfortable staying home and taking care of your baby? You and your husband will have to make that decision when the time comes."

CHAPTER XXI

My uniform began to shrink around my middle. It was the last flight before my maternity leave. Marilyn had assigned both Karyn and me along with eight other flight attendants on the American side on our flight to Madrid. Inez and her group of flight attendants spoke Spanish as well as English. We were on another one of our Airbus 380s. Near the end of our flight, as I was passing by one of the lavatories, a passenger opened the door suddenly. The door unexpectedly hit me in the stomach. This passenger had heard the captain announce that everyone should return to their seats and buckle up in preparation for landing.

"Ow!" I yelled. The force of the door opening knocked me down.

When the passenger realized what had happened, he tried to apologize. "I'm sorry, Ma'am. I just wanted to hurry up and get back to my seat. Here, let me help you up."

"Thank you," I responded as he helped me to stand.

"Are you okay?" he asked.

"Yes, I'm fine. Thank you."

When Marilyn saw what happened, she also wanted to make sure that I could continue the flight.

"Cinnamon, are you sure you're okay?" She sounded worried.

"I'm not sure" was my reply.

The passenger, before returning to his seat, again apologized. At this point, I began to feel a little lightheaded, and my abdomen also started to give me some minor pain. Since Marilyn knew of my pregnancy, she led me to my jump seat and strapped me in.

"Cinnamon, stay!" she commanded, pointing her index finger at me.

"Do you think I'm a dog?" I asked. "Bark, bark. Pant, pant."

"Very funny, Cinnamon. You're to stay put until we land."

I wasn't happy being unable to do the final pickup of trash. That may not have been my favorite part of the job, but someone had to do it. By the time we landed, my abdominal pain and nausea had subsided. I'd gotten up from my seat like the other flight attendants just as the nose wheel buckled and the plane's nose hit the ground making a V groove in the runway. This sudden motion sent me stomach first into the back of one of the middle rows of the seats. This time, the pain was too great. I remembered nothing until waking up in a hospital room, and Inez was conferring with a doctor. When she saw me open my eyes, she came over to me.

"Cinnamon, this is Doctor Gonzalez. He'll care for you during your stay. How are you feeling?" Inez saw the questioning look in my eyes.

"My baby?" came out in a whisper.

Tears welled up in Inez's eyes. "I'm sorry, Cinnamon. The doctor did all he could to save your baby. There was just too much damage. Your baby died."

"No!" I cried. My tears came swiftly. "My baby!"

It took some time for me to stop crying. Inez had also shed a few tears.

"Cinnamon, I need to return home with my crew, but I'll leave Sabrina here for any translations you might need."

"Has anyone told Josh?"

"No, not yet. I'll let him know as soon as we return home."

Sabrina was a big help from the time I'd been in the hospital until my return home. It surprised me about all the paperwork from the time I awoke in the hospital to the time I was discharged. If it hadn't been for Sabrina translating everything into English, I'd have been lost way out in left field or beyond.

Josh welcomed me home.

"How are you feeling, Cinnamon?" he wanted to know.

"Don't ask," I told him, "and I won't tell."

My mood wasn't the happiest, and he expected it. At least, he didn't holler at me for losing the baby.

"Cinnamon, the next time you get pregnant, you will stay home from day one for the duration of the pregnancy, and however long after to take care of that baby." His comment shocked me.

"But, Josh"—came my question—"what'll we do for money in the meantime?"

"You let me worry about that, Sweetheart," he said.

"How can I not worry about money? We just bought this beautiful new house. We need the extra money from my paycheck."

"We'll get by somehow. Now stop worrying. That's an order."

"So now you're giving me orders?"

"Honey, I just don't want you to worry about anything." He gave me a gentle hug.

"Since I'm not going to have a baby, I'll have to cancel my maternity leave."

The thought of it brought tears to my eyes. I'd been looking forward to having this baby. All of the plans we'd made in preparation, and now we had nothing to show for it. This thought made me want to cry even more. Josh did his best to cheer me up.

Yes, he's disappointed at not being a dad, but what about me? I'm very disappointed as well.

When I returned to work, everyone seemed to be sweeter than I'd remembered. Maybe it's because almost everyone knew about me losing my baby.

"Hey, stranger," Karyn said. "Long time no see. How are you?" She gave me a gentle hug.

"I'm doing okay."

"Just okay?" she asked.

"Yes. It's hard, but they say that to work as much as possible will help take my mind off the problems of losing my baby. I'm also counting on you and the rest of our flight attendants to keep my spirits up."

"Now that's the, Cinnamon, I've come to know and care about."

While we were talking, Jaylene came over to welcome me back.

"Good morning, Cinnamon. Are you up to flying?"

"Yes, Ma'am. Have you put me back on the schedule?"

"You're going with Karyn to San Diego and return." Jaylene smiled.

"Is that all?"

"Well, this is your first day back, and we don't want you to overdo it. Don't worry, Cinnamon. You'll be back in the swing of things soon enough," she said. "By the way, your flight leaves in about an hour. So if I were you, I'd get a move on."

"Okay," I told her.

Our 737, as usual, happened to be almost at the end of the terminal. When Karyn and I arrived, Jaylene told me I'd be working in the forward galley serving the first-class passengers. After I stowed my crew kit, Jaylene asked me to take some of the coffee packages back to the rear galley. Apparently, the ground crew put too many in the forward galley by mistake. Karyn was looking for some coffee packages without success.

"Are you looking for these?" I asked Karyn, who had her back turned to me. She turned around with a surprised look on her face.

"Were you trying to hoard all the coffee in first class?" she asked.

"Jaylene told me the ground crew left too many coffees up front and asked me to bring them back to you."

"And all this time, I thought you wanted to take some home with you," Karyn joked.

"No way, Jose" came my reply. "I'd rather have the coffee at that coffee shop across from the airport that we like so well. This coffee will suffice in a pinch, but it's not my favorite."

"That's not going to leave you short, is it?" she asked.

"If we're short, we'll come back here and steal some from you."

"Do I detect a potential thief on board?" Karyn joked.

Just then, the galley phone buzzed and Karyn picked it up.

"This is Karyn," she said. She listened for a few seconds then said, "We're on our way," and hung up.

"That was the master, or should I say mistress. We're wanted up front to greet the arriving passengers."

When all were on board, we, flight attendants, prepared to demonstrate what Jaylene told the passengers over the in-cabin intercom about the safety briefings that are mandatory on all flights. While standing near the front row of first-class passengers, my eyes went to one chubby lady, Ms. Willingham. My hand gave her a little wave between demonstrations. I'd be serving her. This time, I'd been assigned to the forward galley and would not have to go back and forth like the first time I met her. What a pain in the butt she'd been then.

Once we started serving refreshments, Ms. Willingham just wanted to talk to me. When she realized that there were other passengers also wanting refreshments, her hand caught me in passing and said, "Cinnamon, when you get a moment, I'd like to talk to you."

"Okay, Ms. Willingham, I'll be right back."

A few minutes later, my voice asked her, "What's on your mind, Ms. Willingham?"

"It's been some time since I've seen you, Cinnamon. How are you?"

"I'm doing okay. If my memory serves me correctly, the last time we met happened before my marriage to Josh. He's now a pilot for Angel Air."

"That's wonderful, Cinnamon, congratulations."

"Thank you."

"What's your new name?"

"It's Lamberg."

"Cinnamon Lamberg," she said, trying out my new name. "I like it. Have you thought about some little Lambergs?"

"Right now, Ms. Willingham, I'm just getting over a pregnancy that ended in a bad way." Mentioning this out loud just brought back the hurt. "The baby died before it was born." Now I was almost in tears.

"I'm so sorry, Cinnamon. If I'd known, I'd never have asked."

"That's okay, Ms. Willingham."

"If there's anything I can do, please let me know." She patted my hand.

"Thank you."

Upon my return to the galley, Jaylene saw my sad face.

"Cinnamon, what happened? Did one of the passengers harm you in some way?"

"No. Ms. Willingham, without knowing about what happened in Madrid, brought up the subject. It just brought back some sad memories."

Jaylene grabbed a tissue and handed it to me.

"Cheer up, Cinnamon, there will be other times when you'll be happy. Besides, you still have to finish this flight, so please put a smile on your face."

"I'll try."

"Cinnamon, do you know where rabbits go when they get sick?" Jaylene asked.

"No."

"They go to the hare doctor."

I smiled a silly smile at her.

"What animal do operating room doctors use to put people to sleep?"

"Jaylene, are you trying to cheer me up?"

"Answer the question, Cinnamon," she admonished.

"I don't know."

"They use the ether bunny."

"Jaylene, do you really think you're funny, because if you are, it's working."

"Good," she said. "Now get back to work."

CHAPTER XXII

"Another day in the salt mine, another dollar," I sighed upon entering the employee lounge of Angel Air. "Where is everybody?" I said to no one in particular. The entire lounge was deserted. I looked all over. Then in the locker room, one flight attendant appeared with her back to me. She looked familiar. "Jade, is that you?" came my question.

She slowly turned around. It was Jade, but something didn't seem quite right. She began to smile. That's when I noticed she had fangs like Dracula. She inched toward me in slow motion.

"Wait!" I yelled. "You aren't Jade. You're D-D-Dracula."

"My name is Sukura, and you killed me," she angrily said. "You should have stayed in that dungeon."

"What do you mean *dungeon*? Jade was shot in an airplane in this century, not during the reign of King Arthur. Besides, the bullet that hit you wasn't meant for you. That bad guy shot you because of my actions in trying to get away from his choke hold."

"It doesn't matter what you say. You are still to blame for me getting shot. Now I'm going to suck the blood out of you and let you die." She hauntingly laughed, coming closer to me.

"No, Jade! Please don't do this! I'm sorry it happened and want to make it up to you. I'll do anything you want. I promise."

"It's too late for excuses. You're going to die for your crime against me."

"No, Jade! Please don't come any closer. Please Jade. NO! NO!" I screamed.

Suddenly, Josh woke upon hearing me scream in my sleep.

"Cinnamon, wake up!" Josh said, shaking me awake. "You're having a nightmare."

When my eyes opened, I found myself in a cold sweat and crying at the same time. *Thank goodness, it was only a bad dream.* If Josh hadn't been there to comfort me, I'd have been terrified even more now. He put his arm around me.

"What happened?" Josh asked.

"My dream was about Jade. In my dream, she'd become Dracula and wanted my blood. I'd been thinking about her earlier in the day. The thought still haunts me that I'm the one responsible for her disappearance."

"It's not your fault, Cinnamon."

"That's what everybody keeps telling me, but it still hurts. I'm the one who made the mistake of moving that bad guy's arm to the point he aimed his pistol at Jade. If it weren't for me, maybe she'd be here today."

"Stop beating yourself up, Cinnamon. What happened, happened, and there's nothing you can do about it."

"No matter what anybody says, I'll always feel guilty about that day."

"Cinnamon, try to think about some happier times and then try to sleep," Josh ordered.

"Easy for you to say. You weren't even there."

Sleep evaded me for most of the rest of the night. The next morning, I showered with cold water to wake me up. Talk about cold water having a shock value. *I'm awake now.* Josh left a note to tell me he went for takeout breakfast at a nearby fast-food restaurant. By the time he came back, I'd made the coffee.

"Good morning, Sugar," Josh said upon entering the kitchen with a smile on his face. The food had cooled off on his way home, so he stuck it in the microwave to reheat it. "Did you sleep okay after the nightmare?"

My response? "No, I tossed and turned most of the night. I'm sleepy."

While the microwave warmed the food, Josh went to get dressed in his uniform.

"Maybe you'd better stay home and call in sick," he called from the bedroom.

"I've thought about it, but I really can't."

"Well, it's better than being put on sick leave."

"You're right, Honey, but maybe I can sleep on the way to work or maybe drink enough coffee to keep me awake until the end of my shift."

Upon my arrival at work, I went into the ladies' room to splash some cold water in my face. Karyn was applying red lipstick.

"Morning, Cinnamon," she said, looking in the mirror. Then she took a closer look. "I'd say you need some sleep. Look at those bags under your eyes."

"You're right, Karyn. I had another nightmare about Jade and couldn't get to sleep after that. If it hadn't been for that, I'd have slept better."

"Maybe you need to go see a shrink?" suggested Karyn.

"What? Do you think I'm crazy?"

"I'm not saying you're crazy, Cinnamon, but maybe a shrink can help you. You never know if you don't try. Give it some thought."

"I'm not sure that's the right thing to do."

"Then why do you keep beating yourself up about Jade?" she asked.

"Because I feel like I'm responsible for what happened to her and that bothers me."

"Maybe a shrink can help you see that," Karyn said. "Just because you go to a shrink doesn't mean you're crazy."

"You've got a point, but I'm worried about what other people will say when they hear that I'm seeing a shrink. Will they think I'm crazy?"

I'd just finished talking to Karyn about my dream and seeing a shrink when Sammie, another Angel flight attendant, came in. "Hi, guys," she said, smiling.

We returned her greeting.

"Karyn, Marilyn wants to see you."

"Why?"

"She didn't say. She just told me to find you and have you report to her ASAP."

"Is Karyn in trouble?" I asked Sammie, worried.

"Beats me. I'm just the messenger."

After Karyn left, I tried to get Sammie to tell me more.

"Okay, Sammie, Karyn's gone. You can tell me what Marilyn wants with her."

"Cinnamon, I'm telling you the truth. Marilyn didn't tell me anything."

"Okay, I'll take you at your word."

My next stop was to get a cup of coffee, and Sammie decided to join me. We'd just sat down at a table with our coffee when Karyn came out of Marilyn's cubicle in tears.

Sammie noticed her first. "Karyn, what's the matter?" she asked.

"My father just died," sobbed Karyn.

The news spread like wildfire throughout the lounge. Everybody, including his/her little brother/ sister, came in to say they were sorry and offered their help. Some of the flight attendants who were closer to Karyn also shed some tears. Mine weren't far behind.

Marilyn came in and said, "I'll make sure she gets home to her family."

The next day someone brought in a sympathy card for all of us to sign. We also sent a huge arrangement of beautiful flowers to the funeral home from Angel Airlines. Those of us who were able to take time off to go to the funeral went in our uniforms. In the receiving line, we all told Karyn we would do anything to help. All she had to do was ask. She gave each one of us a hug and thanked us.

When Karyn returned a week later, we all did everything we could think of to put a positive spin on everything we said or did to cheer her up.

"Hi, Karyn," I said, giving her a gentle hug. "Welcome back."

"I'm just glad to get out of that house. There are too many decisions still to be made. My family can't seem to agree on what's best under the circumstances."

"Well...," Jaylene said. "Getting back to work should take your mind off your troubles, at least for a little while."

"That's what I'm counting on." Karyn smiled for the first time since getting the news about her father.

On our flight to Atlanta, Jaylene asked me to keep an eye on Karyn. She seemed to be back to her old self again, I'm happy to say.

For some reason, when Karyn returned to work, she brought up once again the idea of me going to a shrink.

"Karyn, I've not had a nightmare since we talked about this before. I'd appreciate it if you'd please drop the subject."

"Okay, Cinnamon, I'm just trying to help."

"I understand, but unless these nightmares continue, it's not something I'd like to think about."

"Okay, okay, end of discussion. Let's talk about something else," Karyn said, holding up her hands as if in surrender.

"Thank you, Karyn."

That's when the topic of our new 787 MAX 8s came up. We still had no idea if or when they'd be put into service. Every time we asked Jaylene or Marilyn, they kept giving us the same answer. They didn't know anything more than we did. Even upper management claimed they didn't know.

CHAPTER XXIII

About three months later, I arrived at work as usual, and Jaylene handed me a cable. It said: Attention Cinnamon Shaffer. In my mind, *Everyone knows my name has changed to Lamberg.*

"Who would send me a cable using my maiden name?" I quizzed Jaylene.

"Only one way to find out, Cinnamon. Open it," she said.

Once I opened it and started to read, my heart began to beat faster. It came from Jin Hee at the American Embassy in Seoul. She'd been our guide when we were in Korea before and had a report that someone had seen Jade. My nerves were shaking so bad that they would no longer hold me up in a standing position. Once I found a seat, Jaylene wanted to know what was making me agitated. I handed her the cable.

After she'd read it, she asked, "Cinnamon, does this mean that you want to go to Korea again?"

Jaylene saw me nodding my head yes as tears ruined my makeup.

"Go talk to Marilyn. She's making up the new schedules. That doesn't mean she'll give you that route. All you can do is ask," she said.

Jaylene returned the cable and had me go directly to Marilyn's office. She was not there. Another employee who happened to be passing by told me Marilyn had just gone to a meeting and wasn't expected to be back for at least another hour. That prompted me to go to her desk and to leave my own note along with the cable talking about Jade. I found a blank piece of paper to write on, then left both the note and the cable so that Marilyn would not be able to miss them.

Shortly after I returned to the lounge, Jaylene said, "Let's go, Cinnamon. Our flight to Seattle will be ready for boarding shortly."

I had to fix my makeup after we boarded one of our old 737s.

Upon our return to home base, one of the ramp agents handed me a note. It said for me to report to Marilyn. My first thought was that my request had been granted.

Wait a minute, my mind said to me, *Maybe they will not honor my request.*

The only way to find out would be to talk to Marilyn. Once I arrived at her cubicle, she told me to sit.

"Cinnamon, you give me more headaches than all of the other flight attendants put together."

"Do you want some aspirin for your headache? What would you do without me?" I asked.

"Cinnamon, what am I going to do with you?"

"Send me to Korea?" I questioned hopefully.

"It's not that simple," Marilyn said, exasperated. "I've got several other flight attendants who also want to go to Korea. Most of them have more seniority than you do."

"What about letting me take a week's vacation?"

"I thought you'd want to take vacation with Josh sometime in the Summer. Does he even know about this cable concerning Jade?"

"It came just before we left for Seattle. So no, he doesn't know anything about it."

"If this is going to cause trouble at home, I'll deny your request for vacation now. I'll look at maybe finding an opening for you to work on your way to Korea. Remember, I said maybe. In the meantime, talk to Josh. Let him know what I've just told you concerning Korea. Here, take this cable to show him."

Josh had come home earlier in the day. "Hi, Josh."

"There's my Sweetie," he said. "What's new?"

"Honey, I've got to talk to you. I need to go to Korea."

"Not that again, Cinnamon. We've talked about this before."

"Just listen to me. This morning at work, Jaylene handed me this cable." I handed it to Josh. "It came from the American Embassy in Seoul. Someone spotted Jade. I've asked Marilyn to get me on a flight to Korea or maybe take a vacation. That's why she told me to talk to you."

"Why didn't you tell me sooner, Cinnamon?"

"Why, because you were somewhere between here and Australia. How could I contact you? Within a few minutes of that cable, Jaylene told me we had to get to our flight headed for Seattle. When we returned, another employee told me to go see Marilyn. She wants me to explain everything and hope you'll understand about the possibility of taking vacation now."

"Cinnamon, it's useless. It's been too long. It would be like looking for a needle in a haystack."

"What else is new? Honey, you don't understand. First, if it weren't for me, Jade wouldn't have been shot… I know what you're going to say, stop beating myself up, but I'm the one responsible for that. I'll carry that guilt with me for the rest of my life. Second, someone spotted Jade. Maybe we can find her through this person. That's the best lead we've had since she disappeared." My emotions began to quiver. "I'd rather take that flight to Korea instead of a vacation. Either way, I need to go as soon as possible." Now my tears were on the verge of overflowing.

"And what happens if you don't find Jade?" asked Josh.

"I'm not sure" came my reply.

"If you don't find her this time, will you give up your search?"

"I can't. Not until I'm sure that she's okay or dead. Either way, I've got to know."

"You're not leaving me with any choice," Josh said, sighed. "Cinnamon, please try to get that flight where you work and not vacation."

I flung myself at him with tears falling and my arms outstretched for a hug.

"Thank you, Honey. I'll do my best to get that work-related flight. Now I'm hungry."

"Me too," Josh said.

The next morning, Marilyn almost bumped into me as we both arrived at the same time.

"I talked to Josh last night, and we decided that it would be in my best interest to take a working trip to Korea instead of vacation."

"As I've said before, Cinnamon," Marilyn replied, "I'll not make any promises. If someone else with more seniority than you wants that route, the only other way would be for you to make arraignments with that other person to change. Otherwise, my hands are tied."

"All I'm asking is that you try to let me know the results as soon as possible."

"I'll let you know the next time I see you," she said.

"Thanks, Marilyn."

Karyn came over to me just after Marilyn left for her cubicle. "Morning, Cinnamon."

"Morning, Karyn, what's up?"

"You're going with me to Miami only I'll be taking vacation when we arrive. You'll be flying home with someone else."

Marilyn had come through for me to take a working trip to Korea. That meant I'd only have twenty-four hours to find Jade. I sent a telegram to Jin Hee at the American Embassy telling her to meet me at the Angel Airline ticket counter and the date and time I'd arrive at Kimpo International Airport. She waited for me at the counter but seemed confused.

"Hi, Cinnamon. What are you doing here?" she asked. "I'm waiting for a Cinnamon Lamberg."

"Hi, Jin Hee. You're waiting for me. The last time we met my name was Shaffer. It changed to Lamberg when I got married."

"Now everything makes sense. Congratulations."

"Thank you. Let's go. My time here is very minimal."

We got into the government car provided by the embassy, and Jin Hee gave the driver directions where to go. We wound up meeting a man at a cemetery crypt that displays pictures of people who have been cremated. Jin Hee introduced me to a man named Lee

Min Ho. She then told him my name. He bowed, and I reciprocated. Mr. Lee then showed us one of the pictures on a wall with several others. He pointed to a picture that looked like Jade. Jin Hee asked him what happened to her. He claimed he didn't know.

"Jin Hee, please ask him how he found out about Jade and where she's been."

She did, and he replied.

"He claims he'd been conversing with a friend, and they began to talk about Jade. His friend told him he knew where Jade might be, but it would cost Mr. Lee some money. They decided to split the reward money in half."

"Ask him where this friend found Jade."

His answer after interpretation was that his friend told him to bring us here.

"Where is this friend?" I wanted to know. Jin Hee asked.

"He doesn't know. He told me this friend will contact him after we leave. At this point, he demanded the reward since he was told that this is where Jade is supposed to be."

"Not so fast, Mr. Lee," I said. Jin Hee explained this in Korean.

Upon closer examination, it looked like Jade's eyes were closed. When I looked at other pictures in this crypt, almost all of those people had their eyes open and in a happier time. It put a question in my mind. Did he or someone else take a picture of Jade while she slept? It consisted of just her face. I told Jin Hee to say to him that we needed to verify his story. She spoke to him. Then she told me he claimed it was the truth and said we could verify his claim with the caretaker whom he would point out just as soon as we paid him.

"First, the caretaker and then the money or no deal," Jin Hee said in Korean.

Reluctantly he pointed out the caretaker, and that's where we went, but he didn't remember Jade being here. We went back to Mr. Lee who still demanded the money.

"Jin Hee, please ask this man if he understands what the word *extortion* means. Also, that Jade is in this country illegally. He and his friend could be arrested for harboring an illegal alien."

She gave him my message. He spoke to Jin Hee, then ran away.

She explained, "He needed money and thought he saw an easy way to get it. He wanted no part of the police. I'm sorry you came all the way over here for nothing, Cinnamon."

"That brings up the question—Is Jade still alive, or did she die? I've got to be sure before I give this reward to just anyone."

"How did you see through his scam?"

"I've known Jade long enough to know when she's sleeping. Also, the strips of ribbon that start near the middle at the top edge of the picture and go diagonally to each side were missing."

"Now what do you want to do, Cinnamon?"

"Maybe the police might have an idea. It couldn't hurt to ask."

"Good thinking. They'd know if someone like Jade has died within the last few months. If that's not the case, then we'll have to keep searching."

At the police station, Jin Hee talked to the officer in charge and explained the situation.

"He told me," Jin Hee said, "that if Jade is still alive and missing, he'll have his men search for her. The police frown on illegal people in Korea."

"Maybe if you explain the circumstances of how Jade became lost, it might help," I mentioned.

"This may take a while, Cinnamon. Why don't you sit over there," she suggested, pointing to a bench near the wall.

I sat and waited and waited and waited. The more Jin Hee talked, the more it seemed to me that the police officer yelled at her. Finally, after about an hour, Jin Hee came over to me.

"Let's go, Cinnamon. We're done here."

"What was all that yelling about? Did you upset him?"

"That's just the way he talks to most of the people who come in here. He wanted to know why it has taken so long to talk about Jade being here illegally in the first place."

"Are you all right, Jin Hee?"

"Yes, I'm fine."

"I began to wonder how much longer you'd be. I've got to get back to Kimpo for my flight home."

We returned to the car and headed for the airport.

"I'm sorry we didn't find your friend," Jin Hee said, "but I'll keep looking."

"I appreciate that you want to help but can't ask you to do that, Jin Hee."

"It's okay, Cinnamon. I'm intrigued by this case."

"Thank you. I'm disappointed but glad I've got someone here who is willing to help."

When we pulled up to the terminal, Jin Hee also got out of the car. We turned to each other and hugged goodbye.

Back home, Marilyn asked, "How'd your search go?"

"I'd say close, but no cigar. The man we talked to tried to make me think Jade had died. The problem happened when we saw the picture he showed us of Jade. It was a close up of her face with her eyes closed."

"What made you suspicious of the picture, Cinnamon?"

"We were at a cemetery where they cremate the dead. All of the other pictures were of people wide awake and who looked happy. Also, the picture of Jade did not have the diagonal strips of ribbon from the top of the picture leading to the sides about halfway down."

"So did you give him the money?"

"No. When we told him about extortion and Jade being in the country illegally, he ran away. Then we went to the police. They gave Jin Hee a bad time because this went to what we call a cold case file when nothing turned up in months after she went missing."

Josh came up to us. "Hi, Gorgeous," he said as he leaned down to give me a kiss. Marilyn left us.

"Hi yourself, big guy. Just getting off work?"

"No, just leaving. I'm headed to Rome."

"Now?" I questioned. "You mean I'm supposed to spend my first night back home alone?"

"I'm afraid so, Honey. Sorry."

"That's not nice," I told my husband.

"Again, sorry. How'd your search go?"

"We didn't find out anything until we talked to the man who claimed he knew about Jade. He turned out to be a con. We went to the police and explained everything, so they are now actively looking for Jade again."

That night at home, I made a ham, bologna, and cheese sandwich with lettuce, tomato, and mayo for supper. After the dishes were washed, I watched TV until bedtime.

My eyes closed and sent me to dreamland almost as soon as my head hit the pillow.

"Cinnamon," called Jin Hee, "Cinnamon, get out of that bed."

"What?"

"Either you get out of that bed now or I'll have the guards drag you out." For whatever reason, she seemed angry. She looked over her shoulder and called to the guards, "Get her out of that bed!" Two guards from King Arthur's time came into the room and dragged me out. On the other side of the door, we were now in an open field with a brick wall on one side in Korea. In front of this wall was a large pole about seven feet tall that stuck out of the ground. The guards tied my hands behind this pole. Once this was accomplished, they stepped aside. About fifteen feet in front of me stood ten military men with modern-day rifles but with King Arthur's armor. On one end stood Jade dressed as their commanding officer.

"What's going on, Jade?"

"I've told you my name is Sukura, Cinnamon Shaffer."

"And my name is not Cinnamon Shaffer anymore. It's Cinnamon Lamberg now."

"It doesn't matter you're going to die anyway. You should have stayed in that dungeon."

"Why?" My tears began to flow. "I didn't mean for you to get shot. It just happened!" My voice rose.

"You're showing very little if any remorse," she intoned.

"If it'll make you feel any better, I'm sorry."

"Too little, too late."

"No, Jade. Please don't do this."

She turned to her guards and gave the command, "Ready, aim." As she said the word *fire*, my eyes opened wide as I sat up in bed crying.

"Why? Why me? I'm sorry, Jade." No one was in the room to hear me. I got out of bed, turned on the lights, and went to my phone.

Mrs. Glade answered sleepily, "Hello?"

"Mrs. Glade," my voice quaking with sobs. "Please help me."

"Cinnamon, is that you?" she asked.

"Yes, I've had another nightmare, and I'm all alone. Josh is in Rome."

My tears were still falling when Mrs. Glade rang the doorbell about half an hour later. She came in and immediately hugged me. After I explained my dream, she took me to the bedroom and stayed there. She sat on the edge of the bed.

The smell of bacon cooking told me it was morning.

Who's in my kitchen went through my mind. Then Mrs. Glade appeared in the doorway.

"Good morning, Cinnamon. Are you hungry? Breakfast is almost ready."

"Yes, good morning, Mrs. Glade. What are you doing in my kitchen?"

"Making you breakfast. What's it smell like?" she asked, heading for the kitchen. "You were pretty upset last night. So I slept on the couch and got up to make your breakfast."

"But…" came my stammer and followed her.

"Cinnamon, as I've told you before, I've no one else to fuss over, and it makes me happy to help you whenever you need it."

"I am sorry I dragged you out of bed last night. It's just not right."

"Cinnamon, it's my pleasure. Now sit and eat your breakfast before it gets cold."

"Yes, Ma'am," I acknowledged. "It's not right for me to drag you out of bed like that. I'm sorry to have done that."

"I'm not. If it weren't for you, Cinnamon, I'd just waste away."

"Thank you, Mrs. Glade," I said, giving her a warm hug. "You're one of a kind."

CHAPTER XXIV

Karyn greeted me at work. She was always here ahead of me. After our morning greetings, I asked her, "Karyn, why do you get to work so much earlier than most of the rest of us?"

"It's a habit from the military school I attended. Boy, were they ever tough."

"You went into the military?"

"I'm referring to high school. My dad decided their discipline was what a tomboy like me needed. He felt he'd lost control of his budding young daughter. At first, I rebelled against the military discipline but then began to accept it. If you did anything wrong, they found a way to punish you that made you think about why you deserved the punishment. The one thing they drilled into you was being on time. I just got into the habit of being early just in case. It kind of spilled over into this job."

"One time, I'd gone past your locker when you had it open and noticed how neat you keep it compared to mine."

"Cinnamon, you can be as neat or as sloppy as you like. It just takes practice to keep everything in its place."

"Can you show me, Karyn?"

"Sure. Let's go see your locker."

"I'm not proud of the appearance of my locker after seeing yours."

"It's easy. Let me show you," she said.

Karyn rearranged my locker in a matter of a few minutes, and it looked so much better.

"Now you need to keep it like this. No haphazard tossing everything in just to get it closed before you leave on any flight. You need to make sure you take a little extra time to keep it neat and clean."

"Thank you, Karyn. I'll try to remember that."

"I'll give you another hint for looking sharp, Cinnamon. I can show you with this extra blouse you have hanging in your locker. Put the seams on the sides together and lay the back out flat on one side. Then iron in a crease. After that, take one side seam and the crease you just ironed in and pull the middle of that material out and iron in another crease. Do the same to the other side and, just below the collar, fold the blouse horizontally and crease the entire back near the shoulders."

"Where'd you learn all this?"

"In that military school. Most of the time, those creases will not show since you'll be wearing a jacket, but when you take it off to serve the passengers, they will notice. You may even get some compliments."

"Again thank you, Karyn."

"You're welcome."

"There you are, Cinnamon," Jaylene said. "How was your trip to Korea?"

Immediately, my mood saddened. "Not so good. The person Jin Hee told me about had false information. Then last night, I had another nightmare about Jade. Since Josh wasn't home to comfort me, I just fell apart and called a family friend to help me."

"Cheer up, Cinnamon," Jaylene said. "Try to look on the bright side. Just think about the fact that one day, hopefully soon, you'll find Jade."

"Thank you, Jaylene," I said while fighting back tears.

"Come on, Cinnamon, let's get to work. It'll take your mind off your problems," Karyn said.

Upon the return from our flight to New Orleans, Marilyn called me into her cubicle.

"Cinnamon, please sit down," Marilyn said this as she went behind her desk.

"It's come to my attention that you're having nightmares about Jade and that it's affecting your work. I've conferred with upper management, and they've agreed that it might be advisable to have you see the company psychiatrist."

"So you think I'm crazy?" My voice rose.

"Wait a minute, Cinnamon!" Marilyn interrupted, holding her palm up, facing me. "No one thinks you're crazy. It's just a suggestion. He may be able to help you get over your nightmares."

"If I go to the company shrink, word will get around that I'm crazy." My heart began to beat faster.

"You're a good employee, Cinnamon. I'd hate to lose you, but you need to put a stop to your nightmares. I can't do that for you."

"I'm sorry, Marilyn. I'd be too embarrassed to have other employees snickering or talking behind my back."

"Would you be willing to go to a psychiatrist on your own away from the company? Nobody needs to know."

"I-I-I'm not sure."

"Since this recommendation came from above, you have a choice to either go to a psychiatrist, or your employment with Angel Air will be terminated."

"You can't be serious, Marilyn."

"It's out of my hands, Cinnamon," she said, then after a pause, continued. "Tell you what I'll do. I'll let you choose the psychiatrist you want to use, and I'll also let you have a week's vacation. If you bring me the results from that shrink, I'll let the people above me know you complied with their wishes, and then I'll shred the results you bring to me. You have my word."

"Marilyn, I'm not at all happy with what you're telling me, but I need this job."

"Cinnamon, you have until Monday to give me an answer either way."

Marilyn then reached across her desk to shake hands with me. I stood and gingerly shook hers.

At home that night, Josh got an earful from me.

"Cinnamon, calm down. Getting all upset won't help anything. How long did Marilyn give you until you have to answer about the shrink?"

"Until Monday."

"Okay. On Monday, tell Marilyn you want to take a vacation and go to your parents' house. That should be far enough away that word won't leek out about you going to a shrink."

"But what if it does leek out? People will think I'm crazy."

"Stop being so stubborn, Cinnamon. If you want to keep your job, you have to go. The only other alternative is to quit. Then people will think of you as a quitter. Is that what you want?" Josh asked.

"No."

"Then go see a shrink. Look, Cinnamon, I'm not happy with you having nightmares, and neither are you. He may be able to help you get over these bad dreams. At least, give it a try. If you don't want to do it for yourself, then do it for me," Josh pleaded.

"Okay." I sighed.

The first thing on Monday morning, I went to see Marilyn and told her I'd like to take a vacation and to see a shrink.

"The only condition is that no one finds out. If they do, I'll quit."

"I'm glad you made the right decision, Cinnamon," she said.

"Just for your information, I'm not happy about seeing a shrink," I said.

"That's understandable. I'll arrange a week of vacation for you."

CHAPTER XXV

I DECIDED TO drive to my parents' home in Cimarron, Kansas, a trip of 862 miles. It would take longer than a plane, but my hope was that my fellow flight attendants wouldn't find out my reason for this sudden vacation. I'd also get to see my parents, which I always love to do, but it was the thought of going to a shrink that bothers me. It kept playing over and over in my mind as the miles went by.

Mom and Dad greeted me upon my arrival home and helped me unload the car. Immediately they sensed my dread even though they didn't know I'd come to see a shrink, and that was what made me sad.

"Sweetheart, what's got you down?" Mom asked.

"I've been told to go see a shrink, or I'll be fired from my job," I replied.

"Why would they do that?" my father asked. "We know you're not crazy."

"It's a long story."

"We're all ears," Mom said.

"Yes, tell us what happened," Dad commented.

"Well..." I sighed—"it all started with an incident concerning another flight attendant whom I'd become friends with. Remember that break-in at my apartment? The same bad guy somehow snuck one of those computer-generated printable guns on board our flight to Korea. He shot Jade, my friend, and...and..."

At this point, I began to cry. "It's my fault. Since then, I've had nightmares about her."

Mom produced a tissue for me. It took some time for me to tell the whole story about my nightmares, but my parents listened without interruption. When I finished, Mom gave me a supportive hug.

"No wonder you're stressed out," Dad said. "We'll do whatever it takes to help, Honey."

Dad found a shrink in town that came highly recommended.

The name on the door said Dr. Alex Tobascus. After I filled out the initial paperwork, the receptionist showed me into the doctor's office.

"The doctor will be in shortly," she said and closed the door.

A few minutes later, a lady walked in.

"Ah, I've got an appointment to see Doctor Tobascus. They didn't tell me I had to share my time with someone else."

"I'm Dr. Tobascus. You must be Cinnamon Lamberg," she stated as she stuck her hand out for me to shake.

"Oh, I thought I'd be seeing a man."

"My name is confusing for most people," admitted the doc. "They think I'm a man because of the spelling. Maybe I should have spelled out my full name, Alexandria." She smiled. "I'd like to start off with some basic information from you, Cinnamon."

The doctor seemed to be very nice as we went over everything she wanted from me.

"Now, Cinnamon, what brings you here today?" she asked.

"I've got a problem with nightmares about a friend." As I went through my explanation, my tears fell in full force.

"Why do you feel guilty?" asked the doctor.

"It's all my fault. If I'd moved differently or at a different time, Jade would not have been shot."

"Did you have a grudge against Jade? Did she harm you in any way?" she asked.

"No, Jade was my friend. I cared very much about her. I'd never intentionally hurt her for any reason."

"You mentioned Jade *was* your friend. Does that mean she's deceased?" the doctor wanted to know.

"No. We think she's still alive some place in Korea. The problem is that she walked out of the hospital unseen by anyone. The doctor who treated her thought she might have amnesia. We've been searching for her ever since. I'm referring to some of the flight attendants who were with us at the time and an employee of the American Embassy."

"How long has that been, Cinnamon?"

"It's been about three and a half years? I'm not quite sure exactly," I said.

"That's a long time to keep carrying the guilt." She looked at her watch and said, "That'll be all for today. We'll continue this at the next session."

My dad made appointments for every day during this week since I'd be returning to my home to Josh at week's end. The next day, I returned to Doctor Tobascus's office.

"Cinnamon," she said, "normally patients come in only once a week. I'd like you to come in next week instead of today."

"But Doctor, I'm only going to be here for the rest of the week. That's why my dad made these appointments for every day. Saturday, I'll be going home."

Dr. Tobascus helped me see that my guilt was the result of the trauma of seeing Jade shot. At the end of the week, she gave me a report to take back to Marilyn.

I enjoyed my time with my parents except for the fact that my mom was under the weather most of the week. She let me take over cleaning the house and cooking the meals we had together. Near the end of the week, my mom regained her health. That took a load off my mind. It meant I'd be able to go home to Josh without having to worry about her. Leaving wasn't something I'd have liked to do because I'd have to say goodbye to my parents. My dad always keeps reminding me that we are as close as a phone call away. That cheered me up.

The morning I left my parents, nausea hit my stomach with a vengeance. It went through my mind about what food I'd eaten. Nothing. I'd had a cup of coffee and nothing else. *What about last night?* went through my mind. My mom's cooking had never made me sick before. Spying a convenience store just before entering the highway, I decided to pull over and grab a cup of coffee, a bottle of water for later, and a candy bar. I paid for my purchases and started to drink the coffee on my way to the car. Just as I arrived at the car, bile rose in my throat. Looking around, I ran to the side of the building where there happened to be overgrown grass and weeds on a vacant lot. Just then, my vomit made a mess in the grass.

What's going on? I've never had that kind of reaction to coffee before. *Maybe I'd better get some ginger ale.* That would always calm down my upset stomach.

CHAPTER XXVI

THE NAUSEATING FEELING that started after I left Mom and Dad continued all the way home. How I arrived safely is beyond me. Maybe Josh had a remedy?

He suggested a visit to the doctor. Some help he was. Being the weekend, my doctor would not be available until Monday at the earliest. That meant going to urgent care. I'd have preferred to go to my own doctor, but this nausea refused to give up.

The nurses and other medical workers treated me very friendly as they went about giving me test after endless test. I explained the last time I'd been pregnant, there was some nausea, but this time when it came back, it made me feel miserable. Then the waiting began. About half an hour later, a doctor by the name of Binger came in to see me.

"Mrs. Lamberg," the doctor said, "the reason for your nausea according to our tests indicate that you're pregnant."

"Are you serious?"

"No, I'm Doctor Binger," he smiled. "Congratulations, Mrs. Lamberg. Now go home and take it easy for the rest of the day. On Monday, you should make an appointment with your obstetrician. In the meantime, I'll give you something for the nausea and a note for your own doctor."

"I have a question, Doctor."

"Shoot."

"I don't have a gun" came my smart-aleck reply. "My husband told me he won't let me work if I get pregnant again. Would it be okay for me to work? I'm a flight attendant."

"Did you have complications when you were pregnant before?"

"No. My pregnancy ended because of an accident."

"What kind of accident?" he asked.

"It happened on a flight to Spain. One of the passengers opened a lavatory door just as I passed by. It hit me in the stomach. Then on the same flight, the nose gear collapsed on landing, and that hurled me into the back of some of the passenger seats. Again, my stomach hit first. They took me to a hospital where they told me the baby died."

"How far along were you?" the doctor inquired.

"About four months. My uniform at that time began to feel tight around my waist. It wouldn't have been too much longer before I'd have had to take maternity leave."

"My suggestion is to talk to your own doctor about this. If it were me, I'd suggest taking your husband's advice about not working during your pregnancy."

"So you're saying that I'm not capable of working while I'm pregnant?"

"No. That's not what I'm saying. I'm suggesting you take it easy. If you want to work while you're pregnant, that's up to you, but given that you've had problems in the past, I'm only saying you should take it easy for your own sake as well as the baby's. Talk to your husband and your employer before you decide if you should work."

On Monday morning, I went with my nerves jumping up and down to see Marilyn. Her first question referred to the fact that I came to see her in civilian clothing instead of my uniform. The news that I'm pregnant was something to make my nerves to continue their aerobics.

"I've been feeling nauseated for the last couple of days and went to urgent care over the weekend. It turns out that I'm pregnant. Josh told me that because of the last time I'd become pregnant that he would not let me work from day one of a new pregnancy."

"So you're saying that you want to start your maternity leave now?" Marilyn asked.

"I'm not sure what to do at this point. All I'm sure about right now is that I'm not feeling well. I'll make an appointment with my doctor after I leave here and see what he recommends. I'd still like to work during this pregnancy even if it means pushing a pencil. Josh surely can't object to that."

"We'll talk about that after you've seen your doctor," Marilyn said. "In the meantime, Cinnamon, do you have that report from the psychiatrist you were supposed to have seen?"

"Oh…yes, it's right here." I gave it to Marilyn.

With that, I left Marilyn and went to my doctor's office to make an appointment. Since it was on the way home, it felt ridiculous to call when I could go there in person.

"Is Doctor Munchler available to see me today?" I asked Jamie, the receptionist. "I've had this feeling of nausea since the weekend and went to urgent care. They referred me to my family doctor."

"I'm sorry, Mrs. Lamberg. The doctor is all booked up for today," she said. "Let me see what openings we have for tomorrow… Ah, here's one at nine a.m., someone just canceled. Would that be okay?"

"Well, if that's the best you can do, I'll take it, although I'd have preferred one today. If you get a cancelation later today, I'd appreciate it if you could fit me in and then cancel tomorrow's time."

"You've got it, Mrs. Lamberg. We'll do our best to fit you in. If not, then we'll see you at nine tomorrow morning."

"Thank you, Jamie."

I'd just arrived home and had pulled into driveway when my cell phone rang.

"Hello."

"Mrs. Lamberg, this is Jamie from Doctor Munchler's office. We've had a cancelation at four this afternoon. Will you be able to come in at that time?"

"I'll be there. Thank you, Jamie."

What a waste of gas. I'd have preferred that call to have come before arriving home, but beggars can't be choosers, or so I'm told.

Anyway, back to the doctors' office I went.

I'd like someone to explain that when you have an appointment, why it takes forever to be called into the exam room much later than the appointment time. Finally, the nurse called me and took me into a room to take my vitals before the doctor came in. Then the waiting began again for the doctor to arrive. Ten minutes later, he came in.

"I began to wonder if you were ever going to come in to see me, Doctor."

"I'm sorry, Mrs. Lamberg. It's been hectic today. I received your information from the urgent care doctor. His tests indicate that you're pregnant. That can be part of the reason you're nauseated."

"I was never this nauseated during my first pregnancy."

"Perhaps it's related to the accident in which your first baby died. In any case, it's nothing to worry about. In the notes from Doctor Binger, he says he gave you a prescription for your nausea. You can continue to take that medicine. If you develop anything unusual from that medicine, please call me immediately. Are there any other questions or concerns at this time?"

"Yes. How do I keep this a secret from my husband? He's determined to make me stop working while I'm pregnant."

"If I were you, I'd talk to my boss and see if you can do some other work that's less labor intensive, something that will keep you off your feet for most of the day."

At home, the phrase *I will work as long as possible while I'm pregnant* kept going over and over in my mind. *Even a desk job would be better than nothing* was my thought. *My question is, how am I going to convince Josh to let me work during my pregnancy when he's determined that I'm not to work for at least nine months or possibly longer after the baby arrives?*

My nerves began doing their Mexican hat dance when Josh came home. We greeted each other with a Hi, Honey, and a kiss. I've got to stand up for my rights.

"Honey, what do you think of me pushing a pencil at work for a while?"

"Does that mean you're pregnant, Cinnamon?"

"Who said anything about me being pregnant? The question was what do you think of me pushing a pencil at work for a while? Please answer."

"I will," Josh said, "as soon as you tell me if you're pregnant."

"Okay! I'm pregnant. Are you satisfied? Now answer the question!" My emotions began to intensify.

"My answer is no." He shot back. "I've told you before. You will stay home for the duration of your pregnancy from day one. Period! End of discussion."

"You don't love me!" came out as a shout along with my tears. I turned and went into the bedroom to pack a suitcase.

Josh followed me into the bedroom a few minutes later and saw me packing.

"Where are you going?" he demanded.

"What do you care? You don't love me," I said through my tears.

"That's not true. I've been in love with you since we first met. Cinnamon, I'm just trying to look out for your health. Can't you see that?"

"There's no reason that sitting behind a desk all day will do any harm to me or the baby. I'd rather be flying, but given what happened last time, a desk job is much safer. Why won't you let me try?"

"You could have an accident at work. That's why. The safety of you and the baby are my main concern."

"You don't care about me. All you care about is the baby and the prestige of being a father."

"That's not true. Cinnamon, I love you and only want what's best for your health and well-being."

"Accidents can happen at home as well as at work." I pointed out through my tears. "What happens if you're flying several hundred miles from home, and God forbid, I should slip and fall in the bathtub and hit my head or the house catches fire and I'm knocked unconscious by something falling on me? If I'm all alone, who's going to help me?"

Josh opened his mouth for a comeback, but nothing came out. After a short pause, in a calm voice, he said, "Cinnamon, I'm sorry.

You opened my eyes as to what could happen. Sometimes you knock some sense into me. Again, I'm sorry and ask for your forgiveness."

"Only if you let me push pencils until after the baby is born."

"You're a stubborn woman, Cinnamon Lamberg."

"That comes from my father."

Josh held out his arms for a hug.

"I'll forgive you this time, but don't let it happen again. Promise?"

"Promise," he said.

"Remember, a promise is a promise," I told him and went into his arms.

The next working day, I kissed Josh goodbye as his flight was about to take off for Argentina, then went to talk to Marilyn about working behind a desk.

"Hi, Marilyn. Have you got a minute?"

"Sure. Come on in, Cinnamon."

"What are the chances of me working for you like I did for Pearl after that accident?"

"Right now, the only thing available is working at the ticket counter dealing with the public or taking their boarding passes at their respective gates. I'd really prefer you work as a flight attendant."

"Josh and I had a big fight over that last night. Do you remember what happened the last time I'd been pregnant? That's why he won't let me fly."

"I'm sorry, Cinnamon, that's all there is right now. If something else comes up, I'll let you know."

Leaving Marilyn's office with my head down and a sad look on my face, Karyn managed to bump into me on purpose.

"Hi, Cinnamon. Why the long face?" she asked.

"Hey, Karyn. I'm pregnant, and Josh won't let me fly because of what happened the last time I'd been pregnant. Marilyn just told me there's no other work for me at the moment. What am I to do?"

"Join me in the break area for a cup of coffee and let's talk about it."

We took our coffee to a table and sat to discuss my problem. The break area was full of other flight attendants and pilots. This didn't give us much privacy. The room slowly began to empty about fifteen minutes later. By then, Karyn had to leave for her flight. Some discussion that turned out to be.

"I'll catch you next time, Karyn," I called after her.

Jaylene came into the room, grabbed a cup of coffee, and came over to my table.

"Mind if I join you, Cinnamon?"

My sad reply, "It's a free country."

"What's the matter, Cinnamon? You're usually chipper," said Jaylene.

"Josh won't let me fly while I'm pregnant because of what happened in Madrid."

"Well, congratulations on your pregnancy."

"Thanks."

"Cinnamon, have you considered any other position in the company?"

"Yes. I'd hoped to help Marilyn like I did for Pearl after that accident when I first started, but Marilyn said that wasn't an option at this point. Now what am I gonna do?"

Jaylene looked all around the room. There were only a couple of flight attendants left.

"I could be fired for leaking the information I'm about to tell you," she said in almost a whisper. "There are rumors that upper management is considering you for a supervisor position. Please don't tell anyone until it happens."

"I'm flattered that I'm so highly regarded, but I'm not interested in being a supervisor. I'm happy just being a flight attendant. It's just that Josh has in one sense of the word *forbidden* me to do my job until after the baby comes. In the meantime, what else is there to do?"

"It's my opinion that you'd make a fine supervisor, Cinnamon."

"Thank you for your kindness, Jaylene, but for me to tell other flight attendants what to do just isn't something I'd be good at. I'm sorry."

"I'll talk to Marilyn to try to find something you can do that'll have the least impact on your pregnancy."

"Thank you, Jaylene."

She looked at the clock on the wall.

"Oh, oh, I'd better hurry. It wouldn't be a good idea for a supervisor to be late for her flight. I'll see you later, Cinnamon," she said as she raced out of the room.

"Have a safe flight," I called after her.

CHAPTER XXVII

Time just dragged by at home with nothing to do. Sure, I'd clean the house, but then nothing would happen. Each day of the first week felt like more than a month. The second week seemed even longer. By the third week, I was climbing the walls. The nights with Josh away were the worst. In the middle of that week, the phone rang.

"Hello."

"Cinnamon, this is Marilyn. How are you holding up?"

"I'm miserable."

"I'm calling to let you know I've been promoted to upper management."

"Congratulations, but what has that got to do with me?"

"I'm taking Pearl's old job, and I'd like you to come work for me. It'll mean working behind a desk."

"I'd love to, but I'll take that job on the condition that after my maternity leave, I can go back to flying."

"We'll see when that time comes."

"By the way, Marilyn, who's taking your place?"

"Jaylene will for the time being. That's subject to change depending on what upper management wants to do. My recommendation is that she take my place on a permanent basis."

"So when do you want me to start working for you?" I happily responded.

"How about tomorrow morning at seven?" she asked expectantly.

My happy reply, "I'll be there bright and early. Thank you, Marilyn."

As I'd told Marilyn, my arrival time was bright and early. That time turned out to be 6:17 a.m. It gave me time for a cup of coffee. When Karyn came in at quarter to seven, she was surprised to see me here this early.

"Cinnamon, what are you doing here this time of morning?"

"Marilyn asked me to work for her behind a desk while I'm pregnant and wants me to start at seven. I'd been chomping at the bit, waiting for something to come along. I'm a little early, but as you said one time, it's better to be early than late."

"Will you be happy sitting on your rear end all day?"

"I'd rather be flying, but Josh won't let me until after the baby arrives. So this will have to do. I don't expect this to last for more than one year at the most. If it does, I'll put up a big stink about it."

"Marilyn had been a friend when she was one of us. Now that she's management, I'm not sure if we can trust her to be friendly."

"Are you saying she might be a tyrant?"

"Don't hold your breath, Cinnamon."

"I'll let you know by the end of the week. By the way, Karyn, where're you going today?"

"I'm headed for Rome with a stop in Madrid."

"Lucky you."

"Hey. It's your own fault for getting pregnant."

"You're right. Anyway, have a safe trip."

"Thanks, Cinnamon."

Marilyn just walked in for a cup of coffee.

"Let's go, Cinnamon. Bring your coffee with you."

Once she had me seated behind a receptionist desk, she explained what she wanted concerning some letters that needed to be typed up and how to use the Dictaphone.

"Cinnamon, I'll be gone for most of the morning. If anyone calls for me, please tell them I'm in a meeting and can't be disturbed. If you run out of things to do, you can tidy up this place."

"If they ask when the meeting will end, what shall I tell them?"

"Be honest with them, then ask for their name and a phone number. I'll call them back sometime after the meeting."

"Okey dokey."

This put a smile on Marilyn's face.

After Marilyn left, I put my typing skills to the test. I'd completed two letters and was almost finished with the third when the phone rang.

"Good morning, Marilyn Benoid's phone. This is Cinnamon, how may I help you?"

"Cinnamon? This is Melanie Willingham."

"Oh, hi, Ms. Willingham, what can I do for you?"

"I'm surprised you're in Marilyn's office."

"It's only temporary while I'm pregnant. That husband of mine won't allow me to fly until after the baby's born."

"We'll, congratulations, Cinnamon."

"Thank you."

"Is it a boy or a girl?"

"We haven't found out yet. It's only been about five weeks. I know you didn't call to hear my life story."

"You're right, Cinnamon. Is Marilyn available?"

"No, Ma'am. I'm sorry. She'll be in meetings most of the morning. If you'll give me your number, I'll be happy to have her call you back when she's free."

Ms. Willingham gave me two phone numbers just in case she could not be reached at the first one.

"I've got it, Ms. Willingham," and repeated the numbers back.

"That's correct. By the way, did you ever find your friend? What's her name?"

"Jade. Unfortunately, no. It turned out that my information was false. I'd like to thank you for helping me get back to Korea."

"You're welcome, Cinnamon. Well, I'll let you get back to work. Please take care of yourself."

"Thank you, Ms. Willingham, I will and have a nice day. Bye."

I'd just finished writing the note for Marilyn to call Ms. Willingham when the phone rang again.

"Good morning, Marilyn Benoid's phone, this is Cinnamon, how may I help you?"

"Is this the Cinnamon we bestowed our Medal for Valor on?"

"Yes, Sir. And your name is?"

"I'm Mr. Stickler."

"Oh, I'm sorry for not recognizing you, Sir."

"Cinnamon Shaffer. I'll never forget that name."

"Since then, I've gotten married. My name is now Lamberg."

"Congratulations, Ms. Lamberg. Would you please connect me with Marilyn?"

"I'm sorry, Mr. Stickler. She's in a meeting at least until lunchtime. If you give me your number, I'll have her call you when she gets back."

Two callback notes. Then it was back to letter number 3. At this point, things began to get hectic as more letters and more phone calls started to come in—more callback notes. I'd have to take lunch after Marilyn came back. The afternoon went by in a flash. The next thing I knew, it was a little after four o'clock.

Marilyn had come out of her office unseen by me.

"Are you still here, Cinnamon? You're off the clock now. Go home."

"I've still got some of these reports to type."

"They can wait until morning," she said.

"But…"

"Goodnight, Cinnamon."

"Okay, see you tomorrow."

Time seemed to pick up speed the busier I became. I decided to bring in a coffeepot to save some time. It took about five minutes to go to the break room for coffee. This way, we could get coffee almost right away and save that long walk, which, near my due date, became hard on my feet.

I decided to wait until my eighth month to take my maternity leave. Marilyn wasn't too happy about my leave because she'd become used to my work and now had to train someone new. Sorry, Marilyn. On my last night before my leave, Marilyn came to me to wish me luck, and we hugged each other goodbye for now.

CHAPTER XXVIII

Little Jerika Lamberg was born at 5:23 in the morning. She weighed in at 6 pounds, 3 ounces and was 20 inches long. She has a little dimple at the end of her nose just like Jade.

Josh and I had talked about baby names at length. While we talked, Josh hit upon calling our new daughter L.J. as a nickname. It stuck.

About a week after I left the hospital, L.J. went with me to my work location. Lucky her, she got to be carried while I had to do all the walking. Everyone at work not only cooed and ah'd over her, but they all wanted to hold her. You'd think she was some kind of celebrity. For whatever reason, my coworkers decided to wait until after the birth of my baby to give me a baby shower. Some gave us newborn clothing, some gave baby blankets, but most gave diapers. Thank goodness my maternity leave still had a few weeks left. It gave me time to write thank-you notes to all who attended the baby shower.

I contacted Mrs. Glade and told her about L.J. being born, and she came over to the house after I returned from the hospital. She, too, fawned over Little Jerika. She just wanted to help with the new baby. I welcomed the help as my skills with newborn babies were nil to nothing. I thought it would be easy, but that thought went out the window along with the breeze. Mrs. Glade made me realize that a baby comes with a lot more work than I'd realized. Now I understand why some women decide to be stay-at-home moms instead of returning to work right away.

As my maternity leave neared its end, the question of me staying home with L.J. or returning to work began to drive me crazy. I talked to Josh, but his answer did not help me make up my mind. Mrs. Glade had the perfect solution. She'd babysit L.J. while both my husband and I were at work. At first, Josh didn't like the idea. After much discussion, he agreed to let Mrs. Glade help, and she refused to accept any money to babysit L.J.

It felt good to be back at Angel Air as a flight attendant again. Being back in the air was more enjoyable than working behind a desk. While my time working for Marilyn helped pass the time, my enjoyment as a flight attendant gave me more pleasure.

My, how times flies. L.J. had grown old enough to go to school.

Since Mrs. Glade didn't want any money to babysit, we decided to give her a new car as hers was old and falling apart. At that point, her car was on its last legs. We found a used car about one-year-old with very low mileage. Someone had traded it in for a newer model.

"Mrs. Glade, we appreciate all the help you've been, and since you wouldn't let us pay you, we decided to replace your old car with this newer one."

When she saw the car, she said, "Oh, Cinnamon, you and Josh shouldn't have." Then she began to cry and hugged us. "Thank you both."

"It's the least we could do for all the help you've been," Josh said.

L.J. had to put her 2 cents in "Aunt Nana, why you cry?"

Mrs. Glade picked her up and said, "Because your mommy and daddy made me very happy."

On Monday, I'd take L.J. to kindergarten for the first time. We made arrangements with the school for Mrs. Glade to pick her up after school while both Josh and I were at work.

About a month later, the feeling of nausea came over me again. I went to my family doctor, and he told me that I was once again pregnant. This time, working for Marilyn wasn't an option. She already had someone else working for her. My only option would be to stay home with L.J. Mrs. Glade would not be needed this time until the new baby arrived.

My ten-year-service anniversary came somewhere in the middle of my maternity leave. Ten years—it didn't seem possible. I'd have to miss the celebration. Since I'd become pregnant, my focus became L.J. instead of working. Our income would be less, but that meant I'd be able to spend more time with L.J. My daughter and I bonded quite well until my eighth month when I'd had to call Mrs. Glade to help.

When Hallie arrived at 9:48, it was in the evening. She weighed in at 8 pounds, 15 ounces, and measured 25 inches long.

My coworkers held another baby shower for me. L.J. couldn't grasp the meaning of a baby shower. She thought it meant that the baby needed a bath, not people giving gifts like at a birthday party. How do you explain to a little girl who is almost six years old about a baby shower?

"L.J.," Mrs. Glade said, "when you were born, your mommy was given a baby shower just like this one for Hallie because new mommies need a lot of baby things. So one of her friends gives her a baby shower. That way, she can get a lot of baby things without spending a lot of money."

"But, Aunt Nana, everything would get all wet."

"No, sweetheart, it's not that kind of shower. A baby shower does not use water. Friends of the mommy-to-be give her presents for the new baby. These are gifts for Hallie."

L.J. came over to me.

"Mommy, why do those people give you presents if they are for Hallie?"

"Honey, my friends know that new mommies need help with new babies, so they want to help by giving presents."

I'm not sure L.J. fully grasped this meaning.

When Josh came home, L.J. ran to him crying about why she didn't get any presents. He explained everything to his oldest daughter.

A few weeks later, I returned to work. For reasons unknown to me, the moment I stepped into our lounge, my mind focused on Jade. When I'd put her out of my mind, she would flash right back into it. *Where are you, Jade? Are you trying to tell me something? Am I going to have another nightmare about you?*

Karyn was already drinking coffee as I filled my cup, then went to join her.

"Morning, Karyn."

"Morning, Cinnamon. How are your kids?"

"Okay."

"Just okay? What's the matter, Cinnamon?" Karyn asked.

"For whatever reason, as I walked into the lounge, my mind went to Jade. Now I'm worried that I'll have another nightmare about her."

"But that happened years ago. Why would thinking about her now give you nightmares?"

"You tell me, then we'll both know. We were friends."

"All of us were friends," Karyn said.

"Yes, but I'm the one responsible for her being shot."

"It just happened. You need to let it go. There was nothing you could've done differently."

"You're right, Karyn, but it still bothers me because she walked out of that hospital and disappeared. If I'd been there, maybe we'd know where she is now."

"Let's think about work. We're both scheduled for San Diego today," Karyn said.

"What type of aircraft are we on today?"

"If my memory serves me correctly, it's one of our older seven thirty sevens."

"And if I'm correct…that flight leaves in…" I checked my watch, "about forty-five minutes."

We finished our coffee, washed the cups, and made a beeline for the gate our flight would originate from.

Karyn was right. Work took my mind off Jade. Everything seemed to be going smoothly as the passengers began to board. Almost all of the passengers were seated when a commotion erupted.

Two different people were claiming the same seat. Angel Air has a policy of assigning seats, so this should not happen. After I checked the seat assignments, it appears that somehow two passengers were assigned the same seat. I called the captain to inform him of the problem. Then before the ramp agent closed the door, I explained our predicament to him. He said he'd get back to me after he checked the computer and boarding passes. In the meantime, Karyn tried to calm the male passenger who claimed the seat that the lady passenger was already sitting in was his seat, as he had a ticket with that seat number. He started to curse loudly and tried to force this woman from the seat.

"Sir, that kind of behavior could get you kicked off this aircraft and possibly banned for life from flying on Angel Air," Karyn said.

When the ramp agent returned, he told me what we could do. We were both at the disputed seat.

"Sir, Ma'am, I'm authorized to offer either of you one hundred dollars as compensation to take a different flight as this one is full," he told both passengers.

Both said no.

"This plane cannot take off until this matter is resolved," Karyn explained to both passengers.

The ramp agent then offered $150. Both again refused. At $200, both still refused to leave. I then whispered in the ramp agent's ear about asking another passenger if he or she would take the offer. He agreed.

I went to the in-cabin microphone and said, "Ladies and gentlemen, we are inadvertently overbooked by one passenger. I've been authorized to offer any one who will voluntarily give up their seat a voucher for one hundred dollars to take another flight."

Josh had to take this flight to San Diego so he could fly to Vancouver in place of another pilot who'd called in sick.

"Cinnamon, what's going on?" Josh asked.

"We've got two passengers assigned to the same seat. The ramp agent was authorized to offer one hundred dollars to anyone who would take another flight. A woman is in the seat, and the male passenger is standing arguing. Neither one wants to give up the seat."

"I'll go with you. Maybe between the two of us, we can persuade one of them to take that offer."

We arrived at the disputed seat, and neither one had changed their mind. The man who was standing had just started to grab the seated woman to drag her out of the seat.

"Sir," I told him. "That is not the way to get that seat."

He turned on me and slapped my face very hard. Seeing this happen to me enraged my husband. Without thinking, Josh grabbed the man and first punched him in the stomach, then on the chin.

"You don't slap my wife in the face without paying the consequences," he said, pointing his index finger at the man.

"Josh, don't!" I yelled at my husband and tried to pull him away.

Karyn tried to step in between Josh and the man. Just then, a couple of police officers came in. After the initial inquiry, the police took the man in handcuffs off the plane. While Karyn talked to the woman to make sure she was all right, I dragged my husband into the Jetway.

"Josh, what were you thinking? Do you want to be fired for fighting with a passenger? That could happen, you know."

"Cinnamon, I only wanted to protect you. No one is going to hurt you as long as I'm around and get away with it."

"Your concern for my well-being is greatly appreciated, and maybe that guy did deserve it. However, that does not give you the right to fight with a passenger especially in front of so many other witnesses. Now I'm worried about your job."

"It was in defense of you, Cinnamon. If I'm fired for defending my wife, so be it. I'd do it again and again if necessary. Anyway, how's you face? It looks a little red on the left side."

"I'm all right. I'll put some makeup on to cover that spot. Now let's get back on the plane, so we can take off."

Josh went into the cockpit as an observer, and I headed toward the back of the plane, checking seat belts to ensure the passengers had adequately fastened them. I then picked up the samples of the seat belt, life jackets, safety card that shows the diagram of the plane and the oxygen mask just as Karyn started her announcement. While going through this procedure, the plane began to be pushed back from the gate to head for the takeoff runway.

Sometime later, when the CEO could get everyone who was involved in that incident together, he held a hearing on the matter.

Karyn joined Josh and me standing in front of Mr. Stickler.

"I've heard the witnesses and Mr. Shiner (the rude passenger) tell their individual stories. I'm not happy this happened. Can any of you tell me how it all started?"

"It began when Mr. Shiner demanded the lady who was sitting in the seat he claimed happened to be his vacate it." Karyn began.

"Somehow, two passengers were assigned the same seat. We still don't know how that happened," I explained. "Anyway, when he grabbed that passenger by the arm, I tried to grab his arm to stop him. That's when he slapped me in the face. Then Josh hit him."

"I won't let anyone hit Cinnamon and get away with it," Josh intoned. "If it happens again, I'll do the same."

Then Karyn said, "I stepped in front of Mr. Shiner to stop the violence."

"Captain Lamberg, what you did was not in accordance with company policy. You, of all people, should resist violence as a fighter."

"I'm sorry, Sir, but when it comes to my wife being harmed, no one is exempt from my wrath. If it happens again, I'll do the same thing again."

"So you've said, Captain. Well…I've no choice but to suspend you for six months without pay for your actions."

"Sir, won't you reconsider that punishment?" I asked. "We have two young daughters to worry about."

"Your husband should have known better than to punch that man in front of the other passengers."

"But, Sir, Mr. Shiner was trying to harm the passenger sitting in that seat."

"Mrs. Lamberg, you're lucky I'm not suspending you for the actions you took in this incident. You're all dismissed."

As we left Mr. Stickler's office, both Karyn and I felt like we wanted to scream because of the punishment given to Josh. We felt it was too harsh.

"Honey," Josh admitted, "what's done is done. We can't change it, so let's just drop the subject."

"But how will we pay our bills?"

"Cinnamon, please let me worry about that. I'll think of something."

Over the next 6 months, Josh took some low-paying jobs…in a fast-food restaurant, then with a major retail department store. It brought in some money but not very much compared to what we were used to. It did help with some of the bills, but we had to cut way back on our spending.

Sometime near the end of Josh's suspension, I began to feel nauseated again. This time, it felt worse than the other times. Most of the time, I'd feel sick and wanted to stay in bed. Josh made me take sick leave about three months into my pregnancy.

I'd still have to get L.J. ready for school and make sure Hallie was taken care of. Mrs. Glade stepped in to help. We hated to impose on her because she'd already done so much for us. Also, she was getting on in age. She couldn't do all the things she used to do, so we didn't ask her. We'd just get by with what she could do and find another way to get those other things done.

I'd gone into labor around 3 in the afternoon. However, my baby decided to stay in my womb because of the warmth. I'd have preferred to get this birth over with. Finally, around suppertime, he must have been hungry. Once he decided to come out, he came in a hurry. About 5:39 p.m., Ozzie came into this world. Before they handed my new son to me, I felt something wet between my legs like I'd been urinating uncontrollably.

She's hemorrhaging! someone yelled.

I don't remember anything after that. Several days later, I woke in a daze.

"Thank goodness," Josh said, "we were beginning to think you'd never wake up."

"What do you mean?" I asked with worry.

"Cinnamon, something went wrong, and you started hemorrhaging."

"What about my baby?" was my first thought.

"He's in the NICU. He only weighted in at four pounds, five ounces. Right now, he's on life support," Josh said.

With worry, my tears began rolling down the sides of my face.

"Cinnamon, the doctor has high hopes for little Ozzie pulling through this. You also need to regain your strength."

"Easy for you to say. You didn't go through all that labor and everything that I had to go through."

"Honey, you need to calm down. Everything's going to be all right," Josh said.

"I need to see my baby!" I cried.

"That will be up to the doctor," Josh said. "You need to have a positive attitude."

When the day came that my strength returned, the doctor explained why I'd hemorrhaged. He then said, "Mrs. Lamberg, I'm going to advise you not to get pregnant in the future for fear of something like this happening again."

I showed no emotion. I'd think about what he just said over the next few days.

"Now for the good news," the doctor said. "If you feel up to it, I'll send in a nurse with a wheelchair so you can go see your new son."

That brought a smile to my face. My spirits soared at seeing Ozzie for the first time. Every chance I'd get, I would go to see my son.

The day I was discharged brought both happy and sad emotions. Happy because I'd be at home with my husband and girls and sad because I'd be away from my son. When the hospital finally released Ozzie, he'd become healthy, and he'd gained enough weight to go home.

L.J. was anxious to see her new brother. Hallie at only a little over a year old, didn't seem interested. Mrs. Glade, on the other hand, wanted to hold little Ozzie.

"You must be tired, Cinnamon," said Mrs. Glade. "Let me hold the baby for a while."

I was reluctant to give him up but relented when L.J. wanted my attention.

Shortly before my maternity leave expired, little Ozzie went to work with me for everyone to fawn over. At the same time, Josh had returned to work, and everything seemed to be back to normal. Normal that is except that now Mrs. Glade had three little children to take care of when we were at work. This worried me because of her old age.

"Cinnamon," she said, "taking care of little ones gives me more energy than staying home alone. So stop worrying."

Where does the time go? With two of my three children now in school, my fifteenth anniversary with Angel Air was fast approaching. Josh wasn't far behind. We decided to celebrate early, and my husband suggested we call and invite Mrs. Glade.

"I'd love to help you celebrate," she said and paused for a long time. "Cinnamon…help…" Then a noise like something hitting the floor came through the phone.

"Mrs. Glade? Mrs. Glade, are you there?" My heart raced at the possibility of something going wrong. "Josh!" I yelled. "Call nine-one-one."

"What's happening?" he asked.

"It's Mrs. Glade. Something's wrong. I've got to get to her right away."

"You can't go in your nightgown."

I hadn't gotten dressed all morning.

"That's why you need to call for an ambulance while I change."

With the key Mrs. Glade had given me when I'd had my fight with Josh before we were married, I opened the door just as the ambulance arrived.

The paramedics worked on Mrs. Glade and told me she was alive. They needed to take her to the hospital. They told me which hospital and left with Mrs. Glade strapped in a gurney. Then I called my parents. My nerves began to act up while waiting for the phone to be picked up.

Finally, someone answered. "Mom, it's me, Cinnamon." My tears began to fall. "Mom, Mrs. Glade just had a heart attack. She's on her way to the hospital."

"Oh my! Are you at the hospital now, Cinnamon?"

"No, I'm at her house." More tears came from me.

"I'll call you when we find out what we're going to do, Honey."

"I've got to close up her house, then get to the hospital. I'll call Josh from there."

On the way to my car, Mrs. Glade's neighbor, Mrs. Kelmore, called to me from her porch.

"Cinnamon, what happened to Alma?" she asked.

"The paramedics think she had a heart attack. They're taking her to the hospital."

"If there's anything I can do, please let me know."

"I'll do that, Mrs. Kelmore," I told her while getting into my car. "Thank you."

At the hospital, I'd been relegated to the waiting room. While waiting for any news about Mrs. Glade, I called my husband, my parents, and Mrs. Kelmore to tell them which hospital Mrs. Glade had been taken to. Mrs. Kelmore arrived just before the doctor came in.

When he did come in, he was looking for a relative of Mrs. Glade. I had to explain to the doctor that I'm the closest thing to a relative that Mrs. Glade had. The doctor let me go see her. In her room, the only noise was the machines helping her to breathe and monitor her heart rate.

"Hi, Mrs. Glade." My voice, a mere whisper.

She opened her eyes. "Cinnamon." she smiled.

That's all she had to say to make my tears flow.

"Stop with those tears. I'm not that sick."

"But, Mrs. Glade, the doctor said you had a heart attack."

"Yes, Cinnamon, but it's not all that bad. I'll survive. You know what your problem is? You don't think positive. Now cheer up. That's an order from me to you."

"Yes, Ma'am."

My parents arrived the next day. Mom stayed with the kids while Josh and I were at work.

When we arrived home, Josh most often took Mom to the hospital to see Mrs. Glade. Once in a while, Dad traded places with Mom and stayed with my children. Mrs. Kelmore visited Mrs. Glade when her time permitted. Most of the time, I'd try to make time to see Mrs. Glade between leaving work and arriving home.

Day by day, Mrs. Glade regained her strength. After a few weeks in the hospital, she was chomping at the bit to go home. The day the hospital discharged her, we were all ready, willing and able to fuss over her.

Once Mrs. Glade was firmly settled in her home, Mom and Dad stayed with her. During the day, Dad came over to help with the kids while Josh and I went to work. As the weeks went by, Mrs. Glade's health improved to the point that Dad felt he didn't need to stay with her. Besides, Mrs. Kelmore lived next door if she needed anything. Mom decided to stay with us while Dad went home.

The flight we were on took us to San Francisco. Karyn had gone with me. Since our flight home would be delayed by a few hours because of a minor malfunction in one of the plane's engines, we were told to go to the employee lounge and wait.

On the way to the lounge, I noticed a police officer with her back to me talking to an employee of another airline. Then the thought disappeared from my mind.

All of a sudden, I hear, "Cinnamon Shaffer, you're under arrest." At the same time, one handcuff closed around my right wrist.

Turning toward the officer, I said, "I'm not Cinnamon Shaffer. By the way, what's the charge?"

"Prove it. Let's see some ID." Then she looked me straight in the eye. "You are Cinnamon Shaffer. If you're not, then I'll eat my hat."

"Do you want salt and pepper with that hat?" I asked and handed over my ID with my married name on it.

She studied the I.D. and passed it back to me with a surprised look on her face. "Cinnamon, you don't remember me, do you?"

"You do look familiar. You're…Liz Bentley?"

She held out her arms for a hug.

"What's the charge? You haven't answered my question."

"Lying to a police officer," she said with a smile as she unlocked the handcuff on my wrist.

"What do you mean lied to you? What makes you think that?"

"It's about the vacation trip to Disneyland."

"You finally went? Did you enjoy the vacation?"

"Yes, Cinnamon, we enjoyed it immensely."

"You can't prove it came from me. My fingerprints were not on any of the items in that package, and it wasn't mailed from outside San Francisco."

"Come on, Cinnamon. Do you think I'm that stupid? I'm a police officer trained to think of the obvious. You're the only one I ever told about wanting to take my family to Disneyland. Thank you."

"You're welcome, Liz." This time, I held out my arms, and we both hugged.

After I introduced Karyn to Liz, Liz said, "You're 'unarrested.' How about a cup of coffee? I'm buying."

Karyn decided to go on to the lounge while Liz's partner called in for a coffee break. Just a few feet away, we found a coffee shop. Liz, true to her word, paid for the coffee. Her partner gave us some space to talk about old times.

"How long have you been married, Cinnamon?" Liz asked.

"Almost twelve years" came my response.

"Any children?"

"Only three," I said and fished out my wallet with the latest pictures of my children. "L.J. is eleven. Hallie is almost six, and Ozzie is five."

"Your children are adorable, Cinnamon."

"Thank you."

"You're welcome. My biggest question is why did you spend so much money to send us to Disneyland?"

"You helped me when I needed help. It just seemed the right thing to do to repay you for your kindness."

"Thank you, Cinnamon," she said as she patted my hand.

"You're welcome, Liz. So how's life been for you and your family?"

"Don't ask. Time just flies by. Jasmine has just one more year left in college. She wants to become a registered dietitian. Ryan just finished high school and hasn't decided on what he wants to do in life. And Andrea is going into her sophomore year of high school." Liz then pulled out her wallet with the latest pictures of her children.

"Wow! It's hard to believe they've grown so much since I last saw them. There're wonderful." You could see the pride on Liz's face.

She thanked me. Then a question popped up in my head. "What are you and your partner doing here at the airport? I thought you guys patrolled the Japanese portion of Chinatown."

"We do. We also patrol wherever we're needed. Sometimes, like this week, we're here at the airport. It's on a rotational basis. The only problem with airport duty is that it covers such a huge area that we have to rely mostly on the TSA agents to do their job."

"It must keep you busy."

"Tell me something I don't know." Liz checked her watch. "It's been nice talking to you, Cinnamon, but duty calls."

"Same here. Let's keep in touch. In the meantime, stay safe Liz and say hi to your family for me."

"Will do." And with that, she and her partner resumed their patrol. I went to the employee lounge.

CHAPTER XXIX

"Cinnamon San," called a familiar voice. Looking around the employee lounge, I spotted a petite flight attendant who hadn't been around for some time.

"Suki San? Hi, how are you? We haven't seen you for who knows when. Where've you been?" We hugged.

"A few years ago, I transferred back to New York. My flight back there is in about two hours."

"How long has it been?"

"I'm thinking it's about sixteen years. Wow, that's a long time."

"So you decided to leave us because of what happened to me in San Francisco?"

"No, Cinnamon, my transfer had to do with the fact that now I'm closer to my family and the friends I'd grown up with."

"We began to think you didn't like us anymore, Suki," Karyn said as she came over at the tail end of our conversion.

"Karyn, you, Cinnamon, and Marilyn are still my friends. Since I've got time before my flight leaves, I'll buy you guys a cup of coffee."

"Bring it on," Karyn said.

"There's always room for coffee when someone else is buying," I said to Suki. We all laughed at my joke.

After we'd gotten our coffee, we sat at a table in the break area of our lounge and reminisced about old times. Suki, like me, had gotten married, but unlike me, her married life was a total disaster.

"When my husband gets drunk, he beats me. I've filed for a divorce, but it hasn't been finalized yet." She sighed.

"Oh, you poor thing." Karyn sympathized.

"My problem is that I now have a daughter, and he wants sole custody of her."

"How can he do that if he gets drunk and beats you? I'd think the court would award you sole custody of her."

"He's a big shot real estate broker with many friends in high places. He's been able to walk all over people like me, and he gets away with it."

"Too bad we don't know somebody like Matlock to fight for you," Karyn lamented.

"If it'll do any good, we'd love to help you, Suki." I hoped my statement would do some good for her. My memory of her helping me in San Francisco meant a lot.

"Thank you, Cinnamon. If I need help, I'll let you know."

We exchanged phone numbers and showed each other pictures of our children. Karyn kind of felt left out since she has not been married yet. She loved Suki's cute little 3-year-old Kimiko. I agreed. She was adorable.

A few months later, Josh took me to Rochester, New York, to attend a pilots' union meeting. He'd become a vice president of our local pilots' union. I wasn't invited to attend, but he'd promised to take me to New York City to a Broadway play afterward. For me to stay in the hotel all day would be boring. My brain told me, *Find a mall to go shopping.* So my boring day wouldn't be so dull after all. *Look out, credit cards, I'm going to spend some money.*

Josh's meeting got over shortly before supper, which we ate in one of the elegant hotel restaurants.

While we were getting ready for bed, I turned on the TV for news. Josh was in the bathroom. The anchor was talking about domestic abuse and showed a picture of a battered woman. A closer look revealed her identity and her name. I yelled to my husband, "Josh. Get in here!"

He rushed in and made me laugh. He'd been brushing his teeth. White foam toothpaste outlined his mouth, and he had a toothbrush in his hand.

"What's the matter?" he asked in alarm.

"It's the news. They say a domestic crime took place here in Rochester. Then they showed a picture of Suki. She's in critical condition."

"What do you want me to do, Cinnamon, cry?"

"Get real, Josh. I've got to go see her in the hospital."

"Why? Tomorrow we're going to New York City."

"Honey, Suki's not only a friend, but she's also an Angel Airline flight attendant."

"Does that mean I've got to get dressed?" Josh asked.

"Yes, and be quick about it." While waiting for Josh to change, my mind raced. Then the only person I could think of that might be able to help popped into my brain. I made the call.

"Hello," she said.

"Ms. Willingham? This is Cinnamon Lamberg."

"Hi, Cinnamon, how are you? This is a pleasant surprise."

"Ms. Willingham, I'm here in Rochester, New York, with my husband. He had a meeting to go to then promised to take me to a Broadway play."

"That's wonderful. I'm happy for you."

"The reason for my call is that Suki, a fellow Angel Air flight attendant, has been badly beaten and is in the hospital. I was wondering if you could please spread the word to all of Angel Air's flight attendants worldwide?"

"Do they know who did this, Cinnamon?"

"The authorities are looking at her husband. Apparently, someone saw him leave the scene of the crime. He's a big shot realtor in New York City and has gotten away with this crime before."

"I'll look into this and have our flight attendants pray for her."

"Thank you, Ms. Willingham."

I'd just hung up when Josh came into the room.

"Let's go." He gestured.

We stopped at the front desk to check on hospitals. The clerk gave us some names and addresses.

"These hospitals are the only ones I know about. Since I'm new here, there may be more. I'm just not sure."

"That's fine. It's a start. Thank you," Josh said.

We raced to the taxi stand and asked the driver about these hospitals. He remembered something about the story and where they'd taken Suki.

We asked at the admitting desk about Suki and were told she is here but only family members are allowed to see her. We went to the waiting room. Soon, a Japanese family came in. The little girl they had with them looked like the picture Suki showed me.

"Excuse me," I asked. "Are you members of Suki's family?"

"How do you know this?" asked the older man.

"I recognized Kimiko from some pictures Suki showed me a few months ago. I'm also a flight attendant with Angel Air, and my husband is a pilot for the same Airline. Suki is a friend."

"What is your name, please?" the man asked.

"Oh, I'm sorry. My name is Cinnamon, and my husband is Josh."

"Cinnamon San?"

"Yes."

The old man then introduced himself as Suki's father and introduced the rest of the family.

"My daughter has most kind words for you," he explained.

"Thank you. She has been kind to me." I then went on to explain what she did for me in San Francisco.

About half an hour later, a doctor came into the waiting room looking for Suki's family. Her mother and father looked on anxious to find out about their daughter. Just before they went to see her, I asked them to give Suki a message from me.

"Please tell Suki San the Angels are watching over her and are praying for her speedy recovery."

"Thank you," her father said as he and her mother bowed. They followed the doctor to Suki's room.

"Come on, Cinnamon. Let's go. There's nothing more for us to do here," Josh said.

"Can we change our plans of the Broadway play to another time, Honey? I'd like to stay here with Suki."

"Why? You can't see her while she's in critical condition."

"You're right, but I'd still like to stay."

"Maybe we can swing by on our way home," Josh said.

"Okay." I sighed. Suki didn't leave my mind until the Broadway show *My Fair Lady* started. The show kept my mind busy, but after it ended, my mind went right back to Suki. The show itself was excellent. I'd never been to one, and I really enjoyed it. At my insistence, we went back to Rochester to check on Suki. Nothing had changed. We were about to leave the hospital for home when my cell phone rang.

"Cinnamon, this is Melanie Willingham. I've started a GoFundMe page for Suki. Where shall we send the funds?"

I gave her Suki's name and told her to send them in care of this hospital and gave her the address.

As the main door to the hospital opened for us to leave, an angry man with a mean look on his face came storming in. I'd estimate his height to be maybe an inch or two taller than me.

He demanded of the receptionist, "Where's my wife?" The volume of his voice could be heard all over the lobby.

We stopped dead in our tracks and turned to see what he wanted. The receptionist asked for his wife's name. When we heard him say Suki, even before he recited her last name, Josh was on him like lightning.

"Just what do you want with Suki?" Josh wanted to know.

"It's none of your business, pal!" He snarled, looking up at Josh.

"It is if you intend to harm her. She and my wife are friends, and I'll not let you hurt her in any way."

While Josh argued with Suki's husband, I called 911 and told the operator there might be trouble at this hospital and that Suki's husband was here. Josh kept Suki's husband busy with arguments. When the police arrived, they asked what was going on.

My husband told them, "I believe he's here to harm his wife."

"This guy is preventing me from seeing my wife. He has no right to do that."

"Yes, he does," said Suki's father as he entered the lobby. "My daughter has a restraining order against him."

The police officer told Suki's husband to put his hands on the counter with his feet back and spread. They searched him and found a gun on him. They immediately arrested him. Before he came here, he'd somehow obtained a gun.

When it came time for Suki to leave the hospital, her husband would be in court.

"You're going to regret this, fella," Suki's husband said. I've got friends in high places."

"So do we," Josh replied.

When we were alone, I said to my husband, "We don't have any big-shot friends in high places."

"Sure we do, Cinnamon. They work for Angel Airlines. They're called pilots and flight attendants."

Not only would Suki's husband have to face charges of beating Suki and attempting to kill her, but he'd also be facing divorce proceedings.

I managed to talk Marilyn into letting me go on the New York run at the time Suki had to go to court. The judge granted Suki 500 dollars for alimony and child support on a monthly basis. We left before the judge gave her husband his sentence. Outside the courthouse, her attorney suggested Suki leave New York City permanently with her daughter.

I suggested Suki and Kimiko stay with us until she could find a place of her own.

Everyone thought that was great except Suki. She didn't want to leave her family.

Reluctantly she agreed.

CHAPTER XXX

Now that L.J. was on the verge of becoming a teenager, she decided she wanted to be called Jerika instead of L.J. After all, Jerika is her given name.

We'd gone shopping for new school clothes for all three kids. Jerika had picked out a wonderful new outfit. Next came Hallie. While I searched for her, Josh took Ozzie to the boys' department.

I'd almost given up on finding something for Hallie when someone behind me said, "Good eye, Mom."

I turned around to see who'd made that comment. To my surprise, it turned out to be Willie.

We hugged, and Hallie said, "I'm gonna tell Daddy on you, Mommy."

"Sweetheart, Uncle Willie is an old family friend from before you were born." Then I gazed up at Willie. "Willie, this is my daughter Hallie and her sister Jerika."

"Good day to you, young ladies. It's nice to meet you," Willie said to my girls.

"Say hi to Uncle Willie, girls."

They did in unison.

"So, Willie, how's the family? We haven't seen you in a long time."

"Billie just turned sixteen, and La Keisha is now thirteen."

"That's great. Are there any more at home?"

"No, that's all. What's Josh up to these days?" Willie asked.

"He's over in the boys' section with our son, Ozzie. How's Laura?"

Willie hesitated, like I'd hit on a sensitive subject. "Laura was killed in a car accident a few weeks ago."

"Oh, Willie, I'm so sorry." I gave him hug.

"Thank you, Cinnamon."

"Did you ever find Jade?" My curiosity got the better of me.

"No. Once I'd married Laura, I gave up on Jade." Willie sighed. "Did you ever find Jade?"

"My searches came up empty-handed just like yours. Every time, after each search with no luck, I'd come home and have a nightmare about her."

"I'm sorry to hear that, Cinnamon."

"I'm okay now. Angel Air forced me to see a shrink, or I'd lose my job. I've now gotten over those bad dreams, but I'd still like to find her."

"Well, good luck in your hunt for, Jade," Willie sighed. "Let me know if you do find her."

"I'll do that, Willie." I smiled. "Why don't you bring your kids over, and we'll all have supper together?"

"Thanks, Cinnamon, but we already have plans for tonight, another time perhaps."

"Okay." My heart was disappointed. "Let's keep in touch and not wait so long to see each other again."

"Roger that," Willie responded.

He left, and I'd gone back to shopping. I found something for Hallie and then took the girls over to where Josh seemed to be having trouble with finding something for Ozzie.

"Hi, guys," Josh greeted us.

Before anyone could respond, Hallie said, "Daddy, Mommy hugged a big black man."

"She did?" asked Josh.

"It was Willie. He's here shopping for his kids also."

"So how is he?"

"He's doing okay. He told me his wife died in a car accident a while back."

"That's too bad," Josh said.

"I invited him and his kids to supper tonight, but he said he had other plans and mentioned some other time."

"Well, you tried. Anyway, I'm having trouble finding something for Ozzie. You're always good at these things. Maybe you'll have better luck."

"Of course, I'll have better luck. I remember the size he wears, Daddy."

Once we'd gotten everything we needed, we headed for the checkout. Willie was at the register watching the cashier ring up his purchases. Josh saw him and skirted the cash registers to wait on the other side for Willie to finish. Just as Willie started for the door, he saw Josh, and they greeted each other.

The two men continued to talk until we girls and Ozzie were finished at the checkout and caught up to them.

"Come on, guys, let's go to the doughnut shop across the street for some coffee, and the kids can have a doughnut," I suggested.

"Yeah!" Ozzie and the girls cheered. Ozzie couldn't wait to get a doughnut.

"I'll race ya," he said to the girls.

"Ozzie," Josh warned. "You'll do no such thing. You'll walk with the rest of us after we check to make sure no cars are coming. Is that understood?"

"Okay." Ozzie sighed.

"Take Mommy's hand," I said to him. "We don't want you to run out into the middle of the street without looking. You could get hurt if you did."

"Ah, Mom, you worry too much," my son said.

"Wonder where he got that from?" I looked at Josh.

While the men sat at a table where they could talk, I chose to sit with my children at a different table.

"Mom, what's this thing about a lady named Jade?" asked Jerika.

"Honey, she was the first flight attendant I met at Angel Airlines. I'd fallen down and hurt my knee on the first day of work. I wanted everything to be perfect on that day. It all went out the window so to speak. When my tears started to fall, Jade came over, introduced herself, and handed me a tissue. From that moment in time, we became friends."

"What happened to her?" Jerika asked, taking a bite of her doughnut.

"We worked together on several flights until one time we were assigned to fly on the Dreamliner. I'd never flown on one before. This flight took us to Korea. A bad man somehow snuck a gun on board. He'd grabbed me around the neck with one arm and pointed his gun at my head. Jade told him to put the gun down just as I tried to jam my elbow into his stomach, and the gun went off."

"How'd he get the gun onto the plane?"

"He told the TSA agents it was origami."

"What's origami?" asked Hallie, stuffing the rest of her doughnut into her mouth.

"Origami comes from Japan. It's a way of folding a piece of paper to make different types of figures like maybe birds or other shapes."

"Then what happened?" Jerika asked.

"When the gun went off, the bullet hit Jade in the stomach, then she fell against the shell that surrounds the seats in first class and banged her head."

"Did she die?" Hallie questioned.

"No. She was taken to a Korean hospital. The doctors thought she'd survive the gunshot wound but didn't know if she'd have amnesia."

"What's amnesia?" Hallie asked.

"Amnesia is when you can't remember who you are or any of your friends. You can't even remember where you are or where you're from."

"So what happened to this Jade person?" Jerika asked.

"One day, she just walked out of the hospital, and no one saw her leave. Since then, we've been searching for her. If she'd come home after leaving the hospital, Uncle Willie would have married her."

"Does that mean she'd be our Aunt Jade?" asked Hallie.

"Technically, the answer is no. She'd be no real relation to us, but to show respect, you would have to call her Aunt Jade."

"Did she die?" Ozzie put his 2 cents in.

"We don't know. She disappeared, and nobody can find her."

"Mommy, are you going to disappear?" asked Hallie.

"No, Honey, I'm not going to disappear."

"What does *disappear* mean?" Ozzie wanted to know.

"It means 'to go away where nobody can find you.' You'll understand better when you're old enough to get married and have your own children."

"Does that mean I have to marry a girl?" he asked.

"That's the general idea."

"Then I'm never going to get married," said Ozzie.

"Why don't you want to get married?"

"Because I don't like girls."

"Does that mean you don't like me or your sisters? We're girls."

"You're okay, Mommy."

"Thank you, Sweetheart, but what about your sisters?"

"No," Ozzie lamented.

"Why not?"

"They're too bossy."

"We are not!" Jerika and Hallie shouted in unison.

"Please keep your voices down, girls." I scolded my daughters. "Ozzie, Honey, no matter where you go, you'll find somebody who will be a boss over you."

"Why do girls always get to be the boss? It's not fair," pouted Ozzie as he crossed his arms.

"Hey Tiger, why the long face?" Josh asked his son as he came over to our table.

"Not all bosses are girls. Look at Daddy. He's the boss of whatever airplane he flies."

"That's right, son. When you get older, you'll understand better about being a boss," my husband said.

"Sometimes being the boss is a shared responsibility, like with Daddy and me. We are both the boss in our house."

"Other times we have to give being the boss to someone else, like a babysitter when Mommy and I go out," Daddy said.

"Are you and Uncle Willie finished talking, Big Daddy?"

"Yes, Ma'am. Let's go home everybody," Josh beamed.

"Mom," Jerika asked, "do you think you'll ever find this Jade woman?"

"Honestly, Jerika, right now, I don't know. It's been a long time since she disappeared. Every day that passes makes finding her that much more difficult, and the hope that she's alive gets less and less."

"What happens if you can't find her?" Jerika asked.

"Again, I don't know. All we can do is live our lives day by day and hope for the best. If it's meant that we find her, then we will. If not, then we won't."

We'd been walking to the place where we parked our car and had to pass a toy store. When Ozzie saw a toy he wanted, he started to enter.

"Where are you going, Tiger?" asked Josh.

"In here," he replied.

"Ozzie, we need to get back home. Kimiko's coming over," my husband said.

"But I want a toy. Besides, Kimiko's a girl," Ozzie whined.

"Boys!" Hallie said, shaking her head. "What's wrong with him?"

"Too many girls. It's not fair," Ozzie complained.

"Come on, Ozzie, we'll get a toy next time," I told him. "If you behave, when we get home, you can have some ice cream."

"In a cone?" he asked.

"Yes" came my reply.

Suki and her daughter, Kimiko, came over about an hour later.

"Help! I'm being invaded by girls," Ozzie complained.

"Hey, Slugger, let's you and me go someplace away from these girls, just the two of us," Josh said.

"Yeah! The sooner the better." Ozzie smiled and was halfway out the door before his dad could say goodbye to everyone.

While my son and husband decided to leave, Suki and I enjoyed coffee and a chance to talk. The girls had fun playing together.

"Thank you, Cinnamon for all your help. Moving away from Kimiko's dad was good for me, but now she doesn't have a father figure in her life."

"You're welcome, Suki. As far as Kimiko growing up without her father, I'm sure you'll find someone else who will care for both of you."

"Because of my ex, it's going to be hard for me to trust another man again."

"Well, no one said it'd be easy. You've still got the rest of your family to help out until you do find someone," I explained to Suki.

CHAPTER XXXI

My sister, Veronica, decided to visit us, and just the way she talked about it made me think she had a secret she didn't want us to know.

On the date she would arrive, my flight wouldn't get me home in time to meet her, so Josh had to pick her up from the airport. He took Ronnie home and got her settled in before returning to the airport to get me. Of course, my sister came with my husband and kids. When she saw me, she outran my kids to give me a hug. It had been several years since we'd seen her. After all the hugs, Josh took us to a restaurant for supper.

The girls wanted to sit on each side of Aunt Ronnie. She wanted to sit across me so we could catch up on all the news from home. The table we were seated at was big enough for eight people, three on each long side and one each at the ends. The girls sat on each side of my sister while my husband, Ozzie, and I sat directly across from her. The restaurant Josh selected was called the Chicken Coop. The main reason for the selection is because our young children are fussy eaters.

Once our orders were placed, Ronnie said, "The big news is the *M* word."

Before we could congratulate my sister, Ozzie asked, "What's the *M* word?"

"Something you don't like," I told my son. "I'll explain it after we get home."

"But I wanna know now," my son complained.

"Mommy said later," Josh admonished. "Do you want to eat alone in the car?"

"No."

"Then please be quiet." Josh scolded.

"Can you tell me what it means now?" Hallie asked.

"You'll get the explanation at the same time Ozzie does," Josh said.

Jerika remained quiet. I'm sure she understood the meaning.

"One of my ideas was to have it on one of your airplanes," Ronnie mentioned.

"Bad idea," Josh said. "The main reason is turbulence. Another is that the aisle would be too narrow. Also, to get started in the back would be too confining."

"What about one of the larger planes?" Veronica asked.

"The larger ones have more than one aisle. Even though they are wider, there're not really wide enough," I explained to my sister.

"Well…it was just a thought. Can't blame me for trying," she said.

Our meal arrived, and our attention turned to eating instead of talking.

The moment we arrived home, little Ozzie asked, "Okay, what's the *M* word?"

"The *M* word is *marriage*," I explained. "That means Aunt Ronnie wants to get married."

"To a man?" Ozzie quizzed me.

"Yes."

He shook his head and said, "The poor guy. I feel sorry for him."

"Why?"

"Because now he'll be stuck with a bossy girl."

"But don't you like Aunt Ronnie? She's a girl."

"That's different," Ozzie said.

"Why's that different?"

"She's family," Ozzie responded.

"Why is my being family different from any other girl?" his aunt asked, tussling his hair.

"Well…sometimes you're fun to be with," my son said.

"Only sometimes?" Aunt Ronnie said as she started to tickle my son unmercifully.

"Don't!... Stop!" Ozzie begged.

"Don't stop. Okay, I won't stop," Veronica agreed and kept tickling my son.

"Ha ha, Mommy, help me! Ha ha," pleaded Ozzie.

"Why? You made Aunt Ronnie mad because you gave her the wrong answer. You said sometimes she's fun to be with. You should have said she's always fun to be with," I explained.

"I'll stop tickling you on one condition," Veronica said.

"Ha ha. What condition?"

"That you give me a hug."

"Gross. Ha ha, okay, okay," my son agreed.

As Veronica let Ozzie get up, he started to run away from her. She grabbed him and said, "Don't lie to me, Ozzie, or I'll tickle you even more."

"But you're a girl."

"While you're arguing with me, you could have given me a hug and been on your way," she said with open arms.

Ozzie relented and hugged his aunt. She returned his hug and said, "Now that wasn't so bad, was it?" Then she kissed him on his cheek.

"Yuck, now I'll have to take another bath," Ozzie complained.

"You'd better be careful what you say Ozzie, or I'll get my lipstick out and plant a big red kiss on your cheek. Then I'll take you outside and call all the girls in the neighborhood and show them your big red kiss."

"You wouldn't dare," Ozzie shot back.

"Oh yeah? Where's my pocketbook? I'll show you," she said, getting up off the floor.

Ozzie ran for his life to get away from his aunt.

"Give him a few years, Veronica. He'll change his mind," I said to my sister.

"Yeah, he'll be chasing anything in a skirt," she acknowledged.

The next morning, Veronica walked into the kitchen with a yawn. "Morning. What can I do to help?"

"Morning, sis. You could call everyone to breakfast."

Just then, Josh walked in. "Morning, ladies."

We both returned his greeting. Then Veronica left to get the kids.

The girls came into the kitchen a few steps behind my sister. Ozzie hung back and was being cautious.

"What's the matter, Sweetheart?" I asked.

"It's Aunt Ronnie. She'll tickle me."

"Not if you're a good boy and come to the table for breakfast," Veronica said.

Ozzie kept a skeptical eye on his aunt as he climbed onto his chair next to her. She made a sudden move as if to attack him, and he almost lost his balance as he slid off the chair.

"Do I have to sit next to her?" he asked, looking at his dad. "Well, if you don't, then maybe you'd like to go to your room without breakfast. Do you want that?" Josh asked him.

"No," Ozzie said.

When breakfast was over, Veronica leaned over to Ozzie and gave him a quick peck on the cheek.

His reaction? "Gross."

CHAPTER XXXII

Josh agreed to stay with the kids while Veronica went with me to see Mrs. Glade. My sister rang the doorbell and stayed centered in front of the door with me off to one side.

Mrs. Glade opened the door.

"Hi, Mrs. Glade. Do you remember me?" Veronica asked.

It took a minute. "You're Veronica Shaffer? Cinnamon's little sister?" she asked. Tears began to fall down Mrs. Glades' cheeks as she hugged my sister.

"Come in, come in," she said. Then she noticed me. "You too, Cinnamon."

Once we were all inside, Mrs. Glade insisted on serving refreshments.

"Veronica, I haven't seen you since…since you were about Hallie's age. You've blossomed into a beautiful young lady."

"Thank you, Mrs. Glade."

"Mrs. Glade, we came here for one significant reason. We want you to come to Ronnie's wedding. She'll be getting married soon." I squeezed in.

"Oh, that's wonderful! Congratulations, Veronica," Mrs. Glade happily said. "This calls for another hug."

Josh and I would travel the 862 miles to Cimarron, Kansas, to my parents' home where the wedding would take place. Well…actually it would be in the Cimarron Baptist Church, which is a short distance from my parents' home. Since Josh and I sometimes had different days off, it worked out for us to take the kids to Mom and Dad's and leave them there until the wedding. Sometimes we got to go together to help with the preparations.

The day Veronica had scheduled me to go for a fitting for my matron of honor gown, I'd also been scheduled to work. In my opinion, this wasn't fair. I went to Jaylene to explain the situation, and she agreed that it wasn't right, but work came first. That meant a call to Veronica to change the schedule for my fitting. She didn't like that idea, but what could I do?

I put in my vacation request for the week before Veronica's wedding to ensure I'd be able to attend without having to worry about being called in to work on that important day. Josh couldn't get that same week but was able to get an extra day off to be at the wedding.

Traveling back and forth between home and Cimarron put a lot of miles on our car. Flying would have been better except that the closest airport to Cimarron was in Dodge City, about eighteen miles east of Cimarron. The problem was that the Dodge City airport is a regional airport for only small planes. That meant no Angel Air craft could land there as the smallest plane, a 717, is too large for the runway. We decided it would be easier to drive than change to a non-Angel flight even though the trip would take a lot longer.

Josh and I finally had some time together at Mom and Dad's house. That's when we met Veronica's soon-to-be husband, Curt Dooley. Mom and Dad invited Curt and his parents and sister, Becky, to dinner the day before the wedding. They live in Mullinville, Kansas, about an hour's drive east of Cimarron.

Curt had joined the Army right out of high school and became a military police officer. The day he was discharged, he managed to find employment on the Dodge City police force as a patrol officer.

After dinner, we went to church for the wedding rehearsal.

Our kids would take part in the wedding. Jerika would be a bridesmaid. Hallie would be the flower girl, and Ozzie would be the ring bearer. Josh would be just a guest. Poor Josh. Of course, I'd be the matron of honor.

On Curt's side of the wedding, Becky would be a bridesmaid. The best man and ushers (or groomsmen) would be friends of Curt's from school. After the rehearsal, Ozzie looked a little sad.

"Ozzie, Honey, what's with the sad face?" I asked.

"It's Uncle Curt," he replied.

"Why, did he do something to hurt you?"

"No. The problem is he wants to marry a girl, poor guy."

"That girl, as you call her, is your Aunt Ronnie. Don't you love her?"

"Yeah, but she'll boss him around. He'll be miserable."

"That's what you think," Veronica said as she came over and heard the last of the conversation. "I should tickle you so you can't stop laughing."

"You wouldn't dare," Ozzie challenged his aunt.

"You wanna bet?" Veronica said and made a lunge for her nephew like she was about to tickle him.

Ozzie ran around behind me to escape.

"Mommy, help me!" he said, giggling.

Just then, my phone vibrated. The number was unfamiliar to me.

"Who's that?" Veronica asked.

"You tell me, then we'll both know."

She looked at the number. Her face told me she didn't know either. It looked like it might be from somewhere overseas, maybe Korea? The only number from Korea that I knew belonged to Jin Hee, but this wasn't her number. So who else would call me? Maybe someone on the other end dialed the wrong number. I didn't answer it.

Veronica changed the subject. "Cinnamon, did you see the look on Dad's face when he said, 'Her mother and I do!'"

"Yes. It's the same sad look he had at my wedding. I think it's because both of us are now on our own. He's had to care for us growing up, and now it makes him sad that he no longer has that responsibility, but like he always says, we're just a phone call away."

The next day, Veronica's wedding went off without a hitch.

About three months later, Veronica and Curt came for a visit. While the men talked, we girls went to see Mrs. Glade. She was happy to see us as usual.

"Your wedding was beautiful, Veronica. It gave me something to do besides stay home alone."

"I'm glad you enjoyed it," Veronica said to Mrs. Glade.

"Too bad we don't live closer so we could see you more often."

"Now, my dear, you need to think about having some little ones. It'll keep me busy."

"You always say that, Mrs. Glade. You aren't getting any younger," Veronica mentioned.

"That's okay. Between you and Cinnamon, both of you make me feel like a million bucks. My age has nothing to do with it. As long as I'm kept busy with you and your families, I'm on cloud nine."

"We'd like to reminisce, but your taxi is waiting," Veronica said.

"You two came to see me in a taxi?" asked Mrs. Glade.

"No, Veronica is joking. I drove us over here. I'm her taxi while she and her new husband are staying with us. Shall we go?"

"Where are we going?" Mrs. Glade asked.

"To the mall," Veronica replied. "Where else?"

"I'd better change. I'll only be a minute, girls," Mrs. Glade said.

A few minutes later, we were headed for the mall. Once inside, we went to one of our favorite stores. As soon as we were out of earshot of Mrs. Glade, I told Veronica in almost a whisper about Mrs. Glade's declining health.

"Mrs. Glade had a heart attack a few months after Ozzie was born. We need to keep an eye on her and make sure she doesn't overdo anything."

"Is she under any restrictions?" my sister asked.

"Not that I'm aware of."

"What about her diet?"

"I've not been told of anything specific. She's pretty much on her own most of the time."

"Does she ever come over to your house on occasion?"

"When both Josh and I have to work at the same time, she'll come over to stay with the kids. Other than that, she stays to herself."

"Don't you ever go over to her house for a visit?" Veronica asked.

"After her heart attack, we stopped visiting with the kids for fear of exciting her too much. Josh or I would still go over to help her with whatever she needed but would not stay very long."

We continued to shop going from one store after another. Near lunchtime, Veronica expressed she was hungry. She talked me into going to the food court for lunch. Then we went hunting for Mrs. Glade.

When we neared the front of the store to go into the mall, we heard a commotion.

"What's happening?" Veronica asked another customer.

"Some old lady collapsed," the woman said.

Closer inspection revealed that the some old lady was Mrs. Glade. Veronica shoved her purchases into my arms and rushed to Mrs. Glade's aid.

"Everyone, please step back and give her some room!" Veronica shouted. "I'm a paramedic. Someone please call nine-one-one. Now!"

Kneeling beside Mrs. Glade, Veronica checked her vital signs, then she began CPR. My guess was that Mrs. Glade had another heart attack.

Once the paramedics arrived, Veronica told them about her efforts to revive Mrs. Glade and offered to assist them in whatever way they needed. All I could do was stand there and shake. My nerves were running around like a chicken with its head cut off only at hyperspeed. Once the paramedics stabilized Mrs. Glade, Veronica got the name of the hospital they were taking her to. Then we hurried to the car and followed the ambulance.

"Cinnamon, why didn't you help?"

"I've been away from nursing too long, and I just…froze."

In the waiting room, I called Josh and Curt to let them know about Mrs. Glade while Veronica called our parents. Josh had to call a taxi since we only have one car, then round up the kids. When they arrived in the waiting room at the hospital, they found both my sister and me in tears.

"What happened?" Josh asked.

"Mrs. Glade just died," Veronica sobbed.

Both of my daughters began to cry. With all but Josh and Curt crying, little Ozzie decided also to cry. It was a sad day for us all.

When we were told which funeral home they'd send Mrs. Glade's body to, Josh mentioned he had to get to work. I'd have to go with him so we'd have use of the car rather than have to pay for a taxi.

Later that evening, Mom called to announce their arrival. While she waited for my dad to make arrangements for renting a car, we told them we'd pick them up and that Mrs. Glade had been transferred to the funeral home. Upon my arrival at the airport, I found my parents sitting on a bench near the rental car booths. Mom could see I'd been crying. It looked to me like it wouldn't take much to make her cry. We all hugged, and I gave my car keys to my dad.

Since it was late, we decided to all go to bed when we arrived home. I had to get up to go to work the next day before Josh arrived back from his flight.

The next morning, Mom took charge as she always did. She had breakfast on the table when the rest of us arrived in the kitchen. The kids came dragging in as usual.

Mom said, "Now that we're all here, I've got something to tell you about Mrs. Glade." She then glanced over at Dad. At first, he did nothing, then gave a slow nod.

"Mrs. Glade," Mom said, with a shaky voice, "wasn't who you thought she was."

Ozzie piped up, "She's Santa Claus?"

"No, Ozzie, not Santa Claus. However, this will come as a shock to you. She was my mother, your grandmother." Mom stood very still.

Veronica and I looked at each other with confused looks on our faces.

My sister said, "You told us we didn't have a grandmother on your side of the family. Then you lied to us?"

"Veronica, let your mother finish her story," Dad scolded.

"Your grandmother," Mom continued firmly, "had been in the witness protection program. This happened before I was born. She swore me to secrecy not to tell anybody. When she met my father, she moved to a Navy base. That's where I grew up and met your father. When my father died, she changed her last name to Glade and moved to her current location."

"It's no wonder she treated us with such kindness," Veronica said.

Mrs. Glade, our grandma, showed kindness more to my sister than to me lately. Now it made sense. Anyway, my watch told me it was time to go to work.

At work, I grabbed a cup of coffee and went to sit at a table in the lounge. At that moment, my hands began to shake, and my coffee started to spill onto the table as I sat. Tears streamed down my face. The shock of knowing Mrs. Glade was my grandmother and had passed away must have worn off.

"What's the matter?" Karyn asked, coming over to the table.

"My grandmother just died," I blurted out in tears.

Karyn sat next to me and tried to comfort me. When Jaylene came in, Karyn called her over.

"Cinnamon, let's go to my office. Karyn, would you go with us, please?" Jaylene asked.

Once we were in her office, Jaylene asked, "What happened?"

"Cinnamon's grandmother just passed away," Karyn said.

"I'm sorry, Cinnamon," Jaylene responded.

"Thank you."

"I'll give you three days off to make your arrangements," Jaylene told me. "Do you have a way home?"

"Josh should be on his way home from here," I said to my boss while wiping my eyes. "We have a certain place where we park the car so that if one of us is on the way to work and the other is on the way home, we can find the car."

"Is he here now, Cinnamon?" Jaylene asked.

"I'll have to call him to be sure."

"Go ahead, call," Karyn commanded.

Josh answered on the second ring, "Hi, Honey. What's up?"

"Josh, where are you?"

"I just left the airport grounds. Why?"

"You need to turn around and pick me up at the Angel Air ticket curb. I'm going home."

"Why? What's the matter?" he sounded concerned.

"I'll explain in the car. Please hurry."

"Okay, I'm on my way." He hung up.

"I'll walk you out, Cinnamon," said Karyn.

By the time we'd walked to the curb, Josh was just pulling up in front of us. Karyn turned to me and gave me a warm hug.

"Let us know if there's anything any of the Angels can do for you."

"Thank you, Karyn. I'll see you in a few days."

Karyn turned to go back into the building as I got into the car. Josh knew about Mrs. Glade's death, but what he didn't know was that we were related to her. It took most of the ride home for me to explain.

"You're telling me that you didn't know about the relationship?" Josh questioned.

"That's correct. Mom kept it a secret until this morning. Veronica and I felt almost like we were related but didn't have any idea that we were really family."

When we arrived home, Josh called his boss to let him know about Mrs. Glade being my grandmother and that she'd passed away. He wanted to be there for us.

At the funeral home, we were ushered into a private room to discuss the funeral arrangements that our family wanted. I didn't know there were so many options, like, cremation, burial in a number of caskets that ranged from inexpensive to very expensive, different types of urns for ashes, different headstones, plots, and so on. We finished with the arrangements and went to lunch while the funeral home prepared everything we'd decided on.

When we returned, Mrs. Glade was in the casket. It looked like she'd decided to take a nap. When Ozzie saw Mrs. Glade in the coffin, he didn't understand that this would be the last time he'd see her.

"Why is Aunt Nana sleeping in that box?" he asked his aunt.

"She's not sleeping," Veronica said, tucking her skirt under her knees and squatting down to Ozzie's level. "Her spirit went to Heaven, and her body will be buried in the ground."

"No. She's just got her eyes closed. Can't you see she's breathing?"

"Ozzie, Honey, you just want to see her breathing."

"You help other people who fall down," Ozzie insisted. "Why won't you help Aunt Nana?"

"At the mall, I did try to help Aunt Nana. If I hadn't, she might have turned into a zombie."

"No way," Ozzie contradicted.

"This is a sleep that even I can't do anything to fix. The only way your Aunt Nana could wake up is if God told her to wake up."

"Then tell God to wake her up," Ozzie commanded.

"I'm sorry, Ozzie. This is something God has control over, not me. He called Aunt Nana to Heaven."

"Then tell God to wake her up." He repeated his demand.

"I'm sorry, Honey, it's out of my hands," Veronica said.

"You're just being mean, Aunt Ronnie," he said and started to cry.

Veronica put her arms around her nephew and picked him up as she stood. "You'll understand better when you get older," she explained. Veronica turned to me and said, "I honestly don't think Ozzie understands all of what's happening."

"Do you want me to take him?" I asked my sister.

"That's okay, Cinnamon. I'll manage."

The funeral home began to receive friends of Mrs. Glade who'd heard of her passing.

At the end of the day, we were all tired and decided to go to Mrs. Glade's home to check on it. Many friends began arriving with food. After we dined on the food, we closed Mrs. Glade's home and went to our house where tomorrow would be a busy day for us with the funeral itself and the burial.

The very next day, the funeral took place in the Foster Road Baptist Church. During the service, my phone vibrated. I looked at the number. It was the same strange number I received the night before Veronica's wedding. Because of the service, I put it out of my mind. Then we followed the hearse to the cemetery. The pallbearers then took the coffin and set it on the stand that would lower it into the ground. We all gathered around the casket for one last time. Then the preacher said a few words and prayed. To me, it looked like there were more people that had come to the grave site.

"Mom, why is it that there seems to be more people here than at the funeral home?" I asked.

"Cinnamon, some people don't like small churches. Others may think there is more room at the grave than at the home. Why, I don't know."

The attorney Mrs. Glade had engaged to execute her will called Mom, Dad, Veronica, and me into his office for the reading of her will. We left our children in the care of Josh and Curt. Mrs. Glade left everything to Mom except one thousand dollars each to my sister and me.

Mom talked it over with Dad and decided to have a home sale to dispose of the contents of Mrs. Glade's house. The house itself would be sold at a later date. Preparing for this sale, tagging and pricing every item, proved to be more than a job and a half, maybe two. That took several days to complete. Josh and I helped when we were home. Most of the time, we had to work. Veronica and Curt helped until they had to return to their home in Dodge City. Once the sale of the contents was over, Mom and Dad contacted a realtor to sell the house. They gave him our contact number and told him he should contact us if he needed any information or anything else relating to the sale. That's when Mom and Dad left for their home in Cimarron.

That evening, my phone vibrated for a third time with this same unknown number. This time, I answered it. "Hello."

"*Yeoboseyo*," the voice on the other end said. It sounded like Jade's voice.

"Jade? Is that you?"

The voice on the other end said, "*Yeoboseyo*," again, then proceeded to speak in Korean. The only word I knew in Korean was *yeoboseyo*, which means "hello" in English.

That voice again sounded like Jade.

"I'm sorry, could you please speak in English?" I responded.

Then I heard a male voice yell in Korean and a female scream before the line went dead.

"Hello…hello? Jade?" my voice questioned. "Jade, is that you?"

No response. Nothing.

"Who was that?" Josh asked.

"I'm not sure. It sounded like Jade, but she spoke only Korean. Maybe it's my imagination, but I thought it sounded like someone was trying to beat her, and then I heard a scream just before the line went dead."

"What do you make of this call?" Josh asked.

"I've no idea unless it was Jade. Hopefully, she'll call back so I can ask her." I began to wonder, *Was my mind playing tricks on me?* "Josh, did I really hear Jade's voice, or was it my imagination?" All of a sudden, my nerves began to vibrate at hyperspeed, and my tear ducts began to fill up.

Jade, was that you I heard on the phone just now? Where are you?

CHAPTER XXXIII

The next day at work, I asked Karyn what she thought about my mystery caller. Jaye and Sunny weren't in the lounge. Just before we left on our flight to Seattle on a Boeing 737, Jaylene came into the break area. We asked her what she thought concerning the mysterious phone call. She had no idea what to think since she had not been on that ill-begotten flight. Karyn suggested we try Marilyn. She'd been our supervisor on that flight. Although that idea would have to wait until we returned from Seattle. By the time we returned, both Jaye and Sunny were in the lounge. The four of us (Jaye, Sunny, Karyn, and I) went to Marilyn's office to tell her about the call I received that might just might have been Jade. We wanted her opinion.

"It seems highly unlikely after all these years, Cinnamon," she said.

"I agree, Marilyn, but it is possible. Isn't it?"

"Yes, it's possible. Just don't get your hopes up until you have positive proof," Marilyn responded.

"I'll call my contact at the embassy in Seoul," I said.

Making contact was easier said than done. I'd have to place the call from home because of the time difference in Korea.

"American Embassy, how may I help you?" asked a pleasant Korean female voice.

"I'd like to speak to Jin Hee please. She works for the embassy," I said politely.

"Who's calling please?"

"My name is Cinnamon Lamberg. Jin Hee is a friend."

"I'm sorry, Ms. Lamberg. Jin Hee no longer works here. She retired last month."

"Could you please give me her phone number?"

"Again, I'm sorry. It is embassy policy that we do not give out personal information to anyone."

"Oh, great," I sighed. "Well…could you please contact Jin Hee and ask her to give me a call? It's imperative."

"The phone she had belonged to the embassy and had to turn it in when she left. She may have purchased a new phone for private use, but I'm not sure about that," the embassy employee said.

"I received a call from someone in Korea at a number I'm not familiar with. Is there any chance you could help me with that?"

"Again, Ms. Lamberg, I'm sorry for not being able to help you."

"Okay, well, thank you, anyway."

"You're welcome, Ms. Lamberg."

"Now what?" I said to no one in particular and hung up.

Then an idea hit me. Maybe Jaye or Sunny would have some ideas or friends that could help. When asked, they agreed. The problem was that Marilyn wouldn't cooperate.

"Cinnamon," she told me, "you refuse to go on a Dreamliner. Also, you are needed elsewhere."

"That was before you sent me to a shrink. I'm willing to try again on the Dreamliner. You just need to give me a chance to prove that I'm over my problems. Not only that, but it'd be like old times if you'd come with us."

"Cinnamon, you're dreaming. Things don't always work out the way we'd like them to."

"You're just being mean, Marilyn."

"No, I'm being practical," she replied in defense.

"Haven't you heard the saying, Where there's a will, there's a way?" I shot back and turned to walk out of her office.

On the way home, my mind kept coming up blank with ideas about going back to Korea.

I greeted my family upon entering and told Josh my problem.

"Cinnamon, why not contact Ms. Willingham? She's helped you before."

"But that was before when I'd helped her. I can't keep asking her to do me any more favors."

"It can't hurt to ask. Try. Maybe she'll help."

"And just maybe, my bosses will be very upset with me for going over their heads. Did you ever think of that?" I put my hands on my hips and gave Josh a smirk.

"Give it a shot. If it doesn't work out, then there's no harm done," my husband commanded.

So reluctantly I called Ms. Willingham's number, and the voice mail picked up. "Please leave a message at the tone." The phone beeped.

"Ms. Willingham, this is Cinnamon Lamberg. I want to talk to you when you have a minute." I left my number before ending the call and told her I'd be available tomorrow night after work.

It took a few days before Ms. Willingham returned my call.

"Ms. Willingham, I've a big favor to ask of you. If you say no, I'll have to forget about it."

"I can't say yes or no until you tell me what that favor is, Cinnamon."

"In reality, I've no right to ask. My favor is to go back to Korea. This time, I'm almost positive we'll find Jade."

A long pause came from the other end.

"I'm not in the habit of interfering with the day-to-day operations of the company," she replied.

"Normally I wouldn't ask you to, but you're the only one who will listen to me." We talked some more at length about family and work. Then I'd given her my total request.

"I'll think it over, Cinnamon, and get back to you in a few days."

"Thank you, Ms. Willingham. You're an Angel."

The next morning at work, I grabbed a cup of coffee and went over to the table where Karyn sat. Sunny and Jaye were also there.

"Morning, ladies."

They returned my greeting in unison.

"How'd it go with you getting back to Korea, Cinnamon?" Karyn asked.

"I've got an ace up my sleeve. I'm just worried that it might backfire."

"What is it?" Jaye asked.

"It might be a good idea if you guys didn't know, then you won't get into trouble if things go wrong."

"Good idea, Cinnamon," said Sunny. "But will you be all right to fly on the Dreamliner again?"

"That's something I'm hoping will be okay. I've had some counseling on the subject and need to test my nerves on that aircraft."

"But what will you do if you find you can't stand to fly on the Dreamliner?" asked Jaye.

"I'll cross that bridge when I come to it."

It took a few days for Ms. Willingham to put my idea into motion. They—Sunny, Jaye, Karyn, and Marilyn—joined me on the Dreamliner bound for the Republic of South Korea. Once on board waiting on our passengers, Marilyn pulled me aside.

"Cinnamon, I'm not happy you went over my head and pulled me away from my desk to fly to Korea."

"Marilyn, you have every right to be angry with me, but I'd appreciate it if you'll be kind enough to listen to why I did this. When we return home, if you want to fire me, I'll understand."

"Okay, explain," she commanded.

"No one would to listen to me. I honestly believe Jade is alive and that she can be found this time. She was your friend before you became management. She's still my friend, and I'm determined to find her no matter what."

"Why does she matter so much to you, Cinnamon?"

"Do you remember my first day at Anger Air? She helped me emotionally get over the accident that ruined my clean uniform and my injured knee. I'll never forget that, and since she was shot because of me, I owe it to her to find her and bring her home."

"But it's been several years. What makes you so sure you'll find her this time?"

"I never told anyone this, but my phone vibrated during my sister's wedding with a number that's unknown to me. I'm sure it came from Korea. Anyway, I'd forgotten about it. Then it vibrated again with the same unknown number during my grandmother's funeral. Then one evening, my phone vibrated for a third time with the same number. This time, I answered it. The woman on the other end said hello in Korean and then spoke more in Korean. Just after I'd asked her to speak in English, I heard someone shouting in Korean and a female scream, then the line went dead. It sounded like Jade's voice."

"How do you know it was Jade? It could have been someone else who sounded like her," she questioned.

"You're right, Marilyn, there's no way to prove it, but this may be the last time I'll be able to look for her."

"Well, all I've got to say is you'd better be right, or you'll be looking for a new job when we get home."

"Thank you, Marilyn."

"Cinnamon, I'm only letting you do this because of Jade. You're right she was my friend. Now let's go greet the passengers."

For the most part, the flight was uneventful. Every time I went near the location where I'd been held captive or looked at the area where Jade had been shot, my nerves shook worse than if I'd had Parkinson's disease. Marilyn had her eyes on me, and near the end of the flight commented on my nerves.

"Cinnamon, you surprised me. You handled yourself very well when you went near the areas you'd been frightened of."

"Thank you, Marilyn. They made me nervous."

Once we were in our hotel room, we changed into civilian clothes. Since it was around 8:00 p.m., we decided to go up to the top floor where there happened to be a snack bar. Marilyn and Karyn each had a beer. Jaye and Sunny had a soju each, and I had a Cheon Yeon Cider. We all ordered sandwiches. Since Sunny and Jaye are Korean, they were also served several small dishes of different types of kimchee.

In this snack bar, there happened to be a piano where a young Korean lady played American songs. Some were country Western, some were hip-hop, and some were love songs. It made us feel right at home. She played for close to an hour before she left. All of us decided to give her a tip of a couple of dollars each for which she thanked us.

We would start our search for Jade tomorrow morning at the American Embassy.

It was a warm summer day as Jaye, Sunny, and I alighted from the taxi in front of the American Embassy. Before we entered the embassy, Jaye told us she knew the receptionist and asked us to wait on a bench just inside. The embassy's airconditon felt good. Jaye went up to the receptionist to ask about Jin Hee. She came back to us with news.

"Jin Hee lives about a mile from here. The receptionist also gave me her new phone number. She told me not to give it out to anyone for fear of getting fired."

"Why would she get fired?" Of course, I had to ask the stupid question.

"Because she gave out personal information that she's not authorized to give. Anyway, the next step is to go to a local phone store and get a couple of burner phones," Jaye said.

Once we did that, we returned to the hotel to connect up with Karyn and Marilyn. While we did this, Sunny went to a car rental company to rent a car for us to use. Sunny returned to the hotel with a minivan.

"How long have you had a Korean driver's license?" asked Karyn.

"I don't need a Korean driver's license," she responded. "I've got an international driver's license. It gives me the authority to drive in whatever country I'm in so long as women are allowed to drive in that country."

Jaye called the number the lady at the embassy had given her. No answer. She left a voice mail with her name and the return phone number.

We'd been waiting almost fifteen minutes when the phone finally rang.

"*Yeoboseyo,*" Jaye answered and waited while the person on the other end spoke. Then Jaye said in Korean, "We'll meet you there." She then hung up.

"Okay," Jaye said, "Jin Hee will meet us at a coffee and bakery shop near the embassy in about half an hour."

"I know the place," Sunny said. "Let's go."

Sunny took the driver's seat. Jaye rode shot gun, and the rest of us piled into the back seats in no particular order. Once we found a parking space, we entered this coffee and bakery shop. Jaye ordered coffee and pastry for all of us. We were surprised that Jin Hee came in later than we did since she lived so close to the place. She ordered and paid for a coffee and pastry before she came over to the table where we were. Once she was seated, we all said our hellos.

As I was the one who got all of us together, it was up to me to start our so-called meeting.

"Jin Hee, a few days ago, I received a call from somewhere here in Korea not once but three different times. I'm almost positive the last one was Jade. It sounded to me like someone beating and yelling at her. Then she began crying before the line went dead. Maybe you can help us find her with this phone number." I passed the number to Jin Hee.

She looked at it and said, "If this is a private number, the phone company may not give us what we want. If that's the case, we'll have to go to the police."

We all agreed.

"Okay, let's go," Marilyn said, draining her coffee. Six chairs pushed back all at the same time. As we all stood, this made a tremendous noise. Everyone in the shop stared at us.

Outside the telephone company, Jin Hee requested, "Please stay here. I'll have better luck getting the information if I go in by myself."

Twenty minutes later, Jin Hee returned.

"They said the number is still active but would not give me any more information."

"Maybe we'll have better luck at the police station," I mentioned.

"If what Cinnamon told us turns out to be correct, we have no other choice," said Karyn. "Jade could be in trouble."

"What happens if this just turns out to be a wild goose chase?" Marilyn speculated.

"Always the skeptic, Marilyn," Karyn said. "I'm inclined to believe Cinnamon. In my memory, Jade wouldn't call like that if something wasn't wrong."

"But Cinnamon just said that she wasn't one hundred percent positive that it was Jade's voice."

"Marilyn, please let us find out for sure. If I'm wrong, I'll pay the price," I pleaded.

"I'm not sure, but we've come this far," Marilyn said. "Next stop, the police station."

We put the same procedure in place at the police station. Karen reminded Jin Hee to tell them about Jade possibly being kidnapped and possibility beaten. Then Jin Hee went inside by herself. Jaye started to get out of the car after more than thirty-five minutes. Just then, Jin Hee came out. Inside the car, she told us what transpired.

"I've been told we have to go to Suwon and check in at the police station there. The phone number you gave me, Cinnamon, is from that area."

"Where is Suwon?" asked Karyn. "And how far is it?"

"We head south for thirty-one kilometers," Sunny said as she pulled away from the curb.

"How many miles is that?" Marilyn wanted to know.

"About nineteen," Sunny replied.

"Well, let's get this goose chase started," I said, trying to inject a little humor into our conversation.

No one laughed. It was time for lunch, so we decided to eat first.

We arrived in Suwon, a city of about 1.25 million people. After taking a few wrong turns, we finally found the police station we were looking for.

"Let me go in alone again," said Jin Hee. "Hopefully, they'll give me the information we need to find Jade."

It took Jin He almost an hour. We began to worry. When she returned to the car, she explained that there were many people wanting information about almost everything under the sun.

"We've got a name," she said. "The name is Park. It's not much to go on."

"What do you mean, not much to go on?" I asked. "How hard will it be to find someone with the name Park?"

"Cinnamon, the name Park is as common in Korea as Smith is in America," commented Jin Hee.

"Oh!"

"This particular Mr. Park lives somewhere just outside the city limits. They think he may be on a farm just south of here."

Jaye asked in Korean which road to take going south. Jin Hee translated into English.

"Let's go to the city limits and talk to some of the locals. Maybe they'll know."

That's what we did. It took fifteen to twenty minutes to reach the city limits with all the traffic. We talked to several people. Some were helpful, and some weren't sure. Then we spotted another police station where Jin Hee went to talk to someone.

She came out with a smile on her face. She told Sunny which way to go in Korean. Then repeated the direction in English. A few minutes after leaving the city behind, we spotted a police officer on a street corner.

"What's a policeman doing this far outside the city?" I asked.

"Cinnamon, police in Korea have authority wherever they go. They are national police like the FBI in America," Jin Hee stated.

"That shows me how little I know about Korea."

We stopped to ask this police officer where to find the Mr. Park we were looking for. He wasn't sure which Park we wanted because there were several families with that name in the area. We'd have to eliminate them one by one.

Half an hour later, we'd had no luck with several Park families. We were cruising slowly past farm after farm with frustrated drivers behind us honking their horns. Sunny kept waving them to go around us. All of a sudden, Karyn pressed her face to the window on her side.

"Stop!" she shouted. Sunny stopped so suddenly that the driver to our rear almost ran into us. She then pulled off to the side.

"I saw something a little ways back. It looked like it might be Jade," she happily cried.

We all got out and started to follow Karyn. At this point, we all saw a man with a whip. He was using it on something brown that had fallen on the ground. That something looked like a frightened Jade. This made my blood boil. With my adrenalin pumping at maximum speed, I ran past Karyn and slammed into this man, knocking him to the ground. Then I punched him on the chin very hard. Pain emanated from my hand and wrist. He threw me aside, grabbed his whip, and got up. By this time, the others were on him trying to keep him from further harming Jade.

He had enough strength to throw them off. I threw myself over Jade to protect her as his whip came down on me, causing me to cry out in excruciating pain. The others again grabbed him.

Someone yelled out, "Call nine-one-one," and then I heard, someone say, "In Korea, the emergency number is one-one-nine."

At the hospital in Suwon, the doctor looked at the x-rays taken of my wrist, which showed it to be fractured. There were welts on my back and the back of my right arm where the whip had connected. Jaye stayed with me to translate into English what the doctor said. In the meantime, Jade was in another room being treated for her injuries. Once my injuries were taken care of, I wanted to go to Jade. But Jaye told me the police wanted to talk to me.

She translated everything the police asked and my answers. Then we both went to the waiting room. Marilyn said they were still waiting to hear the results of Jade's injuries. When the doctor came in, he told us Jade had been beaten before on numerous occasions. Her injuries were worse than mine. At least, we were able to stop the torture she endured.

Sunny told us that since Jade was in Korea illegally, she might have problems leaving Korea once she left the hospital, which would be sometime in the next few weeks.

"Would an immigration attorney be able to help?" I questioned Sunny.

"Attorneys are expensive, Cinnamon," she mentioned.

"Jade may face a problem, but the fact that she was held against her will should work in her favor. Shouldn't it?" Karyn asked. "From what we saw when we rescued her, I'd say it was slave labor."

While we waited for word about Jade, a police detective entered.

"Who is Ms. Cinnamon?"

"I'm Cinnamon, and you are?"

"Detective Shin, from the Suwon police. Mr. Park says you will pay for his medical bills."

"No, Sir! He's very lucky I've decided not to sue him for what he's done to our friend. Please tell him I will not—and I repeat—not pay his medical bills. If he insists, then tell him I'll see him in court."

"That's a pretty bold statement from you, Ms. Cinnamon," intoned the detective.

"My name is Cinnamon Lamberg or Mrs. Lamberg."

"Mrs. Lamberg, you broke the man's jaw."

"What do you call this?" I asked, trying hard to lift my fractured arm, sling and all. "Not only that, but he used his whip on me."

"Mr. Park also said you took his property, and he wants it back," the detective said.

"Detective, the only thing we took from him is our friend. Her name is Jade Pinkerton. She is an American citizen. Mr. Park has been holding her against her will. We want him arrested and put in jail where he belongs," I said.

"Who are your friends?" Detective Shin asked.

I introduced my boss, Marilyn, then all of the other flight attendants, and of course, Jin Hee. Once the detective had all the information from everyone, he started for the door.

"Mrs. Lamberg, you will need to stay here for at least ten days or longer until we investigate all of this."

"Detective Shin," Marilyn called out as he turned to leave, "we are only here for five more days. Then we must return home and work."

He then returned to our gathering and asked us for our passports.

"Oh, that's just great. Now what do we do?" Karyn asked.

"Jin Hee," Marilyn asked, "is there any way you can have our ambassador run interference for us?"

"Sorry, Marilyn, the ambassador is very hard to catch, and since I'm retired, my access to him is even less than when I was employed."

"An idea is forming in my head, but I've got to get back to the hotel in Seoul," I told everyone.

Before I had the chance to explain, a doctor came in looking for Jade's family. Jin Hee who'd been our spokesperson went over to him. They talked in Korean for a while. Then she returned to our group.

"The doctor said she's alert and that we could see her, but no more than two at a time. She suggested that we stay no more than ten minutes each," Jin Hee said.

When it became my turn, Jaye went with me. Jade was sitting up in bed. We smiled as we entered.

"Hi, Jade. How are you feeling?" It's all that came to my mind.

Jade looked confused and then spoke in Korean. Jaye translated for me. "Why is everyone calling me Jade? My name is Park Jin Ju." Jaye then explained in Korean that we were friends from the good ole USA and that she could speak English.

"Jade. Don't you remember? We worked together as flight attendants for Angel Airlines. My name is Cinnamon."

"Cinnamon?" Jade asked.

"Yes, when we introduced each other, I said, 'My name is Cinnamon,' and you said, 'Is that Cinnamon as in the spice or green turnips?' Later, our flight crashed, and I asked you to get the boo-boo box. Do you remember?"

"Boo-boo box?" she repeated.

It seemed to me like she understood everything that I'd been saying. She looked to Jaye for clarification, who spoke in Korean.

"Jaye, would you please ask her where she was born and what she did for a living about twenty years ago?"

Once Jaye interpreted my question, Jade responded in Korean.

"She says that she has no memory of more than twenty years ago. All she remembers is working on that farm we rescued her from. Also, she can't remember where she was born."

"Jade, I'd like to see you again tomorrow if you'll let me," I said.

When Jaye told her in Korean, Jade responded in Korean that she wanted to see Mr. Park. He'd take care of her. To her, we were total strangers. Jaye repeated this in English. Shock registered in my brain but, hopefully, not on my face. It made me sad that Jade's memory hadn't returned.

"Don't you remember anything about Angel Air? I asked. She had no response, just a blank stare as if we were not even in the room.

Back at the hotel, I called Josh. The time difference didn't matter to me.

"Josh," I'd said when he answered groggily. "Are you awake?"

"I am now. Cinnamon?" He paused. "It's five o'clock in the morning."

"I'm sorry to wake you up, but I've got some good news and some bad news."

"What's the bad news?"

"All of us have been told we may have to stay in Korea longer than we'd planned."

"So what's the good news?"

"We found Jade!" My excited and happy voice exclaimed as tears flooded my face. "She's in the hospital. I'll explain all of that later. Right now, I've got something for you to do."

"You woke me up to ask me a favor?"

"Josh, please listen. We're supposed to be home by the end of the week. The police have seized our passports until their investigation in this case is resolved. Don't worry, I'm not in trouble. It does involve Jade and the man she slaved for."

"Cinnamon, what's going on over there?"

"I'll explain everything later. Right now, I need you to contact Ms. Willingham and tell her we need more time in Korea and that the police are holding everything up. Tell her we found Jade. Maybe she might have some influence with the ambassador?"

"Don't you think that's stretching things a bit too far, Cinnamon?"

"Maybe! But it's all we can think of right now. We haven't come up with a plan B yet."

"Okay. Just don't get your hopes up. Let me see what can be done."

Every day, I'd return to visit Jade. One morning, shortly before what we assumed would be the end of our stay in Korea, I walked in, and Jade was sitting up in her hospital bed.

"Good morning, Jade." My smile became as wide as the Grand Canyon.

"Good morning, Cinnamon," Jade happily said.

This was the first time she greeted me in English. It brought tears to my eyes. This is what I'd been hoping for since we found her.

"Have I said something wrong?" she asked.

My head shook no so violently it felt like it might come off. "No. You've said something I've been longing to hear." My tears were still streaming down my face as my shaking legs propelled me to her bedside.

"Welcome back, Jade. What made you remember?"

"You made me think about how we met and how you asked me for the first aid box. The name wasn't something I'd heard before. It just kept going over and over in my mind."

"Jade, can I hug you?"

"Only if you're gentle. My back is very sore from all those whippings."

I hugged Jade as gently as possible. It felt great. The hug would have been better if I'd been able to use both arms. Just then, the door opened for someone else to enter.

"Good morning, Marilyn," Jade said.

A surprised Marilyn returned Jade's greeting. "I've got some good news for both of you," she said. "Something or someone is watching over us. As soon as I'd received the news, I went straight to the doctor. All of us are going home. That includes you Jade."

Upon hearing the good news, my heart rate went into overdrive.

"There's just one thing," Marilyn warned. "We have to be very careful and gentle with Jade. When we get home, we should have her see her doctor. He may want to have her stay at the hospital until her injuries have healed."

My tears happily returned. They came pouring out so fast that they blinded me in my attempt to find a tissue.

"How soon?" I asked, my tears still falling.

"The police detective said we need to be out of the country no later than twenty-four hours from now."

"What about Mr. Park?" Jade wanted to know.

"He's still claiming you are his property and that he wants to press charges against Cinnamon," Marilyn said. "The sooner we leave Korea, the better."

"So the doctor agreed Jade could leave?" I asked.

"Yes, Cinnamon, go find Jin Hee," Marilyn commanded.

When I found Jin Hee, we both returned to Jade's room.

"Jin Hee, did Cinnamon give you the good news?" Marilyn asked.

"Yes. That's wonderful."

"Okay, Jade needs some clothing and a bunch of pillows. Please take Sunny with you and don't take more than two hours. Also, please ask Jaye to come in here."

"On my way," Jin Hee said as she left the room.

When Jaye came in, Marilyn asked her, "Jaye, please call our company at Kimpo and ask that a skycap be ready with a wheelchair for Jade."

"I'm on it." Jaye smiled, closing the door behind her.

"What about Karyn and me?"

"Cinnamon, right now, all we can do is shoot the breeze," Marilyn intoned.

"With what?" I complained. "We don't have a gun."

This silly remark made both Jade and Marilyn laugh. It made me happy that Jade still has a sense of humor.

Karyn finally came in. "Hi, Jade." She waved and smiled.

"Hi, Karyn," she remarked.

"Jade, how did you meet up with this Mr. Park?" Marilyn asked.

"My memory isn't good. I woke up one morning asking for a handout when Mr. Park came along. Since my Korean wasn't very good at that time, I had to use hand gestures. He figured out my meaning and took me to his farm where he fed me. Then he put me to work. He had several other girls about my age working for him.

"Whenever the urge struck him, he'd take one of the girls and have sex with her. That included me. If we didn't do exactly what he wanted, he'd whip us. We were all terrified of him."

"Slave labor?" Marilyn suggested.

"Exactly. We all took precautions not to get pregnant. He gave us all birth control pills and told us if we did get pregnant, we'd have hell to pay."

"Did any one resist his advances and did any girl get pregnant?" Karyn asked.

"If we tried to fight him off, he'd beat us until we were too weak to resist. And yes, one girl got pregnant. He beat her senseless, then took her someplace far away and dumped her."

"What were your living conditions like?" Marilyn asked.

"He put us up in a bunkhouse, which we had to keep clean with our beds made. The only problem was that he kept us all starving. What food he did give us barely kept us alive."

"That's terrible," we all agreed.

"Cinnamon, what happened to your arm?" Jade asked.

"When I saw your Mr. Park swing that whip at you and you cried out, the rage in me told me to stop him. First, I ran into him and knocked him down. Then with all my might, I slammed my fist into his jaw. I've since been told his jaw is broken. I hit him so hard it fractured my wrist."

Karyn picked up my story. "With the rest of us trying to hold him down, it was a struggle. Boy! That guy is strong. He managed to get up and use his whip on Cinnamon when she threw her body over yours to protect you."

Jade began to cry. "Thank you for helping me, Cinnamon."

It was time for hugs all around. We had to remind ourselves to be gentle because of Jade's injured back.

Just when we started our hugs, Jaye came in. "Me too." She wanted to claim a hug with her outstretched hands. "You're looking good, Jade."

"Thank you."

"Jade," Marilyn said, "there have been a lot of changes since you disappeared. Pearl retired, and I've taken her place. Willie got married to someone else and now has two kids, even Cinnamon is now married and has three kids of her own."

I fumbled in my wallet for some pictures.

"They're adorable. Congratulations, Cinnamon," Jade said.

"Thank you, Jade." Then I asked, "How were you able to call me and how did you know my number?"

"I found a little book with everyone's phone number that had been in my pants pocket. When Mr. Park saw me looking at it, he took it and beat me. I'd forgotten about it until years later when I saw it out in the open. That's when I tried to call for help. Some numbers had been changed or were out of service. Other times I got a busy signal. Every time I tried to call anyone, I had to be careful that he didn't see me. The time you answered after my first two calls to you, Cinnamon went unanswered. When you answered, he caught me and beat me."

"When you called, the number was unfamiliar to me, I was at my sister's wedding rehearsal and thought maybe someone had just misdialed. The second time was at my grandmother's funeral. My mind told me someone wanted to play a joke on me and to forget about it."

"Why'd you answer the third time?" Jade asked.

"Curiosity? My husband and I were home when your third call came in. My thought was that maybe I could put a stop to these calls and answered it. I was shocked at hearing your voice. Even though you spoke in Korean, the scream and sudden disconnection told me you were in trouble. I had to do something, and…and well, here we are."

By the time Jin Hee and Sunny returned with clothing for Jade, a nurse had removed Jade from all the equipment attached to her, including her IV.

Marilyn told Jin Hee to wait outside the door to prevent anyone from entering while Jade changed into the new clothes. We had to help her with the new underwear as well as a white blouse, black pants, and black loafers.

With Jade dressed, a nurse brought in a wheelchair. We lined it with the new pillows Jin Hee purchased. Then we had Jade sit in the chair, and we wheeled her out of her room.

Just outside her room, Detective Shin came up to us with some papers and returned our passports.

"These papers are for all of you to fill out when you get home and mail them to the address on the top of each page. Please be prompt in returning them. Thank you."

Marilyn accepted these papers, then we pushed Jade out of the hospital and into the minivan Sunny had brought up to the door for loading.

Once Jade was on board with all those pillows for her comfort, the rest of us piled in all around her and took off for the airport. I called Josh to tell him to have Willie meet us.

With all the traffic, it took us over an hour to arrive at Kimpo International Airport and the Angel Airlines terminal. As we pulled up to the curb, we signaled the skycap for the wheelchair that Jaye had asked for. Again, we plied the wheelchair with pillows before we let Jade get into it. The skycap offered to push the chair for us. We told him thank you, but we would push it while Sunny went to return the minivan to the rental company.

Inside the Angel Air lounge were some non-Korean flight attendants that knew Jade and welcomed her back. Somehow while we waited and talked, Marilyn managed to get our little group scheduled to work on the way back. We'd boarded our plane for home, and our flight lasted thirteen hours.

Now on the ground, we taxied to the appropriate gate and had to wait for all our passengers to deplane before we could have the ramp agent bring in a wheelchair for Jade.

When he arrived, Jade said, "Well, it's about time."

I think she was tired. The flight seemed to take longer than usual. We were all anxious to get home. We arrived at the baggage terminal, and there stood Willie with a massive bouquet of flowers.

"Welcome home, Jade. These are for you," he said, handing them to her with tears waiting to fall.

"Thank you," she said. "They're lovely." At this point, she wasn't sure who Willie was. We reintroduced Jade to Willie. Later, I'd learn that someone already mentioned to Willie that Jade might not remember him. Josh also met us.

"Cinnamon, what happened to your arm?" he asked with a hug and worried look on his face.

"I'll explain it all when we get home."

Word spread faster than a speeding bullet at Angel Air when it got out that Jade was on her way home. Our little group headed for the Angel Air lounge where most of the flight attendants Jade had worked with waited for her arrival.

Ms. Willingham was there, as she's the primary stock holder in Angel Air, and the CEO of Angel Air, Mr. Stickler, also wanted to greet Jade. Even Pearl, her former supervisor, came out of retirement to greet her.

"The missing Angel has returned. Welcome home, Jade." Applause and cheering erupted. "Would you like to say a few words?" Mr. Stickler asked, handing the microphone to Jade.

"It's good to be home," she said, then the tears began to roll down her face. "The Angels have been watching over me. Thank you." More applause and cheering.

Marilyn picked up the microphone. "For those who wish to hug Jade, please be gentle. She has an injured back."

Then one after another, all of the flight attendants who remembered Jade came to hug her and welcome her back. Jade was overcome with emotion as to how much her fellow employees cared for her. I'd asked Marilyn on the plane not to say anything about me. After all, this was Jade's homecoming, not mine.

I took Jade to my home after the reunion. Since she had no family and her apartment had long since been leased to someone else, she had nowhere else to go. Jerika knew I'd be arriving home soon and stayed up to greet me.

"Mom!" she exclaimed when she saw me. "What happened to your arm?"

"Hi, Honey. I'll explain everything in the morning. Right now, I'd like you to meet my friend, Jade."

After the introductions, Jerika went to bed. Josh decided that he also wanted to go to bed. Jade and I talked in the living room for a while, and I decided to tell her about my nightmares.

When I finished, Jade said, "That's terrible. Why did your dreams have me doing something horrible to you, Cinnamon?"

"It's because of what happened on that flight to Korea. When you were shot, I blamed myself for what happened."

"I'm sure whatever happened wasn't planned. I honestly don't remember anything about being shot."

"You also hit your head when you fell."

"My memory is a complete blank," she said sadly.

"Anyway, everyone assumed that when you felt well enough to leave the hospital, you did so when no one was looking. That's why we had such a hard time finding you. By the way, because of those dreams, Marilyn gave me a choice of going to see a shrink, or she'd fire me."

"You don't say. You mean it affected your work that much, Cinnamon?"

"Yes. It gave me problems." A yawn escaped my lips.

"Does this mean you want to go to bed?" Jade asked.

"It wouldn't hurt."

"One more question." Jade wanted to know. "Who was that Willie guy who gave me those flowers?"

"Believe it or not, Willie had planned on giving you a diamond ring upon your return from Korea. It fell on me to give him the bad news about you. He searched for you for over a year and then gave up. He married another woman, and she gave him two wonderful children. Shortly before we found you, she died in a car accident."

"Is there a chance we can see him tomorrow?" asked Jade.

"If we don't get to bed, it will be tomorrow."

"Okay, Cinnamon, I can take a hint. I'm just happy you didn't give up on me. Thank you, Cinnamon."

The next morning found me in the kitchen getting breakfast ready. Josh had to get to work early. The kids came straggling in while Jade still slept.

"Hallie, Ozzie, we have a guest who came in late last night. She's recovering from an accident, and I don't want you to bother her. You may say hi to her but leave her alone, okay? Jerika met her last night before she went to bed."

"Mom," Jerika asked, "is she the black lady you've been looking for?"

"Yes, she's a dear friend, and all of you are to call her Aunt Jade."

"What kind of accident, Mom?" Hallie wanted to know.

"Do you remember Aunt Suki? She had some of the same problems. Only, Aunt Jade's were worse."

"Okay, Mom, you promised to tell us what happened to your arm," said Josh.

I went over to my husband.

"All right, everybody, pay attention. The man who was being mean to Aunt Jade got a punch from me right about here"—I pointed to Josh's jaw—"I struck him so hard that it fractured my arm and broke his jaw."

"What's *fractured* mean?" asked Ozzie.

"It means that 'the bone in my arm cracked.' It's not broken but hurts just as much. It'll heal in time."

"How long?" Hallie asked.

"I'm not sure. I'll have to see the doctor first."

"Morning, everyone," said a pleasant voice from the kitchen doorway.

We all returned Jade's greeting.

"Hallie and Ozzie, this is Aunt Jade. Jade, my two youngest Hallie and Ozzie."

"It's nice to meet you," Jade acknowledged.

After breakfast, I called the doctor to make an appointment for Jade and myself. We were told to come in around 10 o'clock. Since Josh was at work, I had to enlist Jerika's help in getting Jade into the car.

After many tests on Jade, the doctor decided that she needed to go to the hospital to heal. She balked at the idea. She'd been under the impression that she'd meet Willie.

The doctor took the cast off my arm to take some x-rays and, afterward, gave me another cast. He told me to come back in about two weeks for reevaluation. Once everything settled down with Jade in the hospital, I called Willie and told him Jade wanted to see him and gave him the name of the hospital.

"I'll go after work," he said.

Just then, Jerika called me on her cell phone.

"Mom, Hallie and Ozzie want to go home."

"Okay, I'll be there in a few minutes." I hung up and gave Jade the message about Willie. It put a smile on her face.

"Jade, my kids want me to take them home. I'll be back when I can."

I'd gotten as far as the door when Marilyn walked in.

"Jade, you have some company," I told her and turned to leave.

Upon arrival in the waiting room, my kids were anxious to leave. I told Jerika that she'd have to babysit her siblings and that she'd be responsible for whatever happened. She agreed. When we arrived home, I told Hallie and Ozzie they had to mind their sister. They said they would.

Upon my return to the hospital, Willie kept his promise and came to see Jade.

"Hi, Jade. I hear you wanted to see me."

"Yes. It's my understanding you had a diamond ring for me but gave it to another woman."

"That's not exactly what happened."

"Would you mind explaining?" Jade asked.

"I bought a diamond ring that I intended to give to you when you return from Korea. When Cinnamon told me what happened, everything changed. I spent more than a year looking for you in Korea with no luck, and I'd lost all hope of ever finding you when Laura came into my life. She helped me get over my depression concerning not finding you, and eventually, we married. Shortly before you came back, Laura died in a car accident."

"Why were you at the airport with flowers for me?"

"Cinnamon called Josh to tell me to meet you there."

CHAPTER XXXIV

It's been a month since we found Jade. She's out of the hospital and still living with us. My fractured arm has healed, and the cast removed a few weeks ago.

Willie has been calling on Jade two to three nights a week and has taken her out. I think that has been the best therapy for her. She's returning to her old self again. The only problem that she keeps telling me about is Willie's son. He keeps rejecting her.

"Cinnamon, how do I get through to Billy?" She keeps asking me. "Every time I try to do something nice for him, he turns his back on me. He hates me."

"Maybe it's because he's bitter about losing his own mother and thinks you want to take away his father as well. Has Willie tried to talk to him?"

"If he has, it's been when I'm not there," lamented Jade.

"All you can do is keep trying" was my suggestion. "What about his daughter, La Keisha? Is she rejecting you also?"

"No. She wants to cling to me, but her brother gives her the evil eye when he sees her warming up to me."

"Maybe La Keisha is grieving the loss of her mother in a different way from Billy. Have you tried to talk to him, Jade?"

"Yes, but he just walks away like I'm not there."

"Maybe we could go together to talk to Willie and have you meet with Billy one on one?" I asked Jade.

We did just that. While we were talking to Willie, Billy came along.

"I'm going out," he called over his shoulder.

"Billy," Willie called to his son, "please come here for a minute."

Billy came over to where we were with a look of exasperation on his face. "Billy, I want you to go over to the other side of the room and sit. Miss Jade has something she wants to talk to you about. It will be just the two of you while Aunt Cinnamon and I stay over here."

"Do I have to?" he asked.

"Just do it," his father commanded. "She has promised me it will only take a couple of minutes, then you can be on your way."

"Okay" came his anti-Jade response.

Once they were settled on the other side of the room, Jade began her talk.

"Billy, I'm one hundred percent sure that you loved your mother with all your heart. I'm not here to take her place. No one can do that. I'm just asking you to be friends with me. Your father came close to marrying me once, but things just didn't work out the way we'd planned. Then he met your mother, and they had a happy life together until she passed away. For that, I'm sorry. If I can be of any help to you, I'll do my best, but at the same time, I won't interfere with you or anything you want to do."

"Are you finished now?" he asked, bored.

Jade turned her head toward us like she wasn't sure if she'd gotten through to Billy. Then she turned back to him.

"I've said everything for now. If you have any questions, I'll be happy to answer them."

"Yeah. Why should you expect me to call you mom, and why should I trust you?" he asked.

"I'm not expecting you to call me mom. If you prefer, you can call me Jade. It's up to you to decide if you trust me or not. All I'm asking is that we like each other. I'm not asking you to love me like you did your mother." Jade held out her hand for Billy. He just got up and left without shaking her hand.

"Well, you tried," Willie said.

"It'll take time," Jade said. "He still longs for his mother, and he thinks I'm going to take her place. That's not true. I'll never be able to do that. I'll be happy if he just becomes my friend," Jade announced.

"One problem almost solved and one more to go," Willie said.

"Now what problem are you talking about?" Jade asked.

"It's La Keisha. Lately, she's been staying in her room a great deal instead of joining Billy and me like she used to. I'm at wits end as to what to do."

"I might have an idea. Do you mind if I go see her, Willie?" asked Jade.

"Be my guest."

"You don't mind, do you, Cinnamon? Or are you in a hurry to get home?"

"Go ahead, Jade. We have plenty of time."

When Jade returned about a half hour later, La Keisha came out with her, and she was all smiles.

"Well, wonders never cease." Willie grinned.

La Keisha went over to her dad for a hug.

"I'm sorry for being so grouchy, Daddy."

"That's okay, Sweetheart." We all smiled at that.

After La Keisha left the room, Jade explained the problem Willie's daughter was having.

"Willie, La Keisha is on the verge of becoming an adult woman."

"What exactly does that mean?" Willie questioned. "I know she's growing up, but…"

"It's what happens to a woman every month," Jade said with big eyes. "The problem came about because your wife passed away before La Keisha started having her monthly cycle, and she felt too embarrassed to go to you for answers."

"Oh, now I see, but she could have gone to Cinnamon for answers."

"Yeah, right, Willie. How could she when you don't even come to see us anymore?"

"Good point, Cinnamon. I'll have to come see you guys more often."

"How about dinner tonight?" I suggested. "And bring your kids."

"Okay, what time?"
"Is five thirty all right?"
"We'll be there," he said.

Jade was helping me make dinner when the doorbell rang.

"I'll get it," Hallie cried out. When she opened the door, there stood my sister, Veronica.

"Aunt Ronnie!" Hallie screamed and hugged her aunt.

I just came from the kitchen. When Ozzie saw who was at the door, he slapped his forehead with his open hand.

"Oh, brother, here comes trouble with a capital *T*, and I don't mean maybe."

"Ozzie, that's no way to greet your Aunt Ronnie," I scolded.

"He's just aching for one of my megatickling marathons," Veronica said.

"Oh no, you don't," he said.

At that moment, Jade came into the room, and I introduced Veronica. This gave Ozzie the moment he needed to escape his aunt's tickling. Jerika came back from her friend's home to find her aunt here.

"Hi, Aunt Ronnie," she said as she hugged Veronica.

"Hey, Jerika, how are you?" Her aunt returned the hug.

"Great. What are you doing here, and where is Uncle Curt?"

"Unfortunately, he had to work. I'm here for a weeklong medical conference over at the Hyatt Regency."

"Are you a doctor?" Jade asked.

"No, I'm a paramedic. Every so often, we need to take refresher courses to keep up with the latest technology in medicine and procedures performed by paramedics." Veronica volunteered.

"Hallie, go get your brother, and the both of you wash your hands. It's almost time for supper," I told my youngest daughter.

Just as the doorbell rang, Ozzie came running in.

"Mommy, Hallie just called me a bad word," he said.

"I did not, tattletale," Hallie replied.

"All right you two, enough. Hallie, what did you call your brother?" I asked.

"Squirt."

"Ozzie, *squirt* is not a bad word. Hallie, please don't call your brother that in the future. He does not like it. Do you understand?"

"Well, what should I call him?"

"Please call him by his name."

All this went on while Willie and his two children entered, followed by Josh. Then we sat down to eat.

After we finished the meal and before we could clear the table, Willie had something to say.

"Cinnamon, that meal was exquisite. You fed me too much."

"Thank you, Willie, but it's your own fault for overeating. Besides, Jade helped prepare the meal."

"Speaking of Jade, thank you for your help with the meal."

"You're welcome, Willie."

"I've got something else I'd like to say to Jade if you all don't mind," Willie said.

"We're all ears," Josh said.

Willie moved his chair back and got down on one knee. He produced a small box, which he presented to Jade.

"Jade Pinkerton, will you marry me?" he asked.

Jade started shaking as she opened this small box, which revealed a beautiful diamond ring. "Yes," she said in a soft voice as tears filled her eyes. Then she flung herself into Willie's arms.

Everyone cheered and applauded. Everyone, that is, except Billy, who got up from the table and ran to the door.

"I'm sorry for Billy's reaction," Willie said. "I'll bring him back."

"No, let me, Willie. If I'm to be a member of the family, I need him to like me." Then she went after him.

"What's that all about," Josh asked.

"Billy thinks Jade wants to take the place of his mother and doesn't like it," I said as we all went to the door to follow Jade.

We'd just reached the doorway when we heard Jade scream. "Billy, watch out for that car!"

He turned just in time to see the car hit him. Thank goodness this is a residential street, so the car wasn't speeding.

"Someone call nine-one-one!" Jade shouted.

Veronica and I ran to Billy's aid, "Jade, let Veronica help Billy."

"No, I want to help," she said firmly.

"Okay," Veronica said. "Go get something for a blanket."

As Jade ran into the house, Josh called out, "Help's on the way."

"Son, what were you thinking?" Willie asked.

"Not now, Willie," I said. "Josh, please take Willie to the living room. Jerika, please take the little ones inside."

Jade returned with the afghan from the back of the couch and one throw pillow.

"How's he doing?" Jade asked as she covered him with the blanket.

"I'm not finding any broken bones, but can't rule out if any are fractured," Veronica responded just as Jade was about to lift Billy's head to place a pillow under it.

"Eighty-six the pillow, Jade," Veronica ordered. "If his neck is broken, moving his head could paralyze him."

Then we heard sirens.

Every day that Billy stayed in the hospital, Jade would be there while Willie was at work. When she came home, she'd tell me if she noticed any progress that Billy might be making. On my day off, I decided to visit Billy. Upon my arrival, I'd just entered the doorway to his room, and Jade was crying.

"Why can't you accept me for who I am, Billy?"

"Why should I?"

"All I want from you is to be friends. Nothing more. What do I need to do to prove I care about you?"

"For one thing, you could wear a bra."

"At this point in time, I can't," Jade said. She turned her back to him and lifted her blouse. "Look at my back. Look at the scars. They are still tender. Go ahead, touch them. Don't be afraid. Maybe in a few weeks they'll be strong enough for me to wear a bra. I've had a hard life."

Billy ran his hand over her back. Jade made a few faces where Billy touched the scars. They were still very tender.

"Where'd you get those scars?" he asked.

"I'd been in a hospital in Korea with amnesia. I don't know how or what happened. Then I'd been begging on the streets for food when a man who seemed nice at the time gave me some food, then he made me a slave. If it hadn't been for Cinnamon and her friends, I'd still be in that terrible place." She lowered her blouse and turned back to face Billy. "I don't know why you hate me so much, but if it means coming between you and your father, then I'll leave and never come back. Here, take the ring your father gave me," she said as she took it off and gave it to him.

Jade almost ran into me. She started to apologize and then realized it was me. I put my arms around her and let her cry into my shoulder, then took her to the hospital coffee shop, and let her explain what happened.

"Jade, Billy has not come to grips with the fact that his mother is gone. He sees you as someone who wants to get rid of her so you can take her place."

"You're right, Cinnamon, but it still hurts that he hates me. All I'm asking of him is that he likes me, nothing more."

"Hi, ladies," Willie said as he entered the coffee shop. "I was passing by and saw you two in here." Then he noticed Jade's sad look. "Jade, are you crying?"

"Willie, this is girl talk. Go see your son. We'll be there shortly," I told him.

"Hang in there, Jade," Willie said, patting her hand. "We'll see you later."

We stayed there until we finished our coffee.

"Jade, you need to go to the ladies' room and fix your makeup. Then we can go see Billy, and if you're really going to leave, you can say, 'See ya Tuesday.'"

"What? See ya Tuesday? Why? What's going on, on Tuesday?" she asked.

"Nothing. It's a way of saying goodbye without really saying the word *goodbye*."

"Are you trying to cheer me up, Cinnamon?"

"Do you think I'd do a thing like that?" I asked.

"Yeah."

"Is it working?"

"Yeah, I'm feeling a little better. Thanks, Cinnamon."

With Jade's makeup refreshed, we headed to Billy's room. Just before we got there, Willie came out looking anxious.

"Thank goodness you're still here," he said to Jade.

"Why, what's the matter?" she asked.

"It's Billy. He's asking for you, Jade," Willie said.

"Me? He wants to see me?" she questioned, looking at me, then at Willie.

"Yes, just you. Alone."

"Billy?" Jade asked as she entered his room.

"Come in, Miss Jade. I've got something to say to you."

"Did your father put you up to this?" Jade asked.

"No, it's you," he stated.

"Me? I don't understand. You hate me."

"Please let me say my piece without interruption, okay?"

"Okay."

"When you were here before, you told me about your hard life and let me feel the scars on your back. How many others did you show those scars to?"

"You're the only one other than the doctors who treated me."

"When I felt those scars, it made me think about your hard life. If you were to become a member of the family, would you still insist I call you Miss Jade?"

"Just plain Jade will do."

"Will you get my father, please, Jade?"

"On one condition, I'd like to hug you," Jade said with tears in her eyes.

Billy nodded, and they both hugged. Just as Jade started for the door, Billy grabbed her wrist.

"Here, you forgot this." He held out her diamond ring. "You'd better put it on before my dad sees you without it."

Shaking, Jade returned the diamond to its proper place on the ring finger of her left hand. Then without warning, she hugged Billy again.

"Thank you, Billy" came out in a whisper.
"Why are you crying now?" Billy asked.
"Because you made me very happy," she said.
Willie and I stood in the doorway all that time and heard everything. It even produced a few tears in me.

EPILOGUE

The driver who hit Billy agreed to pay his hospital bills. Also, for the first six months after his release from the hospital, Billy had to use a cane to walk. Through therapy, he began to gradually walk without it.

Once he got rid of that cane, Jade and Willie got married in a small wedding ceremony. Billy was the best man while La Keisha took the part of maid of honor. Josh gave the bride away.

Shortly after Jade and Willie returned from their honeymoon, my twenty-year service anniversary with Angel Airlines was marked with my retirement. Veronica and her husband came for the celebration.

Ozzie said, "Let's go to Queen's Burgers."

"The Queen B is better," Veronica countered.

"No, Queen's Burgers is better," my son demanded.

"Can you imagine going to a low-class cafe like Queen's Burgers when The Queen B is a better restaurant?" Veronica asked me while she tussled Ozzie's hair.

"I agree with Aunt Ronnie."

"No!" shouted Ozzie.

When we pulled up to the nearest Queen's Burgers, we explained to Ozzie that the Queen B was another name for Queen's Burgers.

ABOUT THE AUTHOR

Dorlon L. Pond Jr. is from Mohawk, a small village in upstate New York. He wrote an exposé on Eli Whitney and his cotton gin in school. He then wrote a short story entitled "FIGHT FOR LIFE." Also written were two short three-act plays. In his senior year, Dorlon directed a one-act play for his public speaking class and decided to write a book, but could not come up with the right idea. Twenty-seven years later, an ad in a Las Vegas, Nevada, newspaper prompted him to talk to a casting director where he mentioned he had an idea for, and wrote a movie script titled, "LADYHAWKS." He also played as an extra in the movie "HEAD OF STATE" and then went on to write three more scripts before writing his novel titled, "SHE WENT ABOVE AND BEYOND" about a woman who starts out life in poverty and abuse to become one of the worlds' richest and most loved women. Since that time, he has republished the book under the name of "THE LADY WENT ABOVE AND BEYOND" and written close to twenty short stories, three of which have been published in the Henderson Writer's Group Anthology and has titles for close to eighty more.

Lightning Source UK Ltd.
Milton Keynes UK
UKHW041904191222
414191UK00013B/221/J